DOWN DOWN DEEP

A TWISTED TEXAS THRILLERS NOVEL

CHRISTINA DELAY

NIMBUS BRANDS
PUBLISHING

ISBN ebook 978-1-957870-11-3
ISBN print 978-1-957870-18-2
ISBN hardback 978-1-957870-20-5
ISBN hardback with jacket 978-1-957870-19-9

JESSE

IT'S THE COLORS I'LL MISS THE MOST—THE ROSE PINKS and turquoise blues trimming the city, the burning golds of the lattice work, the slashes of red.

The evening call to prayer fades into the dusk, and a warm, dry breeze brushes my cheeks. I press my ribs into the hard stone of my comped balcony in my comped hotel room. A breath later, and Marrakech's buildings and lively streets fade to gray.

Inside my hotel room awaits a half-finished feature article for work, and my editor has already sent three messages asking for the final draft. It'll be a five-star review for the riad, of course, but it's the intricacies of the article that are fleeing my fingertips. Marrakech is a rich, delicate dessert. Only a few bites are needed, but those bites stay with the visitor forever, and my article *must* leave my reader with that same sensation. I'll settle for nothing less.

It's my last night in the city, and the shadows in the streets whisper as if they need me, but responsibility and the addictive *ping* of a text message are my current bodyguards.

Only five people in the world would message me. My mother, my cat-sitter, my editor, the automatic appointment reminders from my therapist, and Gabe. My cat-sitter has already checked in with photos of Leo lazing about our condo, and of the other four people, there's only one that causes a predictable stutter in my stomach.

My phone pings again, but I ignore it, dangle the waiting message as a reward for finishing the article. Or a punishment, depending on who it is. I turn my back on the city, face my almost-packed suitcase, my worn laptop waiting on the silk-clad bed. The shadows will be there when I'm through working. No matter where I am, what I'm doing, the shadows are always there.

Scents of the night market waft through the balcony doors—spices and fire-cooked meat, animal musk and motorcycle exhaust. Sand dusts the edges of the windowsills, ever present in this desert oasis. I grab my computer and inhale Marrakech—the city, the scents, the sounds—and exhale words. The room fades until it's only me, and I fade until I'm only the work.

The night stales, the world darkens, and the shadows smile.

Sunlight stabs my eyelids, and I rub at my eyes. They're gritty, as if I fell asleep in my makeup, and the sheets are tangled around my ankles. A two-toned voice, long and drawn out, thuds off my skull. Other voices join the first, and soon the air fills with the sounds of morning calls to prayer.

The room comes into focus. My laptop is closed and on the table. The sand on the windowsill has grown over night, like an hourglass running out of time. And my hand hurts.

I sit up, disoriented, massage my palm with my good hand, and try to piece together last night. I worked on the article and then...nothing.

My stomach sinks, and exhaustion falls over my body like a weighted blanket. Not again. I'd hoped that this year, with all the therapy... Doctor Hart had said we were making progress.

"Your definition of progress and mine are very different," I mutter to my therapist, who is an entire ocean and continent away.

The room phone rings. I inch across the bed and grab it on the third shrill, the leftover dregs of the blackout dulling my senses.

"Miss Jesse, your car has arrived to take you to the airport."

The front desk clerk. My car. Airport.

I push my bangs off my face, and the clock next to the phone slowly comes into focus.

"Shit," I respond, slipping back into English. "I'll be downstairs in ten minutes."

Double shit. I pride myself on speaking the language of whatever country I visit, even if it is only a basic, butchered version. The point is to try. But my brain is already focused on grabbing all my belongings, stuffing them helter-skelter in my bag, and pushing away whatever happened last night to be explored at another probably useless appointment. I splash water on my face, drag my fingers through my cropped hair, and it helps none.

"Shower at the airport lounge," I order my reflection and dash out of my room, bags grasping at my shoulders for dear life.

It's not until after I slide onto the white leather back seat of my private car and we're expertly navigating the beautiful chaos of Marrakech that I remember the message.

I pull my phone out of my bag, and grin.

Thinking of you in exotic lands, while I sail known seas. - Gabriel

He doesn't know it, but he'll see me next week. It's been a couple of years, though we keep in touch through random texts. I touch my recently shorn hair—I'm not sure he'll even recognize me.

Twenty-four hours later, the humid, jet exhaust-filled air of Bush Intercontinental wraps around my neck and my face and brushes away the recycled air of first class. I slip into my driver's car, the black sedan waiting for me at the curb, and throw my carry-on onto the seat next to me.

"Welcome home, Ms. David," Brian says, his English accent the most familiar thing I've come across in two weeks.

"*Ssalam.*" I bow my head, getting the accent just right.

"Shalam," Brian repeats, massacring the consonants.

I raise an eyebrow at his rearview-mirrored glance.

"Not even close?" he guesses.

"The Moroccan people would say their version of *bless his heart* behind your back." I flash him a smirk and pull up the pictures on my phone.

But instead of looking at the pictures, he grabs my wrist, studies my swollen hand. "Who did this to you?" his voice drops an octave.

I yank my hand back, my bruised bones protesting the movement. "I fell in the shower," I say, and even as the words fly from my mouth I hear their clichéd lies.

He presses his lips together, studies me a moment, then puts the car into drive and pulls away from curb. "Please be more careful with yourself, Ms. David."

I catch his gaze in the rearview mirror, give him a slight nod.

He's picked up on it, I'm sure. The various bruises and wounds I come home with, the excuses that hold about as much water as tissue paper.

If I knew the source of the abuse, would I tell him?

At every red light, I struggle for normalcy. I show him all the people I met, the here-today, gone-tomorrow relationships that fill my travel articles, my phone's memory, and the picture frames in my condo. Brian's been my driver for five years, and besides my editor, he's the longest, not-long-distance relationship I've had. I'm not naive enough to believe it's *friend*ship, but it's something more than nothing, and that's enough to hold onto.

Twenty minutes later, I grab my carry-on, wave goodbye, and stumble through the heavy glass doors of my building. Muffled sirens leak through the glass as I check my mailbox. The luxury condo was billed as soundproofed from the traffic of Houston's Galleria area, but no soundproofing is strong enough to overcome that noise.

I like the noise—reminds me of Beijing—surrounding me like a cocoon, hiding me in discordant notes.

I step off the elevator onto my floor. Javier, a single-dad refugee from Columbia, climbs down his building-issued maintenance ladder. "Jesse, you're just in time. I need an artist's eye. What do you think?" He nods at the garland he's hung around our floor's lobby. His six-year-old daughter helps by hanging ornaments on the little Christmas tree in the corner.

"I'm no artist, but from here...*que linda*. Beautiful." A smile spreads, almost painfully, across my face. I like Javier. I like how he's never given up, how he's reinvented his life to keep his child safe. I like how he loves her, even when she's *having a moment*.

This is how a parent and child should be.

I fumble for the keys to my condo, the first one on the left next to the elevator, prop my suitcase against my leg, and balance two weeks' worth of mail.

"I see *tu mamá* the other day." Javier's tentative voice winds softly around my ears, no doubt remembering my outburst from the last time my mother was here and convinced him to let her in my condo.

My heart stutters. My mail falls to the floor.

"You didn't—"

He raises his hands. "No, no. She was downstairs. I told her to leave."

I let go a hard breath, but my chest is still tight, my muscles still clenched. He bends down, helps me pick up my mail, and rests a hand on my shoulder. "She left. No worries." His smooth tone calms me, and I have to wonder how much he's guessed versus how much he understands from his own shady past.

"*Gracias*." The *r* rolls off my tongue, my accent perfect, but inside, I'm wound into an impossible tangle. *She left*. But that doesn't mean the stain of her footprints isn't here.

The door shuts behind me, and I flip the deadbolt. Velvet footsteps pad down the marbled hall, and the only love in my life runs around the corner.

I kneel, drop the mail, and scoop Leo into my arms. "How's my baby?" He wraps his paws around my neck and gives me an ear kiss, his calico fur vibrating under my touch. "I missed you too. Did Mrs. O'Neil take good care of you?"

Leo jumps from my arms and bumps against my leg. I give him a kitty treat and thumb through the mail, noting the package from Luxury Lines which contains my cruise ticket and information for their twentieth anniversary celebration cruise. Doesn't look like any of it's been touched, but with Momma's lock-picking skills, I never know for certain.

I follow my routine, checking to make sure the lock on my safe hasn't been tampered with, my password book is still hidden, my computer's login record shows the last access was mine. So far, everything's been left alone.

My shoulders unwind. I move to the wet bar and pour a whiskey. I tell myself that I'm safe, that all is well, even as a sense of shame snakes through my chest. No one else analyzes their home the way I do.

But they don't have mothers like mine.

"Hey Google, play a John Coltrane mix." The relaxing sounds of the sax fill my living room, and I sag against the bar, sip my drink, and let exhaustion take hold. For a few days, I can rest. My next trip is all mine. I'm not on deadline, I'm not on assignment—other than the homework my therapist gave me.

Leo winds around my leg, gives a sweet *mew*, and limps to my leather couch.

He's limping. Everything in me freezes as all my caveman instincts go into high alert.

"Leo! What happened?" The next second, I'm cuddling next to him on the couch, checking his limbs, pressing his fur to see if he has any pain. He stretches out for tummy rubs and purrs, seemingly all right.

Except he was limping.

I take a hard look at my living room, and something curls around my stomach.

The blanket on my chair is rumpled, not the way I left it. The framed picture of me and Gabriel is propped against the lamp, the cardboard kickstand at the back of the frame ripped off and flung to the floor. There's a pillow on the rug under my favorite painting, the one of a person split in two with a shining light connecting the halves. It's crooked. One corner barely higher than the other, as if something was thrown at it. I look at the pillow, at the arm chair directly across from the painting.

Momma's been here.

I try to tamp down the panic, try to push away the worry, but it's pointless. *What did she do this time?*

I pull my lip balm out of my pocket and rub it into my lips, the ritual soothing my nerves. It could've been Mrs. O'Neil, but she never ventures further than Leo's dish in the kitchen, and the electric shocks shooting through my chest are too familiar to ignore. I fumble for my phone, ignore the text from my editor. I sign into my bank accounts, my credit cards, my fingers trembling over the screen. Everything looks in order.

What. Did. She. Do?

This is exactly what my therapist has drilled into my head. *Don't let her in your safe places.*

But I didn't. I don't. She pries her way in, despite all my efforts. I drop my head to my hands. I won't cancel my credit cards, my debit cards, have them issue me new numbers. Not again. It'd put a kink in my next trip, and Momma would have already maxed everything out if that's what she was after.

I unpack one suitcase and pack the next, layering in flowing pants, fitted tops, boyfriend jeans, my favorite leather cropped jacket, ignoring the drum beat in my temples pounding out *what did she do, what did she do, what did she do*. I throw in some dresses, exactly one athletic swimsuit, fire off a few emails, and text my editor—who ropes me into writing an article on "The Secrets of Grand Cayman," even though technically, this is a vacation. The only secrets I'm interested in discovering on this cruise are the ones about Daddy's death. Those have stayed buried deep, deeper than even my high-priced therapist has been able to dig.

There's a kick in my chest. One that speeds up and clashes with the drum beat in my head. Luxury Lines's anniversary celebration leaves in two days, recreating its virgin voyage from twenty years ago. The same Caribbean cruise, the same ship, the same itinerary leading to the day Daddy died. The same cruise where I lost all my memories and my reasons why. I'd even booked the same cabin.

When the opportunity appeared, Doctor Hart had jumped out of her chair with an enthusiastic cheer. This was my chance, she'd said, to recreate the trip on which Daddy died. The trip that started my blackouts. The blackouts that get worse every anniversary. She calls my blackouts an anniversary effect, and maybe, *maybe* by recreating the original trip, something will trigger a memory. It sounds like hogwash to me, but at this point, I'm desperate.

A lifeline dangles in front of my nose, and after years of therapy and confronting my issues, it's come down to this—I need answers from the day of his death to get closure and fully heal.

I need to remember the memories I've blocked.

My phone rings with the lyrics to Reba's "Fancy." Momma. My thumb hovers over the *ignore* button, but she'll just call back again and again. If I don't pick up, she'll make the forty-five-minute drive from Rosharon and show up on my doorstep with a mixed-up bag of love and abuse. No, thanks.

I punch my thumb on the *answer* button—"Hi, Momma"— and weariness slides out of my voice.

"You sound tired. I been tellin' you for years, all this travel-ing's gonna make you old before your time." Her voice plows into me, more of a culture shock than walking through the arrivals gate at Bush Intercontinental.

"Yes, Momma, I know. Everything okay?"

"Fine, just fine." Her voice is more chipper than usual, and it sends up warning flares. "I'm in the middle of packing. What *is* the appropriate attire for dinner on a cruise ship?"

My stomach twists into a hard knot. A slow, steady stabbing starts picking at my temples. My apartment seems to stretch out, snap back together, then stretch out again.

How did she know? I'd hidden everything. Researched online in incognito browser tabs. Kept the trip off my calendar. Even bought my cruise ticket in person so there'd be no trace. How could she—? My heartbeat trips. The pile of mail on the counter hunches over like a traitor on trial. The oversized cruise booklet with my luggage tags tries to hide at the bottom.

"What?" Momma continues. "We should be together on your daddy's anniversary. Even better, we can toast to his life at the place of his death. What do ya think of that?" Her cackling laugh reminds me of a trained monkey I met in Burma.

My throat is dry, too dry for the humidity that invades every part of southeast Texas. "It's too late to add you to the sailing. The trip is in two days." I hold onto sinking hope that she buys that lie.

"Wrong! I called the cruise line. They said they could add me onto your room when we check in. Isn't that grand?"

"Momma, it's really not the best—"

"I'm coming, Jesse-*girl*." Her tone flips, her voice deepening, all hints of play and excitement long gone, and for a moment I'm seventeen, and Momma is peppering the side of my boyfriend's truck with a shotgun, pounding nails into the rusted aluminum siding of our trailer to seal my window shut, waiting for me outside school, never giving me a chance to defy her.

Never giving me a chance at all.

I sink to the floor, holding the phone against my ear, and Leo nudges my elbow. I lean my forehead against his, soak in the soft vibrations of his purr. Across the room, I swear I can see Daddy's face, staring at me from the shadows, shaking his head at Momma's bullying.

"I'm showing up at that port and will meet you at security." Momma's voice pummels my head. "I need to say goodbye to him too." Her voice breaks a little, and the rare show of emotion twists me up, steals all my arguments. "You aren't leaving me behind. Not this trip, not this time."

I curl around Leo, hugging the cold marble, wishing I could disappear. And the shadows reaching for me—they darken a little more.

DAY ONE

Down, down deep,
In the big ocean blue,
Swim two little fishies,
A me and a you.

1

GABRIEL

The ship pulled into the Port of Galveston at six in the morning, and Gabriel Gutierrez was already awake, in uniform and on his second mug of percolated, Argentinian coffee, freshly roasted from his sister's own kitchen. He hoarded her coffee beans, hiding them from his fellow officers, breaking ship rules to have a heating device in his room to properly prepare his brew.

Outside, the sounds of the crew bringing in the ship clanked against his ocean-level room. His quarters were bigger than most other crew quarters, with a seating area, a working desk, a bedroom with a door, and a full-size bathroom, but still at crew level. Being staff captain had certain advantages, but not like being captain.

Captain Knight's quarters were on deck eight, had floor-to-ceiling windows, a large balcony, a huge room for entertaining that included a flat-screen TV, a long dining table, and a kitchenette. With his own Luxury Lines-approved coffee machine.

Gabriel wanted to captain his own ship for many reasons, but most of all? That coffee machine.

He took one more long sip of his coffee, draining it empty, and hid his paraphernalia. The cruise ship stuttered as its engines turned off, then went still. After days of being at sea, the quiet ship was eerie. Ships were meant to brave waves, not rest peacefully at docks.

In ten minutes, he was due on deck to help the mass exit of confused and bewildered passengers find their way to their disembarkation stations. He'd gotten used to the shell-shocked look most guests had when returning home from a long vacation. He'd not gotten used to the relief he felt every time they arrived back at home port sans any accidents or casualties.

He pulled up the next sailing's manifest, due to embark in ten hours, sticking to his well-ingrained habits. Ten short hours to clear the ship of passengers, clean, restock, refuel, and welcome the next sailing's passengers, all while keeping a smile freshened on his face. He thumbed through the passenger list to the D's, and slowed down, searching for her name, even knowing she wouldn't be on there.

She never booked a sailing this close to The Accident.

It'd be twenty years this week, but in twenty years, he'd never forgotten that lost little girl, standing by herself on the dock as they called the search and rescue mission off. She forgot him though. And although he sought her out every subsequent sailing she came on, and their relationship had gone from comforter to stranger to something more, she'd never once remembered that he was the guy. The guy who'd convinced his senior officers to stop looking and stick to the schedule, the guy who'd told his superiors the little girl's father was dead, the guy who held her with his own tears on his cheek as the captain told the mother and the girl that her husband, her daddy, had been claimed by the sea. He could still feel Jesse's sharp elbows jabbing his ribs as she cried on the dock, as a crowd of insensitive onlookers gawked at the most tragic moment in her small, short life.

He was the guy who'd kept that secret from her all these years.

His thumb paused over the list of Davids, and there. There she was.

His heart ticked at the base of his throat. *Impossible.*

It had to be a different Jesse. He checked the cabin number— not her typical cabin. He could text her, but if it wasn't his Jesse, all the good his text would do would be to remind her of the date, remind her of his death. No, he'd wait to see if it was her. Besides, if Captain found out that he and Jesse texted, that their relationship went beyond staff and passenger, his ass would be fired.

He took one last look in the mirror above the built-in desk, straightened his navy-blue uniform with the polished brass buttons, and left his secrets locked in his ship-owned stateroom.

2

JESSE

I lean back to take in the Luxury Lines cruise ship looming over the pier, casting a shadow that grazes the tip of my toe. A shadow so thick if I had a shovel, I could dig through two decades of grime and mistakes, back to where I buried all my answers.

I glance at Momma, being wheeled next to me in a new wheelchair. She does her best to look as if she belongs—innocent and vacation-happy like the rest of the kitschy cruise terminal crowd surrounding us—but she's never happy.

And she's not innocent.

"Glad you could make it. What's with the wheelchair?"

She gives me a long look, one that makes me think I'm missing something, then shrugs. "Stopped by while you were out of town—your neighbor let me in. Tripped over that damned cat of yours." She indicates the boot on her foot.

I don't believe it for a second. "Mrs. O'Neil knows better, and Leo tucks tail and runs at the sight of you." Not that I blame him. Of the two of us, he's smarter and wiser. But his limp... The vet said everything looked fine, but cats don't limp for fun. "Did you kick him?"

She shrugs again, and a smirk plays with her overzealous lip liner.

A slam of anger hits the back of my mouth. She kicked my cat? My nails dig into my palms, but she either doesn't notice or doesn't care.

"I see you've dressed for the occasion." She tugs at my shapeless khakis, hanging around my hips, and her smirk rots into a familiar grimace.

I step away from her touch and fiddle with the closed buttons of my blue polo. I'd left the loose fabric untucked, trying to stay invisible. My clothes are my armor, and to be safe around Momma, my armor needs to be about ten feet thick.

Car exhaust and baggage handler shouts pollute the Galveston winter breeze. I take a calming breath, fill my lungs with sticky air, and push Momma into the terminal. We skip ahead of the line using my press pass and wait at the security check. After traveling the world and dealing with airport security, cruise security checks are a bit of a joke—a simple metal detector check and baggage X-ray machine. But still, a whisper of nervousness ticks at the base of my skull.

The security guard helps Momma from her wheelchair and she hobbles through the metal detector. He waves a wand over the wheelchair and, when nothing beeps, waves me through the security check while Momma resettles in her chair.

It's not until I've retrieved our carry-ons from the baggage X-ray machine that I let go of my breath.

Momma twists her wedding band around a swollen finger. "Think we'll have any trouble getting on board?"

My focus swerves and wrecks into the top of Momma's at-home coloring treatment, and I squeeze her wheelchair handles. "You said you checked. You did, right?" I wait for her nod, unclench my lip from the death grip of my teeth, and swipe lip balm over the gnawed flesh. The booking agent holds out her hand for our boarding documents and my credit card to pay for Momma's last-minute arrival.

"So happy you could join us again, Miss David," the booking agent says. "Is this your sister traveling with you?" She indicates Momma, less than a seventeen-year difference from my own twenty-nine.

Momma wheels up, ecstatic. "I'm her mother, but how sweet you are." She can turn on the charm when she wants, and when she does, I get to time-travel back to her youth, to the young girl who bewitched Daddy's heart. Before life hit, before responsibility rotted away her beauty. Before me. Those are her words, echoing through my skull on an endless repeat.

"I'll just need to run your card for the taxes and port fees for your mother here, and you two will be all set." The agent's voice raises at the end of every sentence, as if she was trained that this was the best way to show enthusiasm.

I nod for her to go ahead and busy myself with repacking our boarding documents.

"Miss David, I'm so sorry but do you have another form of payment? Your credit card has been declined."

"Declined? Not possible." I'd been careful, safe. I'd checked that account yesterday. "There's a ten-thousand-dollar limit on that card. Run it again."

"I did, ma'am. Twice."

There's a hard thump in my chest. Just one. Then it goes silent, and my gaze draws to my mother.

She doesn't respond, except for a slight twitch in her lips and a *tap, tap, tap* on her wheelchair. Around us, families and honeymooners move quickly through the check-in line, no problems, no hitches in their plans. They get to enjoy the excitement of vacation, with none of the stress.

"Miss David? I need another method of payment. Otherwise, I cannot allow your mother to board." Apology coats her words, but behind it, the frustration of an overworked customer service agent beams through. Travel enough, and you pick up on subtleties.

Fine with me almost makes it to my tongue, but then I remember that brokenness that came through Momma's voice over the phone.

I press my lips together, pull out my wallet, and hand over my debit card, even knowing that by the end of this trip, Momma will have overdrafted my account and I'll have six messages from the bank.

Despite the dark clouds Momma brings, the blue sign with the arrow that says "To Cruise Ship" beckons me, like a lighthouse shining through a storm. This is *my* vacation, my chance to get to the bottom of my missing memories. Stopping the blackouts and recovering my memories is worth more than my bank account, more than tumbling back into debt, more than the pressure building in my throat.

I push Momma in her wheelchair up the ramp to the ship. Far below, the waves grope the painted white sides, gray and full of debris, demanding life. *And down down deep, the little fishies swim...*

"Miss David?" A familiar voice hits me, and my gaze drags along the deck to a pair of polished shoes, travels up starched uniform pants, and meets the tall, muscled frame of Gabe.

My pulse quickens, and I find myself falling into years of wanting him, reaching for beyond-the-friend-zone.

"I saw your name on the manifest and couldn't quite believe it." His gaze travels approvingly over my new haircut, and he gives me a half-bow, unable to show too much affection in the big brother eyes of Luxury Lines.

I get it. I step away from Momma's wheelchair, half-bow back, and am rewarded with a smile that is all mine.

Momma takes a shaky breath, the shudder rattling the aluminum bones of her chair. She leans back, craning her neck to get a better look at Gabe. Under her rubbed-on rouge, her skin pales, her eyes darken. Like she's seeing a ghost or an ex-lover for the first time post-breakup.

Gabe darts his gaze to Momma, hesitating a second at her expression, before composing himself. "We've your state-room this way. No need to stand in that line." He steps back and directs us toward the front of the ship, away from the rest of the passengers headed aft.

"Thanks. This is Momma's first cruise in a very long time, and I'd hate to show her"—I gesture at the cattle call—"the standard tour."

"Of course. No need for that at all." His voice holds a warmth I've grown used to over the years. It settles around me like a life-saving ring, one that's pulling me back to shore. "Mrs. David"—Gabe addresses my mother—"we are very happy to have you aboard. What brings you back to the sea?"

"I know you." Her voice has gone ragged and worn.

Gabe shoots her a confused smile and shakes his head ever so slightly. "I'm sorry, ma'am, you must be mistaken."

Her eyes narrow to tiny slits of blue lasers, but she lets go a breath, shakes her head, and answers his question as if seeing him hasn't rattled her. "An anniversary. We're celebrating an anniversary."

Her words dig at my chest, catch my breath. I step back behind her chair and give it a push, needing to distract them from this conversation.

Gabe falls next to Momma, keeping her company as I navigate her through the ship.

"Fantastic. What anniversary?" He darts his gaze between us.

My breath tightens. I've known Gabe for years, most of my adult life, but this? This isn't something I want him knowing about. Not until I'm able to work through whatever happened that day.

"My wedding anniversary." Momma doesn't quite lie. Her hands butterfly in her lap. "It would have been twenty-nine years this week had Ellis not...if he'd been here." She twists her ring around her finger, and the clouded diamond struggles to catch the light.

I flex my hands around the chair, needing her to stop.

"That is something to celebrate. I'll have champagne sent to the stateroom. You can toast as we leave port." Gabe uses his keycard to activate an otherwise-inactive elevator while filling the air with practiced, careful conversation, leaving out the flirtatious code we've worked on over the years. "The clouds should break soon, so we'll have a phenomenal sunset."

Our elevator descends to a lower deck, and the doors open onto a small lobby and a narrow corridor, just big enough for Momma's chair.

An ocean view balcony suite is one of my many perks on board. My frequent travels with the cruise line, and my influential readership as a travel writer for the world's most prolific travel magazine, have earned me a spot at the captain's table whenever I desire. I never have, but the suite is one advantage I usually take without any hesitation. Usually.

Gabe opens a cabin door, holds it open for us, and I wheel Momma ahead of me.

The small stateroom is shocking at first, more cramped than a New York City hotel room. A queen-sized bed nests under a porthole window, nothing like my typical suite. Outside, the ocean churn is close enough to make my throat close. Clouds scuttle across the sky, thinning and breaking apart, and a brief ray of sun hits the ship. Momma's chair bumps against the glass coffee table in the center of the room.

"Is the room to your satisfaction?" Gabe folds his hands behind his back and waits by the door.

"Yes, it's perfect." The room has been updated in the last twenty years—new carpets, new curtains, new couch—but the number is the same and the layout is the same and the memories start to stretch their seams.

"This is *not* going to work." Momma has paled a shade or two under her cake-face. Her gaze darts around the room, like a caged wild bird, frantic and breathless.

She remembers.

She tries to make a turn in the wheelchair and fails.

Gabe's eyes go wide, and a thick vein pops up the side of his neck as he realizes the room isn't ADA accessible. "My most sincere apologies. Let me see what I can do." He leaps into action, grabbing the phone from the vanity, before I can make him stop.

No. No, no, no, she can't do this to me.

"Momma, this will be just fine." I try to calm the situation, keep my voice cool, despite the earthquake shaking through the months of planning, of expensive therapy sessions, of gathering fragments of courage to come back to this room, this moment.

"Where is your concern for my wellbeing? How do you think I'll shower in that tiny space with this boot?" She folds her arms, and a flash of triumph travels around her face. "You'd think since *your* cat is responsible, you'd be a little more willing to take care of me." She knows I can't argue without looking like the worst daughter on the planet. Not with her *needing* a handicapped-accessible room.

I set my jaw and turn from her, taking the few minutes I have to soak in the memories this room offers. The little couch I'd slept on, the sleep-worn pillow, the rough sheets. The past burns at my stomach lining. I step close to the bed, steal a glimpse of the view, of the sun that spills through the clouds.

"Miss David?" Gabe's voice breaks the sun's hypnosis, and I turn around. "Our owner's suite is available to you. We would love to upgrade you at no cost."

I smile against the disappointment, the sabotage of my plans. "We would appreciate that." I grab Momma's chair and wheel her around. The edge of her footrest catches Gabe's leg, and his face breaks out in pain. "Oh my goodness, Gabe! I'm so so sorry," I exclaim and reach for his arm. I only let go when Momma looks between us and grins.

"I'm fine." Gabe waves away my apology, but his voice pinches. He presses his lips together, sucking the dark red flesh between his teeth. For a moment, he appears lipless.

Blood rushes out of my head, pours to my feet. The room swims. Daddy's water-bloated face floats to the surface, lips eaten, gums exposed, with a tiny crab clutching the tatters of his cheek. One of the few memories I have from his death.

"Jesse, are you well?" Gabe's voice travels through the darkness, distant and unreal. I'm aware of his hand on my back, but it's in a dimension I can't reach.

I inhale through my nose, hold the breath, and fight to not see Daddy wavering on the edge of my periphery.

"Could I get some water?" My breath disappears, my lungs become a vacuum, and my chest tightens, too tight. I can't breathe and the wreckage of all my plans plows over me in a giant, sea-debris filled wave.

Gabe wheels Momma out of the way and reaches for a bottled water on a shelf high above the vanity as I sink to the bed. He hands me the water, but his gaze catches mine and an unspoken *are you okay* passes through his eyes.

"Thank you." I brush my hand against his arm, reassuring him, and uncap the bottle. "Would you mind taking Momma to our new room? I need a few moments."

"Of course. It'll be cabin eleven oh one. We'll meet you there." Gabe takes control of Momma's chair and rolls her into the hallway. The door clicks shut after him. I drink half the bottle, the plastic crinkling under my fingers, and take a few moments, using the opportunity to apply some lip balm. The strawberry flavor settles on my tongue. I rub my sweaty palms on my pants, stand, and sink Daddy's image back to its dusky depths.

I hate that Momma made Gabe jump through hoops to get us a better suite, but there's nothing I can do about it.

Momma always gets her way.

3

JESSE

Our new owner's suite is a blank slate complete with a fish-shaped towel animal waiting for us on the bar. I shove the fish safely into the sink, walk onto the balcony, and lean over the wooden rail, dangling my champagne flute over the edge. The curve of the ship down to the tip of the deck below reminds me of a playground. I could slide along the bend and catch the rails, just before plummeting into the ocean.

Momma perches in her wheelchair, focused on the fire-and-water sunset. "What were you thinking, booking that cabin? Are you here to torture yourself?" Her eyes have retained some of that earlier wildness, a slight glint of craze circling her irises.

"I'm just trying to remember what happened." I click my fingernail on my champagne glass, digging the edge under the protective hard shell to the tender flesh hidden underneath.

"Trying to remember? *That's* why you're here? There are better ways to remember than encasing yourself in a tomb." She pats my hand. "If remembering's what you're after, I have some ideas. Been thinking about how to help you for a while now." She presses together her smile and sticks out her chin, but the side of her lip quivers the tiniest bit.

"Your ideas are what worry me." My thought slips between my teeth, quiet and murmured. My arms involuntarily draw in, protecting my most vital parts.

"How many times do I have to tell you? Speak up. Your mouth is full of mush." Momma swats at me and stands. Her blue and pink flowered dress flutters around her ankles as she throws off her faux frailty and fake boot and pushes her wheelchair out of the way. She reaches for me, but I duck away, escaping the pinch of her fingers.

"Momma." My voice reaches a high pitch, high enough to make crystal sing. "I *knew* Leo didn't trip you." Which means she kicked him. She. Kicked. My. Cat.

It's been a while since I've felt like murdering someone.

She rolls her glassy eyes. "That stupid cat isn't worth his skin. Let's get inside before someone sees me." She walks with a firm stride into the cabin. At some point in my preteen years, she'd adopted Daddy's military walk. Solid steps, as if her legs were made of thick wood and cased in steel instead of simple bone sheltered in skin like the rest of us.

I hesitate on the balcony, and the port glides away. The crisp salt air strengthens and rustles my cropped hair. The open water ahead grows larger.

"Jesse, I said get inside." Momma's voice crawls through the cabin carrying a warning. "One." *Tap. Tap.*

Did she pack the cane? My heart slams against its veined restraints, each escape attempt mirroring that sound. *Tap—bam. Tap—bam.*

"Two." The curved, marble tip forms in my mind. *Tap—bam. Tap—bam.*

I drink the rest of the bubbly courage and walk inside under the pretense of refilling my glass. *Not* obeying Momma's orders.

I can think that all I want, but we both know better. Momma is a force of nature, but not one you'd notice until it was hours too late. She's the suffocating humidity of the South, always present, always looming, forever inescapable. Prime territory to breed all sorts of minuscule, blood-sucking creatures. Death by a thousand bites.

Inside, she stands by the bar with her arms crossed, waiting to make sure I've obeyed. "Bring my carry-on into my room." She nods at the small bag she could carry herself and turns into the one and only bedroom. With the one and only door and the one and only lock.

I pat my top lip, dig my nail in, and press the Cupid's bow of my upper lip into my teeth. An ant bite of pain calms me, puts me back in order. It doesn't matter that she takes the master bedroom. It doesn't matter that I'm relegated to the sleeper sofa like a child. I can find other places on the ship safe from her reach. *It doesn't matter.*

I drop her bag in the doorway, refill my glass of champagne at the neighboring bar, and unpack my own small carry-on, laying out two sets of evening wear. The first, a gender-neutral pantsuit. The navy blue, trim cut accents my green eyes and slim figure and is guaranteed to irk Momma.

But my second option calls to me. A black satin slinky number, so girly it scares me, but in the way donning a racy costume for Halloween would scare me. The dress is a dare. Backless, paired with a diamond choker that drips down the center of my spine and too formal for first dinner, but I never know if I'll get the courage to wear it again. I trail my fingers across the material, smoothing away the wrinkles.

Truth or Dare?

This trip is all about treading into choppy, opaque waters.

Black dress it is.

Momma stomps out of her bedroom, reaches past me, and pulls an empty duffel out of the front pocket of her suitcase.

She's up to something.

"I'm getting dressed," I announce, ignoring her momma drama. She might be my monkey, but she doesn't have to be my circus.

I shimmy into my dress and fasten the choker around my neck. The long, platinum chain with a single diamond pendant bounces off my spine, then tickles my back. After brushing on a light foundation, blush, and dark eyeliner, I coat on a few layers of mascara. I roll my hands over my collection of lipstick. Which color, which color? Soft Plum will give my outfit a sophisticated Goth look, matching the spikes I've moussed into my hair. French Kiss is delicate and girly.

I'm not feeling very delicate this evening, and girly isn't ever what I'm going for. Something else. Something stronger. Something sexy.

My fingers caress Starfire, a brilliant red with a touch of glimmer. Perfect. I rub a thick layer over my lips, covering the fragile flesh in protective paint. I step back and look in the mirror.

The black satin hugs my small curves. My short, dark hair has transformed into its sexy minx persona. My lips curve at the edges. I don't look girly.

I look like a warrior.

"Jesse-girl. Need you for a second."

I flash an eyeroll at my reflection, grab my champagne flute, and cross into the master bedroom. She's unpacked her carry-on and littered the bed with her passport, a handful of peppermints, and a pay-by-the-minute cell phone. No clothes. Her silver and marble cane rests on the comforter beside her stained tote.

She looks up, sees me waiting at the door, pauses over my outfit, and thumbs at her suitcase. "Get to it then. We aren't here to look pretty." Her non-commentary on my dress hurts more than I want to admit.

I run my gaze up the generous, Dollar Store material of her dress. "Get to what?"

"Don't you sass me." Her words whip at my spine, and she trails her fingers along the smooth silver of her cane. I know what the tips of her fingers feel. I've only sneaked a touch a few times in my life, but I remember the seduction of that long, silver metal. All cold and smooth. Silky as water. Hard as bone. Much different from the concussive weight of the marble head.

"Sorry, Momma." I don't mutter. I don't drop my eyes. I meet her clear gaze and speak each syllable. Crisp every consonant. The deep crevices around her mouth quiver and compress. Forgiven. I lift my fingers from the thin champagne glass, one at a time, releasing the tension from clenching the glass too hard at the stem.

"My suitcase." She flicks her hand at her bag. The sparkle in her eyes isn't attractive. It's bone-freezing scary. "Unpack it."

It's a test—the first of many that I really, really, really should have seen coming. But somehow, I'm unprepared.

I plop the champagne flute on the counter and kneel so fast a shot of pain darts through my knee. My purse falls to the carpet, its contents spilling, but I don't dare stop under her searing gaze. Her suitcase is a study in disarray, but I pull out each shirt, set of pants, and shapeless dress with care.

Momma eases back on the bed. "Think that captain has a clue?" She licks her lips, wiping at some of her hot pink lipstick.

"About manipulating him to get a better suite? Gabe is the staff captain, and no. He was too busy to have a clue." My phone vibrates with the last email I'll receive until we get to Jamaica in two days, but can I stop to answer it? No. No, I cannot. "If you wanted an upgrade, we could have gotten you a different room." *And I could have stayed in the state-room I'd booked and centered all my plans around.* "I'm sure they would have given me a good deal on it."

"I'm not giving this damn ship a cent." Her gaze narrows. "And neither should you. The room change was necessary." There's an undercurrent to her tone, one that electrifies the air.

"I don't think it was necessary." I look up at her expression, and fear hits in sharp tingles that shoot out from all my old wounds and forgotten bruises. My elbows draw in, and we both stop breathing, the air too thick, the cane too close.

Her fingers dance between the cane and her side, wavering between control and a different kind of control.

"Okay, Momma. It's okay. You're right. It's a good room." My heart goes into AFib, but my voice is a monotone. Calm, steady. Desperate.

Her faraway look flees. She releases her breath. Her hands flutter to her chest, and the shaking starts in her legs, vibrating the flowers on her dress. I grab her arm and help her sit on the luxurious master bed my writing career paid for.

"The suite was a great idea." I stroke her soft arm with my nails, and she relaxes. "Your plan worked like a—" I almost say charm, but that's cliché. Overused. "It worked like the perfect beginning to a perfect story." Better. Not great. Too bad I can't revise words after they escape.

She sniffs. "And we haven't paid a penny?"

"Besides your taxes and port fees—and we had to do that to get you on board—not a penny, not a dime. Not even a doubloon." I make an attempt at humor.

She wipes at her nose and takes a deep breath. "I wasn't sure about this when you called the other night. But now that I'm here, you're right. This will work."

Call? I didn't call.

"I got you something." She pulls out a tiny gift bag, wrapped with a pink ribbon.

I push aside my confusion and untie the ribbon. Inside sit three new tubes of lip gloss, glittery and higher quality than her typical grocery store find. Too girly for my taste, but it's enough to know that she thinks about me when I'm not around.

Sometimes, Momma surprises me. It's these moments that give me just enough hope to not run away from her forever.

She waits for me to look up and pats my cheek. "We're going to have a great trip. You still taking your medicine?"

I break the seal on the light pink one and shake my head. "Momma, I've been off those for almost a decade. I've had a clean bill of health since I was twenty."

"Right. Just checking on you. Hard to turn the mothering off." She shoots for a smile that doesn't quite hit, but I appreciate the effort.

I roll the gloss over my lips. It won't blend well, but gifts from Momma are few and far between, and I won't waste this one.

Momma smiles with approval. Behind her, the master bedroom window makes the dying sunset a center stage affair. "My pretty girl. We are going to get you laid this trip," she sasses, and her hip does a very un-motherly thrust.

"Momma!" I flinch my shoulders away from her, needing even more of a barrier than my warrior-outfit can provide.

"None of that. You work too hard. Even a girl needs a release every once in a while." She smacks her lips, leaving a swipe of pink on her teeth.

"I don't, I can't, I don't even know what to do with that." I wave her away and kneel back at the suitcase, careful not to wrinkle my dress.

"You'd better," she continues, layering on the pressure as if she's a fault line. "Since you're you, one-night stands are 'bout the best you can hope for."

The flare of hurt is unexpected. I should be used to it by now, but it singes my heart before I can pinch the flame out. Momma is right. Me being me, a relationship is a dream.

She rustles some paper and spreads the ship's layout she printed from the website on the gold bedspread. "What's our cabin number again?"

"Eleven oh one."

"Perfect," Momma whispers and drags her finger along the paper. Some off-colored tint in her voice pulls my gaze forward. Along the floor, up her dress, pausing on her lips. Lips pressed into a smile that is part-happy, part-manic, and completely terrifying. Her blue eyes are fever bright, and there's a glare from the overhead lights that makes her seem more mannequin than alive.

A slow, chilled certainty crawls up my arms, and somehow I know, like I know when I've written a headlining article, that Momma's not here just to celebrate a death anniversary. She's here for more.

And it's the open-endedness of that 'more' that has me curling in and searching for an unattainable safe space.

4

GABRIEL

THE LAST OF GABRIEL'S CREW TRICKLED OUT OF THE staff meeting room—a white-walled rectangle of blue and gold carpeting, decorated with panoramic pictures of crew members on the ship's helipad. The pictures stretched back twenty years and were hung with the carelessness of someone assigned to do a task. No interior decorators in crew-only areas.

Gabriel pulled out his pocket watch, engraved with *Papá's* favorite saying—now his mantra—*Be your best man.* He traced the lettering like a worry stone, the once-rough indentations worn smooth over the years, and the predictable twinge in his gut followed.

More reliable than the large clocks around the ship, the glass face showed fifteen minutes until first dining seating. Giving him ten minutes to hustle to main dining and inform Jesse's server of her unofficial VIP status. Anything he could do to make this trip easier for her, he would.

In all the years that had passed between them, his guilt over her dad had never eased, and it added an uncomfortable element to their friendship that made him hesitate every time they were alone. Which wasn't often. Corporate policy against fraternizing with guests made it difficult to do much of anything where Jesse was concerned.

Gabriel fastened on his showboat smile and left the empty staff meeting room. The ship rolled under his feet, a late winter storm rocking the waves. The familiar adrenaline at catering to the cruise ship guests and representing Luxury Lines at every turn, literally every step, coursed through his veins. He nodded to a few of the passengers who stumbled into each other, unsteady on their landlubber legs. The Promenade was scattered with crew members selling drink packages and promoting spa specials. Most of the shops were closed, clear glass with friendly security bars rolled down over entrances. Any area that sold liquor or alcohol was closed until seven tonight, when they would reach international waters. Laws were a strange thing at sea. Strict in a controlled ocean, but once the ship reached unclaimed territory, ship's law took authority.

His phone gave a loud chirp on his hip. "Speak," he said into the phone-slash-radio.

"Sir? This is Laurence, cabin steward on deck two."

Gabriel stepped through the frosted glass doors and into the closed dining room for privacy.

"Go ahead." Gabriel set his jaw and looked around the main dining room, gaze scanning the three-tiered room for any signs of disorder. This had better be good.

"My passenger says someone stole his service dog. Personally, I think he lost the ankle-biter." Something in the steward's voice told Gabriel that he'd already enjoyed the experience.

"We're at sea. How could he lose his dog?" Gabriel's focus shifted from the conversation back to main dining, his old maître d' responsibilities haunting him.

"Not sure, sir," Laurence paused and waited until Gabriel's attention was back on the conversation. "But he needs it for his seizures." Laurence gave the final word the weight it deserved.

The impact of the situation descended on Gabriel's shoulders. They rose to meet the challenge. First emergency of the week had arrived.

"I see. Room number?" Gabriel's voice snapped with the authority of a sail in the wind.

"Twenty-four ten, sir." The sharpened edge to Laurence's words had disappeared, now that he'd passed the baton of responsibility.

Gabriel clenched his stomach muscles, forcing himself to stand a little taller. "I have one thing to take care of, and then I'll speak with him personally. He is in his room?"

"Yes, sir," Laurence said, relief sweeping through his voice. Gabriel was about to hang up, when the steward took a deep breath.

"Is there something else?" Gabriel asked.

Hesitation. That was never good.

He resisted the urge to reach through the phone and wiggle the steward's tongue for him. Patience was a virtue he hadn't quite mastered. "I have very little time, as I'm sure you are aware," he reminded the man.

Behind him, the dining room *clinked* and *clanked* with the setting of salad plates and silverware.

"Sorry, sir. The guest who lost the dog? He's a nudist."

Gabriel's jaw hit the polished gold buttons at the neck of his uniform. "A nudist. With seizures. On a cruise ship."

"He wears a robe when walking the deck, but in his cabin..." His voice trailed off, and Gabriel detected notes of trauma.

He closed his eyes. Deep breath. "Please inform the guest I will be dropping by. And please gift him one of our most luxurious spa robes as our apologies for his lost dog. Put it on my account."

"Yes, sir."

"Laurence." Gabriel's voice held a tint of panic he hoped was only audible to himself. "Gift the robe now. As in the *very* next thing you do."

"Yes, sir," he said, a hint of laughter in his tone's undercurrents.

Gabriel rolled his shoulders back, one at a time, shaking off the task he had to look forward to and focused on the one he was now almost out of time to complete. Failing to take care of Jesse simply wasn't an option.

The maître 'd opened the dining room doors, and guests filed in. Many had dressed for the occasion, from shirt and tie to button-up polo. Sundresses and resort-style pant suits for the women. A couple wore luxury bathing suit cover-ups—forbidden in the dining room, but for first dinner, when many guests had yet to receive their luggage, the crew allowed the attire affront to pass without comment. Gabriel quickly checked with the hostess as to Jesse's table and maneuvered the tight spaces between the chairs to a rare table for two with a windowed view. He flagged down her assigned server.

"What can I do for you, sir?"

"You have a very special guest you will be taking care of this week." Gabriel assumed his do-not-ask-questions tone. He liked to run his staff with a careful balance of dictatorship and democracy, but Jesse deserved the dictator. The server straightened his spine. Gabriel checked his name tag. "Emmanuel, I expect you to take very good care of her." His own *Papá* came out in his voice, fatherly and stern.

"Of course. Always." Emmanuel jittered in his eagerness to impress. Gabriel had gotten used to it over the years, even come to appreciate his authority.

Around them, the dining room came alive, servers delivering bread, water, salads. Bartenders took drink orders. There was a quiet roar that lay under the dinner conversation, but despite all that, Gabriel dropped his voice. "Some nights she will not follow dining room dress code." That stopped Emmanuel's jittering. "Despite this, you will not make her feel judged at any moment during your time with her."

Emmanuel licked his lips. "Yes...sir. Of course, I wouldn't make her feel uncomfortable."

Gabriel paused. He'd gone too far. Luxury Lines staff would never cross that line. He pressed his lips into a thin line and nodded.

Emmanuel's gaze flicked beyond Gabriel's shoulder.

"Why, Gabe. How wonderful to run into you again." Jesse's voice caressed his spine.

The smile spreading across his face did not have to be fastened on. This one was as natural to him as the nudist's daily wear he hoped was covered by now.

"Miss Dav—" He turned, and the words dried out in his mouth. Jesse was a sexy pixie, covered in glitter and a black dress that hugged Every. Single. Inch.

His heart rolled behind his ribs, and the ten years that used to separate them, back when he was nineteen and she was nine, they no longer mattered.

It was surprise, that was all. Surprise at seeing her with makeup on, in a form-fitting dress. Surprise at all those tight, tight, tight curves. Surprise at seeing her again, as a woman, instead of the little girl that had wedged herself into his memories.

"Gabe? We'd like to sit down now." Jesse's voice dripped in pleasure and confidence.

"Yes, here you go." He pulled out her chair. She turned her back to him, and his words burrowed even deeper. Silky skin covered the soft ridges of her spine. How deep did that *V* cut into the back of her dress go? A single diamond pendant rested against her skin, as if she needed the bait. *Remember who she is, Che. You've known her since she was nine. Off limits in every possible way.*

He turned and wheeled her mother to the table. "Do you lovely ladies need anything else this evening?" Gabriel grasped for some of the professionalism he'd lost and regathered the comfortable barrier around his body.

"Some of that bubbly you brought us earlier would be just fine. On the house, please." Mrs. David snapped her fingers.

"Momma!" A slight flush in Jesse's cheeks softened her look, making her seem like a lost virgin in a fairytale. Jesse hadn't told him much about her mother over the years, but he'd picked up that they weren't close. So what were they doing together now, on this ship, so close to that horrid anniversary? Mrs. David's earlier words haunted him. *We're celebrating a wedding anniversary. I know you.* Had Mr. David died on their wedding anniversary? Even worse, did she remember him? Sweat broke out under his arms and around the neck band of his uniform.

Not for the first time, he wished he could go back to that day. To stop worrying about the ship's schedule and instead convince his superiors, somehow, to stay another few hours. To make sure.

Gabriel placed his hand on the back of Jesse's chair. "It'd be my pleasure." He turned to Emmanuel and whispered the order, then took his leave. Before he could make an even bigger fool of himself in front of the staff...and Jesse.

He played dodge-the-guest out of the dining room and walked into the now empty waiting area just outside the frosted glass doors. He took a deep breath, but even that wasn't enough to dispel the lingering effects of that dress. Or Jesse. A walk on the deck with the spray of the sea and the cold, pre-Caribbean air was just what he needed. It had the added benefit of delaying his next task.

Cabin 2410. The ship's newest nudist colony.

Gabriel walked through the sliding deck doors. The deck was empty. The rain had chased everyone else indoors. The slick wooden slats with their beaded raindrops, the sway of the ship, the crash of the waves, the flash of the storm. It wasn't Paradise, but at the moment, it was the heaven he needed. The change in temperature was enough to steal the breath out of his lungs for a few seconds, reminding his body that the Garden of Eden was very present. The forbidden fruit had been left lying innocently all over this ship as if God himself had reached down and shaken the tree. But it *was* forbidden. No matter how bite-able the fruit look—

This wasn't helping.

He stopped and leaned over the deck rails. Not that far below, water crashed against the side of the ship, flirting and frothing.

Gabriel needed shore leave. Soon. Maybe he could put in for an extra week. It'd be a cut in pay, but that was preferable to losing his job, and possibly Jesse, because he allowed his second mate to captain the S.S. Gabriel for a minute...or all night long.

He sucked down some salty sea air and let the salt cleanse his soul, refocus his purpose. Then he stood straight, adjusted his uniform, and brushed the sea spray off his shoulders. At the other end of the ship, as far from the main dining hall as he could manage on the open seas, he walked through the sliding glass doors.

5

GABRIEL

Cabin 2410 stood in front of Gabriel, the deep, mahogany stain of the wood as imposing as a castle gate. He closed his eyes and knocked once. Hard and loud, with a quick prayer that Laurence had delivered that robe.

The door clicked and slowly opened. The lights were off, and except for a pair of naked, pasty feet in the small triangle of light from the open door, Gabriel couldn't see anything. The guest sniffled.

"Good evening, sir. I'm Gabriel Gutierrez, the cruise staff captain." There was a waver to his voice that was anything but confident.

"Have you found my dog?" The dark shadow sniffed again, the voice high and nasally.

"We are doing everything we can."

The dark wailed, and the pasty feet turned and hurried back into the cabin. The door slammed shut against Gabriel's big toe. He bit his tongue to stop the *damn* from tumbling out and moved his foot out of the way. The door clicked shut.

His jaw moved from side to side, teeth grinding against indecision. *Stay or go?* This was the most important part of his job. Reading the situation and beating the odds of being wrong.

If he stayed, he'd have to comfort and console.

If he left, he could pass this off to Laurence.

Be your best man.

He stopped grinding his teeth and clenched down. He rechecked his phone to remind himself of this guest's details, clicking into Luxury Lines's secure app that allowed him access to every guest's and staff member's personal details. Evan Reese, Luxury Lines's one and only nudist.

Gabriel raised his hand to knock again.

"Staff Captain Gutierrez?" A feminine voice, soft and accented with a slight French lilt, startled him, making his back flinch.

He turned around. Luxury Lines's newest Chief Security Officer, Delice Andre, stood in front of him, about chest high. But what she lacked in height, she made up for in gumption and an impressive military and detective career. That is, if he didn't count her being fired from said detective career.

"CSO Andre, I didn't expect to see you here. How is your first day going?"

Her dark hair was pulled back into an army-approved bun and her new, navy blue uniform was a striking contrast against her dark skin. She flashed a smile, one full of new-job hope. "Everyone's been very helpful. All was running smoothly until I got the report about Mr. Reese's lost service dog. I'm here to take his statement." She indicated her notepad, fresh out of the plastic wrap.

"Very good. We can do this together then." Gabriel raised his fist to knock again, paused, and lowered his voice. "You're aware of this guest's special situation?"

"Seizures?"

His lips thinned. "Yes, but also...he's a nudist." He gave her a split-second to absorb the new information. Nothing like a nudist to haze a new senior officer. "Prepare yourself." *Knock, knock.*

When the door opened this time, the cabin was flooded in light.

Mr. Reese stood in the small entryway, barely wrapped in a fresh Luxury Lines robe. The sash sagged threateningly in the middle of the guest's generous belly. Little curls of springy black hair poked out of the wide opening of the loosely closed fabric.

Gabriel dragged his gaze away from the biggest threat in the room and focused on the guest's face. Snot glistened just under his nose. His double chin trembled, and tears collected at the corners of his eyes. A midnight-black toupee, reminiscent of an elder Elvis Presley, leaned precariously on his forehead. Something about that Gabriel couldn't reconcile. A nudist wearing fake hair.

Gabriel blinked and stepped back into his cruise director's role, hoping the guest didn't pick up on his split-second perusal.

"Mr. Reese, this is CSO Andre. She's our head of security and would like to take your statement."

He nodded, wiped at his nose, and stepped aside, letting Gabriel and Delice inside the cabin. Dog toys were strewn about the room, along with other personal effects. No clothes. Behind Mr. Reese, lightning flashed through the porthole window. Water splashed against the side of deck two and splattered the glass, fragmenting the flash of the storm. The seas would be rough tonight.

"I'm sure this is difficult," Delice began, with just the right touch of compassion and efficiency. "But can you please recount your activities since boarding? Perhaps that will give us a clue about where your dog may have gone."

"Jelly." Mr. Reese wiped at his nose with the sleeve of the robe. The action tugged at the rope, loosening it even further.

"Jelly?" Gabriel repeated to make sure he had heard correctly. He and Delice exchanged a look.

"My poor little Jelly." Tears spilled over and tracked down the guest's cheeks.

"Is Jelly the dog?" Delice asked.

Mr. Reese nodded. Then something in his expression changed. Gabriel had seen it before. The tightening of muscle, the hardening of eyes, the thinning of lips. Most of the time, from parents who flipped from worry over their lost child to extremely pissed off. It was the winch tightening to catapult a cannonball of blame.

He braced himself.

"If you do not find my baby, I will sue this line for *everything* it's worth. I will have your job!" Mr. Reese jabbed his finger, not at Gabriel, but at Delice, and his voice cracked from the effort.

Something kicked, low in Gabriel's stomach. *That's new.* He was used to being assumed as the authority in the room, not ignored.

Mr. Reese's hard façade wobbled. He sank to the small couch and rubbed his face with his hands.

Delice's expression shifted into dealt-with-this-before. Gabriel's muscles unwound a bit. *It's nice, for once, to share this burden with someone else.* But the beating going on at the bottom of his stomach got in a few more hard kicks.

"I am very sorry, Mr. Reese," she said. "We are doing every-thing we can to find your—to find Jelly. Do you have any pictures? We can print it in the ship's newsletter, the Mainstay."

"Gave it to the steward." He covered his mouth and slowly shook his head from side to side.

Gabriel shot a look at Delice. Laurence hadn't mentioned a picture. From the look on her face, she hadn't seen it either.

"Good. We will have it printed in the daily Mainstay until Jelly is found. She—"

"He."

"Excuse me, he cannot have gone far. More than likely some child found him and is entertaining him in their cabin." Delice offered up the only explanation that could possibly offer Mr. Reese comfort.

Mr. Reese nodded, sniffled again. "Yes, yes. He is so friendly, he would probably do that," he said.

Gabriel's gaze fell on a dog blanket on the bed, next to Mr. Reese's pillow. The blanket was curled up, as if the dog had made his nest just before disappearing. Gabriel took a deep breath, weighing the best way to handle the next item to be discussed. This situation had potential medical and legal implications. "Now, Mr. Reese, I realize Jelly is your service dog."

"Yes, I have seizures." Mr. Reese gestured at the vanity, the counter stuffed full of medications.

"Is there anything you medically require in Jelly's absence?" Gabriel measured every word, crafting each to minimize risk. If he said the wrong thing, the cruise line could be held liable. Which meant he could lose his job. Which meant his little sister would lose the money he sent home every month. She depended on him. His mistakes as a teenager had cost her not only *Papá*, but *Papá's* income.

Mr. Reese took a second, thinking, then shook his head. "Jelly lets me know when I'm about to have a seizure. He's my ten-minute warning to get help. Nothing can replace him."

"I see." Gabriel's jaw slid side to side. The implications of the dog being lost were severe. He rolled words around his mouth, trying to find the one that would hold him and the cruise line least responsible. "If you don't mind, I will have your steward check on you frequently throughout your stay with us. At least until we can find Jelly."

Mr. Reese's forehead relaxed, and his shoulders lowered a fraction. "Thank you. I appreciate it." He turned to Delice. "And I'm sorry I—"

"Nothing to apologize for, Mr. Reese." Delice held up her hand. "We'll take care of you, and we will find Jelly."

Gabriel tried not to cringe. Promises should never be made to guests unless there was full certainty that they could be kept. He should know—he'd lived with the regret of his broken promise for twenty years.

Mr. Reese wiped away the rest of his tears with his sleeve and stood.

It was the last straw for the robe.

The plush cotton fell open, seemingly a stitch at a time. The gape of the V-neck widened, like a quake that had split apart the earth, one expensive-thread-count side from the other. The cotton fluttered to either side of Mr. Reese, revealing stretched skin over layers of hardened fat.

Delice made a choking sound.

Gabriel tried to stop looking, but it was worse than a train wreck. His gaze traveled lower, reaching images he could never unsee. He ripped his gaze away, but it was too late. The image had been seared into his retinas, his memory.

What was worse was Mr. Reese either had not realized or did not care he was on display.

Gabriel focused on Mr. Reese's face and backed toward the door, Delice on his toes. Mr. Reese gave her a quick accounting of where he'd been with Jelly, his unmention-ables jiggling from side to side as a consequence of his repeated hand gestures.

Gabriel didn't process a word. He hoped Delice had.

"Thank you, Mr. Reese." Gabriel fumbled for the doorknob at his back. "We will cock-er-check all those areas. I'll have Laurence stop by in a little while to see if you need anything." He swung open the door, and they escaped into the hallway.

"I'm hoping that's not normal for this job." Delice's voice was a little higher than it had been before. It put Gabriel on notice. As CSO, she must be prepared for any situation, at any time. There was no room for a learning curve in her position.

His past CSO had been content to sit back and watch every-thing from Control's monitors. Seemed this one would be more hands-on, and he wasn't sure how he felt about that.

He rubbed between his eyes and adjusted his jacket. "Welcome to Luxury Lines, Ms. Andre." He started down the long corridor of staterooms, leaving her to collect herself. At the other end, a steward stood with crossed arms and a crooked smile on his face. It could only be Laurence. Gabriel gestured, and as the steward joined him near the stairs, he subtly checked the man's name tag to confirm.

"Did Mr. Reese give you a picture of his dog?"

Laurence's face crinkled, and he shook his head.

Gabriel rubbed at the sore spot between his eyes. "He thinks he did. Can you check with him again? Get another copy if possible."

Laurence saluted and hurried off, but Gabriel wasn't sure if the gesture was sarcastic or respectful.

He was thankful Jesse was on board this sailing, because he could already tell she'd be his one bright spot to look forward to each day. It was going to be one of *those* sailings—cursed from the start.

Gabriel checked in with two of the bars to make sure the bartenders had all they needed, now that the ship had moved into international waters. The Promenade was sparse at this time of night. Half the guests were dining, and the other half had retired, were enjoying a show, or had found their haunt for the evening.

The ship's background music was playing pop holiday songs. Garland hung from every balcony, and two giant fake trees anchored each end of the Promenade. Christmas was three weeks away, but the ship had been decorated in tinsel since Thanksgiving.

He headed toward the middle of the Promenade, where *cha-chings* and electronic celebrations filtered up a winding glass staircase from the casino. The stairs were lit with a changing purple, blue, and hazy green strobe light. The casino was one of two places smoking was allowed on board, and an invisible cloud of lung-destroying smoke snaked up the otherwise pristine glass steps. Gabriel took one more deep drag of clean air and descended into the casino.

She was sitting at the bar, her ankles crossed so that her back curved just enough to cause a little gap in the side of her dress. The diamond pendant had fallen to the left of her spine and it swayed slightly, in time to her breaths or the ship's, and Gabriel couldn't give a damn which. The diamond sparkled in the changing light, catching a purple glow, then blue, then green. By the time the light had changed back to purple, Gabriel was leaning on the polished glass of the bar next to Jesse, the gold buttons of his cuffs clinking against the counter. That damned jewel on its bed of soft, soft skin would be his undoing.

"Good evening, Mr. Staff Captain." She trailed a polished nail around the rim of her drink. Whiskey on ice. Concern rushed through a chink in his armor, like a draft of warm, welcoming air. That was her usual day-two by-the-pool drink.

"Evening, Jesse." The bartender flicked his gaze at Gabriel, at his casual use of her name. He rolled his shoulders back, the restrictions around his job feeling extra tight. Gabriel's heart thudded sporadically. He had to be ever so careful in public with her. If their close acquaintance was reported, his career would walk the plank, his dreams to be captain would be thrown overboard, his sister's main source of income would dry up.

He'd always taken care of Jesse on board, but not more than any other elite guest. He checked on her, made sure her wait staff cared for her to the best of their ability, sent fresh eggs to her room each morning, handpicked her flowers...all things he needed to do to make sure her time with Luxury Lines was unmatched. Okay, so maybe he did a little more for Jesse than any other guest. But not enough so that his special interest was noticed.

Not even by her.

Most of their relationship existed in text messages, emails, interviews for her articles, innocent flirting in chance encounters, and that one time he'd almost kissed her. But he hadn't. Safer to have that barrier.

So what the hell was he doing?

The secrets he'd kept from her over the years—when it became apparent she didn't remember he was there on *that* day—he couldn't tell her *now*.

Gabriel dragged his focus from his hands and glanced around the casino, looking for any call of duty, any excuse to leave. Passengers pulled on the slot machines, the electronic *chinks* of invisible money threading through the smoke. An intense round of Black Jack had collected a crowd. But no excuses presented themselves. He pulled his hands into fists to keep them from straying and caught Jesse watching him.

"I trust your dinner was enjoyable?"

No, not watching. What she was doing was too seductive to be called watching.

"Dinner? The food was very enjoyable." That fragile finger traced the circle of the glass, around and around. Blood rushed from his head to...lower. "Momma, on the other hand"—she shrugged, and her gaze wandered—"I miss traveling alone." She took another sip and caught a piece of ice between her teeth. Her lips wavered around the ice cube, a shiny balm as red as a fiery sunset.

"You do?" Gabriel thanked God once again for the ability to have his mind be completely focused on one thing—like a pair of crushable lips—and still be able to function in his role as staff captain. He blinked to break the imaginary thread between his body and her luscious— "Most people love company on vacation."

"Oh, this isn't a vacation." She clinked her ice cubes around her glass and took a large swallow, leaving a perfect lip print on the glass when she sat it back down on the bar with a loud *clink*.

That draft of concern widened into a strong breeze. "I take it your mother isn't an easy travel companion?"

She took out her lip balm and rolled it around her lips. "Understatement of the millennium. Momma gets what Momma wants." The last sentence was muttered, and her naked shoulders flinched in, like something had surprised her. She shook her head and straightened on the bar stool. "So tell me, Gabe. What's there to do tonight that can entertain a girl?" She looked him up and down in a quick bat of her long lashes. *Ave Maria*, was she asking what he wished she was asking?

Gabriel's body tensed, and he ran back to his comfort zone, wrapping Cruise around one shoulder, Staff around the other, and tying the invisible cape with the frayed ends of Captain. He pulled out his phone and scrolled through the list of the evening's activities, even though he had them all memorized. Gave his traitor hands something to do. His mind? Lost cause.

"Well, you have the casino. You could make the welcome show if you hurry." He ticked them off, one by one, and she scrunched up her nose to each suggestion. "And, of course the nightclubs."

"Dancing?" That seductive look was back and totally, completely, irresistible.

"Yes." His voice cracked. He licked his lips and tried again. Jesse's gaze followed his tongue and stayed fastened on his mouth. "First night out, so there should be a good crowd. In fact"—Gabriel double-checked the app—"yes. Swig is having a special event that starts in twenty minutes. A silent party." *Take the bait, take the bait.*

"A silent dance party?" She gave him an are-you-screwing-me look. *Screwing with. Screwing. With.*

Gabriel mentally kicked himself. "Everyone wears head-phones and listens to the DJ individually. No talking allowed. It looks fun. Of course, I've never participated."

"You've never danced in your own ship's event? That, Mr. Staff Captain, needs to be remedied at once." She scooted her tiny rump off the vinyl bar stool and sashayed through the casino, expecting him to follow.

He couldn't, of course.

Of course, he couldn't.

He waved at the casino director, gave him the I'll-be-there-in-five signal, and hurried after the black satined distraction that could screw his world a billion times over.

6

JESSE

Gabe abandons me after playing the gentleman and walking me to the nightclub. I wish he'd stay. He's the only man I've ever felt safe around. When he's with me, I feel more real. Like I can fight Momma's crazy and come out unscathed on the other side. Like Daddy can't touch me. But even though I'm real, Gabe's mist. I can see him, hide within his protection, feel the chills he creates along my skin, but I can never hold him.

He'd never risk his position for a one-night stand. He'd definitely never risk his career for me.

His square, strong frame retreats into the cloud of smoke puffing from the casino, and I turn away from the distraction that he is, my thoughts running straight back to Momma's words, my emotions snuggling into the hurt.

You being you, a one-night stand is about the best you can hope for.

Tomorrow, I'll start my search. I'll get Gabe to let me in to all the places I can remember from that first cruise twenty years ago. I'll unlock the rusted deadbolt in my head, and then I'll find what it is Daddy wants, what he's been whispering to me from the shadows all these years. I'll stop the blackouts.

It sounds too easy. I know it won't be. But I escaped Momma's house at seventeen, I put myself through college and got my degree in three years, I forged a successful career in a business of rejection—I can do this.

My unformed plan is enough to keep me from collapsing in a hyperventilating puddle outside the nightclub. Tomorrow, my work begins.

Tonight...

A group of young, perfectly legal boys head into the night club ahead of me. A flash of my much younger self with my college boyfriend stalks my memory, and a soft breath of panic begins to curl inside my chest.

"Please." My beg pants against his ear.

He grabs my hips, dives into me. I arch my back under the pressure, driving him deeper and deeper.

My rocketing orgasm burns in the atmosphere and falls back to earth in a quick, cold descent...then...nothing. The next thing I know, it's morning, and small splatters of blood speckle the sheets and pillowcase. I'm alone.

I never saw him again.

It was the first time I had a blackout that lasted longer than a few minutes. It was also the first time I voluntarily checked myself into a mental hospital.

"Miss? Are you alright?" A young, accented voice snaps me to the present. The nightclub's bouncer stands behind a podium, a little light like an angler fish hanging over the wood. "Would you like to come in?" He gestures to the swinging doors of Swig, complete with a martini glass taller than me etched into the window.

Would I like to go in?

At the very least, it'd be another distraction. My therapist would call this *avoidance*.

It sure as hell is.

The glass door sways to the motion of the boat. A handprint smear on the window catches the light, and for a moment, I believe a ghost has stepped into the club ahead of me, leaving the stain of its past for all to see.

I blink a few times, rein in my imagination, and nod.

"Yes, thank you. I *would* like to go in." I twirl my flapper-styled purse around my finger, swishing away my ghosts, and saunter past the bouncer into the too-quiet nightclub.

A dark, narrow hallway empties into a square loft that over-looks the dance floor. The ship bobs under my heels. A couple of already-had-too-much barflies stumble around the carpeted floor. A crew member weaves in between clumps of people, passing out headphones from a tray as if they are cocktails at a gala. I grab one from the waiting tray, hook it over my arm, and head to the bar until the festivities begin.

"Jameson on the rocks," I order.

"I got this." A deep, male voice rumbles at my side.

I turn around, rest my elbows on the bar, and take a good look at my whiskey supplier while we wait.

Handsome.

That's the first word that enters my brain.

The second is not-my-type.

He's too confident. *Too* handsome. The last thing I want is a guy who thinks he's prettier than me.

Strong bones, strong muscles, strong gaze. Dark hair with a sexy, manicured scruff. If I hadn't already lost my play money at the casino earlier, I'd bet it all that his facial hair isn't the only part of him manicured.

Chiseled. That's the third word that flits across my brain.

If I were younger, I'd do what it took to be wrapped up in those powerful arms. If I didn't know what I wanted, I'd take my time on those full lips, nibbling and sucking. If I didn't know how disruptive my blackouts could be, I'd tangle myself in those long legs.

If...

I need a man I can get away from. A man who won't over-power me. Who can't. I'd rather a man I trust, who understands me and loves me in spite, or ideally because, of who I am. I'd rather Gabe.

But as Momma always tells me, *keep dreaming, Jesse-girl.*

Keep dreaming.

The bartender slides over our drinks. Behind him, the bottles of liquor are back lit by changing colors of red, green, and purple. Overhead, pinpricks of light designed to look like stars shine down on us, illuminating the otherwise dark room.

"I'm Dan." Mr. Too Perfect grins a Colgate smile and passes my drink.

"Of course you are," I mutter and take a sip. "Thanks for the drink." I raise my glass in a toast and sidle away. It's rude but can't be helped. I didn't ask him to buy my drink, and it'd be worse to lead him on. Worse for him. Definitely worse for me.

I take a large swallow of the whiskey, and the peppery comfort slides down my throat. The boat dips under the influence of a particularly large swell, and little gasps and surprised laughter pop around the waiting dance crowd as they lose their footing and collide into one another.

Not me.

I ride the swell and walk down the stairs to the dance floor. The DJ announces the start of the silent party. I drain the rest of my whiskey and set the glass on a nearby table. Clusters of friends and glittery girlfriends move toward the dance floor, situating their headphones around their ears as they go, and in between them, is Daddy.

He's a ghost, wisping through the undulating crowd. He's whole. Skin not in tatters and an intact smile—a welcome change from my nightmares.

I bite my lip, and Daddy disappears into the shadows, chaperoning me even in death. A strobe light flashes, and the dance floor exists only in brief, sporadic seconds. Bodies pulse to the silent music, the beat an obscure force that seems to move from hip to hip, commanding all my focus, all my attention, forcing me to forget about Momma and the lost secrets of the past.

Is this how the deaf experience music? As an unfeeling observer who can only watch as the tide of desire, drawn by the current of impossible-to-reach music, washes over everyone. I remain apart for a little while longer, detached. But I need to connect, to be a part of the crash of undulating hips.

I unhook my headphones from the crook of my arm, pull them over my ears, and join the sea of writhing bodies. Because I'm not deaf. And I'm certainly not unfeeling.

The music pulses through my ears, and the whiskey heats my blood. I don't care about the lyrics, just the beat. It's a heartbeat, hot and rushing, each *boom boom* answered by some primal instinct that must respond, must move, must seduce.

The rhythm snakes through my body, thrusting my hips from side to side. I raise my arms and become a black flame, flickering in the dance crowd's fire, hypnotized by the thud of the drum. A warm hand traces my spine and wraps around my hip. Gabe? I freeze for one flicker of the strobe light before reality dropkicks my heart. Mr. Staff Captain would never be so inappropriate. I turn around and meet my partner.

He has that messy, boyish look and green eyes that sparkle with lust. Tousled brown hair falls into his eyes. Not too handsome, not too strong. Close to my age, late-twenties, give or take a few years. He circles me with his arms and pulls me in, feeding my fire, and picks up one side of my headphones.

"Dance with me," he commands into my ear, his deep voice tickling sensitive places, before dropping the headphones back into place.

I let my body answer, moving closer to him, letting the beat direct us, guide us, drive us. His hips meet mine, and we slide against each other in perfect rhythm. His fingers play with the edge of my dress, sneaking underneath at the places where the curve of my hips make the satin gape open. He works his knee between my legs, and I let him. My body moves against his, with no other thought than to obey the beat. That's all the beat wants. Obedience.

We stay together through the next song. His fingers trail my spine, and he locks his gaze with mine.

He wants me.

I can have him.

If I want more.

I break our gaze, because that *if* tightens my gut and constricts my lungs. Breath shortens in my chest, not from the dance, but the *if*.

I turn and slither up and down his body. He wraps his fingers in mine, and we move into a more intimate dance. His breath warms the skin on my neck, prickling my flesh as he dips his mouth nearer to my skin. He brings our connected hands in front of my body and uses my own fingers to press my hips against him.

My stomach dips, and I lose my rhythm. I'm not ready for more.

I move away, break our linked hands, and face him. To say goodbye. But he doesn't let me go.

The thick crowd of dancers pushes against us. A girl in a short dress draped in silver threads salsas with a beefy male, crew members planted to make sure all guests are having fun.

I put distance between me and my partner, but he pulls me closer. His hands are flat against my bare back, and they catch the diamond pendant hitting my spine. It pulls at my throat, choking me, too close to a pair of hands, strangling me.

I've never been strangled, not that I can remember, but my memory's not to be trusted, and the grip is too familiar, too close to a pain my brain won't address. It signals red lights and sirens, screaming at me to *get away*. I jerk out of his grasp, and before he can respond, I'm pushing through the crowd, bumping into the salsa-couple, leaving my partner alone and confused on the dance floor.

Sweat slicks my skin. My lungs shrink. I dart to the back of an alcove and brace against the wall, the ship's slow up-and-down sway a lullaby for my nerves. I pull the headphones off my ears, silencing the music, focus on one spot on the wall, force my breaths in, out. I go through my muscle relaxation, tightening my hands and releasing the tension, repeating the movement with my arms, my thighs.

The dance floor shutters closed, open, and everything calms. My skin feels too small, my bones too fragile, but I'm back in control. I shove my baggage into a reserved corner of my brain, press my hands against my chest. *You're okay, Jesse. You're okay. Now, focus.*

My dance partner has made his way to the edge of the dance floor. Confusion thins his mouth.

I flag the bartender down as I yank my lip balm out of my purse and roll it around my lips.

"Two whiskeys please, on the rocks." I catch my dance partner's gaze while the bartender makes our drinks. He darts his eyes, embarrassment coloring his cheeks. I wear an apologetic smile on my face and reel him in again, raising the drink I ordered him. I nod my head to the left, where a bench seat awaits, partially enclosed by a dark velvet curtain.

He stares for a few seconds before a smile spreads across his face, and he heads my direction.

I channel my assertive side, throw a swagger into my hips. I'm all too aware that I'm grasping at ice-slick confidence, but at this point, I'll take what I can get. *God, I wish I wasn't wearing this dress.* Ideally, if I'm going to be with someone, I want to be *me*, not this costumed version of who I am.

"Thought you abandoned me." He slides onto the cushioned bench seat next to me and rests his arms on the black marble table.

"Sorry about that. Needed a break." I slide one of the whiskeys over to him. "And a drink."

He eyes the liquid like he isn't sure what to do with it.

"You *are* legal to drink?" I say it sarcastically, like I don't really care, but I do.

His gaze flicks to mine, and he leans in, his lips dangerously close to my neck. My skin shivers in expectation. He doesn't disappoint.

His teeth graze my neck, and he ends on a kiss just below my ear. "I'm legal," he growls. "Just wanted to make sure you didn't slip something in it."

Cool. Role reversal.

"I'm Michael." He slips his hand into mine.

"Jesse." I stroke my thumb across his knuckles, fidget in my high-heeled toe pinchers, and feel like I'm wearing a glittery lie.

His lips move to my jaw.

And the lie ceases to matter.

7

GABRIEL

Gabriel left Captain Knight's quarters at too-close-to-midnight, their ritual first-day toast done. One finger of whiskey poured over the side of the ship to say goodbye to passengers past, and one finger drunk in salute to the new sailing, a fresh start. With that, the slate was wiped clean and no matter the grievances of the last week, this week held nothing but potential.

Crew weren't allowed in elevators on Luxury Lines, so he took the stairs to the Promenade level where he could cut across the ship to his room. It was quiet this time of night. They were a small, upscale line with an older crowd. Not a lot of late-night revelers to manage, which he should be grateful for. But lately, it had started to wear, as if the years of retirees were rubbing off like tarnish on a polishing cloth. At thirty-nine years old, he felt like he'd already lived every new experience life had to offer and he was just waiting for the end.

He stepped off the stairs onto the soft carpet of the Promenade and hesitated. He could turn left, go to his quarters and stick to his responsible routine, or...

Swig was rocking, a deep bass boom vibrating the walls, the silent dance party having given way to a midnight rave for the under-thirty crowd. Was Jesse still there? Not that he could do anything other than observe, but he could be there, on the edge of living. He could talk with her, be around her, watch that shy smile light up the room. He could, for a little while, pretend this job hadn't ceased to be a career and had instead become a life sentence.

He turned toward the club.

A drunk couple laughed and stumbled around the corner.

Gabriel kept his head down, giving them privacy, but that laugh...

He jerked his head up and slammed right into Jesse's glazed smile. Some guy was wrapped around her, nibbling her neck. Jesse's back was stiff, her jaw set in a stubborn square. Did she want this?

A brief flash of anger tore through Gabriel's bones. He wanted to be that guy. He wanted her in his arms, his mouth on her neck, devouring her.

Jesse's expression flickered from seductress to something else as she met his gaze. He wished that what he saw in her eyes was regret that the other guy wasn't himself. But it was clear she had given consent.

Cold crept through his chest, as if his heart had finally given up on him. Gabe couldn't blame her. He'd broadcasted loud and clear that there was an impassable gap between them, one that his career wouldn't allow him to cross. But *che*, he'd wanted to.

He stepped to the side to let them pass, gave her a slight bow, and tried to keep the pain off his face as Jesse and her guy stepped outside, the sliding doors letting in a strong breeze and a blast of cold.

He watched them walk away until he couldn't see them anymore, until the reflection of the glass doors showed only him, standing alone in the hallway, the brass buttons of his uniform gleaming.

Almost forty years old, and he'd never fallen in love, never had a relationship that lasted longer than a couple of months. He'd sacrificed everything for this cruise line and for what? Money? The promise of an eventual promotion he only wanted for its coffee machine privileges? His sister depended on his income, but there were other ways to make money. Other cruise lines, other jobs where he could put his skills to work, other places that weren't slowly killing him, week after week after week.

The drive he'd once had to be the best...he'd lost it somewhere along the way and now he was adrift in the sea, battered by the waves.

Did he have to lose Jesse too?

Gabriel tightened his hands into fists and turned away from the club. He walked back to his stateroom, unlocked the door, and shut the sounds of the ship behind him, the silence his only companion.

Was this his life? Was this all there was?

He hung up his uniform, climbed into bed, and attempted to breathe through the weight of a life unlived.

Ten minutes later, his phone beeped with a passenger incident signal.

8

JESSE

Lightning flashes in the distance outside the glass doors. The look Gabe gave me as we passed was anything but professional. *What if I'm wrong?* I shake away the thought. Gabe's on a playing field to which I have no ticket.

The doors slide open, and a blast of winter Caribbean air hits us. The wind yanks at our clothes, the ship dips, and a gust of frigid rain whips around us. Michael moves so that he's standing behind me, arms wrapped around my waist, doing his best to cover all my exposed parts.

We do an awkward crab walk down the deck, passing by windows with warm lights and drinking couples, before turning the bend at the back of the boat. The wind dies to nothing, blocked by the bulk of the cruise liner. Back here, there are no windows, just the white-painted skeleton of the ship laid bare. The boat dips low into the water, and the ocean seems to rise up, foaming at the mouth.

I've been here before. Daddy picked me up so I could see over the rails better, and we watched the Texas coastline float away. We laughed at the dolphins chasing the boat, and Daddy whispered in my ear a tale of mermaids, his hand wrapped around my leg, holding me close so I didn't fall over.

Nausea coils in my gut, and I have to push it down, pretend everything is normal as Michael locks his arms around me, as Daddy's ghost tickles the soft hairs of my ear, whispering that story again, singing the song he made up, just for me. I can't remember the ending. Just the beginning. Always the beginning. If I could get to the end of the song, I'd remember everything, I know it. *Down, down deep in the big ocean blue, swims two little fishies, a me and a you.*

"So, Jesse, where are you from?" Michael tries, interrupting Daddy as he leans back against the rain-splattered railing. He shouldn't do that. Daddy doesn't like being interrupted.

I turn in Michael's arms to face him, and my bare back chills in his absence. "Don't."

"Don't what?" He's full of that boyish innocence, not yet stained with the dirty business of living.

"That's not what we're doing." I struggle to separate him from Daddy. Michael's real. Daddy's dead. Ghosts can't hurt me.

"And what's that?" His lips tilt into something between a smile and a grimace.

"Getting to know each other. Let's just"—I cringe, because what comes next can't be helped—"enjoy the moment." So. Cliché.

He gauges my expression, making sure I'm not lying. "You're not like—"

I cup my hand over his mouth, careful to avoid touching his lips, stopping the next unavoidable cliché. "You're not even scratching the skin of how much I am not like most girls." I add a coy smile, so he doesn't pick up on my seriousness. Behind him, Daddy smiles through the rain, watery and broken, not quite whole.

Michael moves my hand and tries to kiss me, and my stomach revolts. Lips. I don't kiss lips. I turn my head and run my hands under his shirt, up his smooth, lean abs. Teeth graze my jaw, my throat, nibble along the cords of my neck. His hand reaches for the thigh-high slit of my dress as he lifts me up to my tiptoes and pulls me roughly against him, fingers tracing the line of my silk panties and I'm held hostage. Over his shoulder, the black, bottomless ocean's broken teeth reach up to eat us. To devour our faces. The very thing that makes us recognizable from one to the other.

Michael tilts my chin up, his lips teasing my jaw, my cheek, the corner of my mouth, but I can't tear my eyes from the ocean. His mouth moves to mine, and there's a quick explosion of *does not belong* as he forces his tongue inside.

I struggle against him.

He won't stop, and then he's saying something, screaming something, and I can't stop.

The ocean and the flesh-eating fish and Daddy's white, decomposed face, teeth and gums exposed beneath his sucked away lips take over my world. But something else, a long-forgotten memory, swims to the surface.

The sun hit Daddy's legs that first morning on the cruise ship, the light dappling his bare calves and turning him golden. I spied on Momma and Daddy while they were sleeping for an hour that morning, memorizing their twin masks of innocence and peace and safety. On vacation, I was safe.

The memory changes. Terror wells up inside and bubbles surround my face, lifts my hair as if I've jumped into the water, and I'm swimming, swimming, faster, faster or he'll catch me. Don't stop. Don't let him catch me.

And down down deep, the little fishies swim, the little fishies swim, all the little fishies swim...

I'm flung across the deck. My tailbone hits the hard wood. I slide. Bang against the metal wall.

My heart rams against my chest, as if I've been swimming for my life, adrenaline crashing through my blood. I want to yell, I want to scream, I want to cry.

My vision clears, and awareness falls on me like a storm. Michael's hand covers his mouth, and he's yelling something. Something like "psycho bitch," but my hearing hasn't quite caught up with what I'm seeing. I hear myself apologizing, but I don't know what I did.

And then I do.

Blood splatters his shirt, hits the deck, and a sickness slithers through my veins, cold and scaly. He moves his hand to yell some more. His lip is massacred. Chewed and bleeding, a shred of his lower lip lays against his chin like a tiny pink caterpillar.

Footsteps pound the deck, rush to where we are. My stomach takes a dive, but something else rushes through me. Something twisted I immediately hate. I want to tear it from my body, rip it out from the roots, and at the same time, I want to hold on to it tight. A small spark falls down down deep and when it lands, something like thrill and pleasure and coming home chomps through me.

Two crew members round the corner, take in the scene, and restrain Michael. They radio for the CSO to join them on deck.

More crew members join them, start asking questions. I let them think their words don't make sense. Michael is to blame. This was self-defense.

I let them think I'm shaking from shock.

The spark flickers. The bright taste of blood coats my tongue.

For the first time, I have a piece of the puzzle.

For the first time, Daddy leaves me alone.

DAY TWO

"Swim," you say,
So I flip my fin,
And another little fishie,
Jumps right in.

9

GABRIEL

Gabriel's uniform was half unbuttoned, and cold wind rushed through every opening. The ship rocked, the waves reached a dangerous swell, and lightning flashed on the horizon. They were sailing into a storm, one the captain had warned him about, one they couldn't avoid.

The scene before him felt unreal, like he'd walked onto the set of a horror movie. A spray of blood splatter fanned across the deck, beading up against the water-resistant wax. A medic leaned over the guy he'd seen Jesse with earlier, and Jesse...she leaned against the side of the ship, her dress torn, her chin and neck covered in blood, and a dazed, not-quite-here look coating her face. He'd seen this look on her face only one time before.

This was what Jesse looked like when her world had been ripped apart.

A low, dark emotion rolled behind his chest's walls, and he fought with himself. He fought to run to her, to scoop her up in his arms, to take her to his room to keep her safe, keep her hidden. He fought to maintain composure, to stay within the boundaries of his job.

He fought the urge to kill for her.

It'd be easy, too easy, to walk calmly across the deck, pick that *pendejo* up, and fling him overboard.

Gabriel had a lot of regrets.

Unlike his *Papá's* death, this murder would not be one of them.

"What happened?" His voice surprised him, cold and calm, a taut string of control that, if tested, would snap.

The two crew who had been the first to arrive straightened, keeping a firm grip on the guy struggling in their arms.

"That bitch attacked me." The guy slurred, sputtering and spitting blood, his voice shaking, his muscles straining. If they let him go, he'd fly at Jesse.

And then Gabriel would have to kill him. Cause and effect. There would be no choice, no decision made. It was ice in the face of fire, the mountain against the century wind. Inevitable destruction.

Gabriel flexed his fists, trying to keep it under control. "Sir, I must ask you to restrain yourself."

"But she—"

"Please." Gabriel's voice didn't lift, didn't rise in anger. It deepened, it dove, it bored down and tunneled through rock, eating away at the very foundation of this guy's self-righteous act, leaving a shell. A fragile shell Gabriel would pummel into dust. With pleasure.

He flicked his gaze to the nearest crew member.

"We were making the rounds and heard screaming. We ran over here, and Mr. Hart was standing over Miss David." The crew member sucked on the inside of his cheek.

Luxury Lines crew were trained from day one to never, never cross guests. The guest was always right. Rarely did crew have to go against their training. Gabriel understood his hesitation in the most clinical sense.

Every other sense wanted to throttle him for not immediately jumping to Jesse's defense.

"Standing over her how?" That thin line of control stretched through his voice again, weakening.

The other crew member answered. "Like he was about to attack Miss David."

"*She* attacked *me*," Mr. Hart roared.

Gabriel stepped in front of him, got close enough to see the jagged edges of where his lip used to be. "I highly doubt that." The control snapped and what was left was only that dark tunneling rage.

"What is going on here?" A female voice, not Jesse's, brought him back.

He took a step away from Mr. Hart, then another, putting necessary distance between them. He looked to the newcomer.

"CSO Andre." He nodded at her, all professional courtesy once again. Delice stood at the edge of the scene, eyes wide as she took it all in. Her uniform was perfectly buttoned, not a hair out of place in the bun plastered to the top of her head. "That is exactly what I am trying to figure out."

Delice looked him over, her eyes roving up and down, then raised her eyebrow. As if she found him lacking.

Gabriel's jaw clenched so hard his back molars ached.

"Mind if we move this inside? Seas are a little rough to be doing an interrogation, don't you think?" Her tone bothered him, as if she was pulling rank.

He pressed his lips together and nodded at the crew, who dragged Mr. Hart inside the nearby crew-only access door and pushed down his darker half.

Delice looked from him to Jesse, and her complexion lost depth, as if the blood in her cheeks had been replaced by ice. Her focus narrowed, her lips tightened, and she went utterly still. Like a bunny who had caught the scent of a predator.

She blinked, and her expression returned to the professional mask he'd met earlier this evening. Something had made her face spasm, and Gabriel glanced around the deck to see what, or who, had caused his new CSO to look so disturbed.

"We'll meet you inside," he said to Delice.

She gave a sharp nod and followed the crew and Mr. Hart.

Gabriel turned to Jesse, her crumpled body breaking him in two. He should have stopped her. The moment he saw her drunk, with another man, he should have stepped in. He should have stepped in years ago.

He knelt in front of her. "Jesse?"

Her reaction was slow, barely able to meet his gaze.

"Honey, are you all right? Did he hurt you?" He grazed her arm, just barely, trying to bring her back to him.

A slow shake of her head, her gaze fixated on some spot just past his shoulder.

If Mr. Hart didn't hurt her, then why was she acting like this? Why did she bite him?

"Did he try to hurt you?" Gabriel tried again.

Jesse's gaze finally broke the distant stare and met his, her light green eyes blinking against the spray of rain. "Yes." It was a whisper, a small breath of a word, but it was enough for him.

She moved her hand and rested it on his arm. "Take me away from here. Please, make him go away." Her voice wavered around each breathless word, as if she was afraid to speak.

Gabriel jerked back. Those words...did she remember saying those words to him so long ago?

His heart thundered. Did she remember him?

It'd been twenty years, but Gabriel remembered being taken aback by those words. Make who go away? Because it couldn't be Mr. Hart.

"He's gone, *cariño*. He's gone. You're safe now." Gabriel reached out to pull her toward him, then stopped, fighting his instinct to protect her. "Is it all right if I help you stand?"

She looked at him, eyes wide as the sea, and nodded.

He wrapped his arms around her thin, bare shoulders, helped her stand, and held her close as he guided her inside, shielding her from the storm.

The metal door clanged behind them, and the high-pitched whine of the storm shut off like a mute button had been punched. Jesse stayed close to his side, and he wasn't sure if it was because she felt safe, or because she was in shock. Inside, amidst steel pipes thicker than his torso, the first responders, Delice, and Mr. Hart waited. The ship's doctor applied surgical tape to Mr. Hart's mouth until more intensive medical care could be administered.

And then there was Delice.

She was a ball of restrained electricity, bouncing on the balls of her feet.

He and Jesse stepped out of the shadows and into the light.

Delice looked from him to Jesse, and something in her expression tightened, darkened, froze. "You two want to tell me what happened?" She asked, her gaze darting from Mr. Hart to Jesse, her voice so controlled, so detached, so professional, that Gabriel was almost fooled.

Almost. But not quite.

Jesse shifted against his arm, and her movement cut through the room like a rock thrown into a pond. Mr. Hart, who had been the perfect patient, jerked away from the doctor's hands, pushed himself against the side of the ship's belly. He opened his bandaged lips to say something but clamped his hand over his mouth as if it hurt. Good. He should hurt for a long time.

The doctor set him back down and continued working on the bandage.

"I don't know what happened," Jesse said, her voice hoarse, and she touched at the bruise forming around her neck, her fingertips coming away with blood. "I've had too much to drink."

Delice bristled, her hands balled at her hips. Gabriel stepped in before she could voice her reaction. "That's okay, Miss David. Just tell us what you remember."

She looked up at him, those big green eyes bloodshot and puffy, but trusting. She spoke to him, only to him. "He wanted to go for a walk," she said, "and I remember him kissing me. I pushed away, but he didn't stop. He didn't stop."

10

GABRIEL

For twenty minutes, he'd watched Delice interrogate both Mr. Hart and Jesse. He'd stood back, hands cramping from being held in tight fists for so long, and restrained himself from stepping in to defend Jesse, protect her, save her from the CSO's clutches. From where he stood, Delice hadn't seen what the rest of them had seen. She'd seen not an assaulted woman defending herself, but a suspect. She'd seen shades of gray in a black-and-white situation. Delice hadn't been on the job long but he could already tell, she was a bulldog that needed to be leashed.

Finally, a crew member escorted Jesse to her stateroom as Gabriel followed his new CSO into the ship's main security room. The official name was Control, but the security crew had affectionately renamed the room Skynet, doing so on a colored sticky note that he was duty-bound to remove every time he saw it. Even though it made him smile, that rebellious note. If it was *his* ship, he'd allow the crew to do little things like that—have a personality.

This time of night, Skynet was empty, dark, and cramped, mostly lit by the blue glare of a few computer screens and smelled of crappy coffee and sweat-stained polyester.

"Let's take a look at that security tape," Gabriel said, wanting to write the report, get authorization to kick Michael Hart off the ship at the first port, and get to bed. Tomorrow was going to be a long day, and it was only a few hours away.

Delice leaned over a computer monitor and tapped into the ship's security footage history, finding the appropriate file. All public places were monitored to keep guests safe and crime to a minimum. Most times, the crime was petty theft or stealing alcohol from the bar. Easily dealt with.

Gabriel sucked in a breath as Jesse and Mr. Hart walked into view. They leaned against the back of the ship. Even in the grainy footage, Jesse was old Hollywood glamorous. Her skin like a diamond, competing in beauty only with the savage lightning in the background. The couple disappeared partially behind a steel beam, but Gabriel caught glimpses of Mr. Hart's hands groping inside her dress. Tracing Jesse's bare back. Playing with her necklace.

It sparked a dark flame inside him, blackening his insides with the soot of some emotion he didn't want to analyze. Jesse was *his*.

Then Mr. Hart's hand tightened around the diamond and pulled, pulled, pulled. Jesse was tossed through the air, hit the side of the ship, and slid down, the blood on her chin nothing more than a beauty spot.

Gabriel's breath caught, as if he was watching in real time. He leaned forward, fighting the urge to leap through the screen and save Jesse.

Delice clicked the stop button, and he thought maybe she was staring at him, but he couldn't drag his gaze from the screen, from imagining that *culo roto* dead. From replaying Jesse's fragile body tossed across the ship, a bloody beauty.

His thoughts whirred around being worried for her, hurting for her, and thinking that even covered in blood, she was beautiful. Somehow more beautiful. The blood was her medal, earned after winning a fight for her life.

Delice cleared her throat, grabbing his attention, and led the way to a full Mr. Coffee, her generous hips rocking back and forth like an unbalanced ship on rough water.

"There's something off about that woman," Delice said, pouring a cup of coffee and offering it to him.

He accepted and took a sip, even though Delice's words kick-started his defensive lines and the burnt roast didn't hold a matchstick to his sister's beans. His sister's roast was a taste of home. This was whatever was the opposite of that.

Delice watched him take a sip, her gaze somehow penetrating, a penlight for his secrets. She narrowed her eyes and pressed her lips together, as if she were considering him. "Let's finish up in my office." She nodded her head at the small corner office, two temporary walls bolted into the ship.

Once inside the tiny space, her door shutting them off from the one crew member in the monitor room, she turned on him. "Tell me, why are you here in the middle of the night?"

Gabriel leaned against her desk and crossed his arms, tried to keep his cool. "One of the security team informed me. Miss David is a frequent guest and an important supporter of Luxury Lines. The crew member thought it best I be involved."

Delice narrowed her eyes, and picked up a pen, fidgeting with it. "I don't care if she's the prime minister of England. What I care about is the truth, and my gut tells me Miss David isn't innocent." Her tone was way off, as if *she* was irritated with *him*. What right did she have to waltz in here on her first day and start questioning him, his authority, the way things were done around here?

"Miss David is unique, well-traveled, and a very important guest." He straightened and took a step inside Delice's personal space, backing her against a file cabinet, and breathed her in, a surprising floral scent mixed with sweat and cheap fabric. "You need to go with the facts, not your so-called gut. You should also know that Jesse David is one of the most respected travel writers in the world. To us, she's more important than the prime minister, and if you care anything about your job, you'll see her as such as well."

He'd entered that place again, where everything was cold, his emotions were frozen, and logic crunched under his feet.

"The video footage clearly shows a woman being assaulted," Gabriel went on, the muscles around his mouth drawn in tight.

Delice tapped the pen against the file cabinet, doing a sorry job of looking at ease.

Gabriel took a breath, stepped back. What was it about her that got under his skin so quickly? Surely he wasn't this power-driven beast that reared up and attacked every time it felt threatened.

Delice scooted past him and pulled the footage up on her monitor. She fast-forwarded to the end and paused the tape. "That right there, how do you explain that? What woman, who's just been flung across the air and supposedly assaulted, smiles?"

Gabriel didn't bother looking. "You of all people should know that trauma's not a predictable emotion. The smile proves nothing. I've seen parents who've lost their children break into hysterical laughter. She is the victim here, and by first bell, I want a report on my desk to take to the captain, authorizing the removal of Mr. Michael Hart from this ship."

She was shaking her head before he finished. "Mr. Gutierrez, I was hired to do a job, and that job is to keep everyone aboard this ship safe. I'm telling you, there is more to this situation than what's on the surface. Until I know where the threat lies, *both* Miss David and Mr. Hart will be kept under close observation."

Gabriel's jaw slid back and forth, and he huffed out a breath. "So that I'm clear, you don't plan to treat Miss David, who was sexually assaulted and acted in self-defense, as a victim? And you plan to keep her attacker on board?"

"I'm the *first* person to stand up for sexual assault victims." Delice's voice reared up and attacked. "But this incident doesn't fit the profile. Nothing about this sits right with me." Her voice was forced-calm, something he recognized. "Until we know the truth of what really happened, yes, I plan to keep them *both* on board." Delice put on her bulldog face, shoulders back, fists clenched, lips curled.

He needed to get out of here before he did something he *would* regret later. "Thank you for the clarification. I needed to be one hundred percent sure of what I wrote in my report to the captain." He turned on his heel and stalked out of Skynet. He didn't bother waiting around to see her reaction. He didn't care.

The long, steel corridor of the ship's interior stretched out before him, dull fluorescents making the walls look tired and old.

Their new hire was stepping on all the wrong toes. Delice was the new kid on the block. You didn't walk into a room full of old friends, point the finger at one of them, and expect not to be pushed out of the in crowd.

He checked his pocket watch—almost three in the morning. His wake-up alarm would go off in three hours. He shut his mouth around a yawn, stood for a moment in the hallway, closed his eyes, and gave up.

The sliding doors were locked, and a sign on the glass warned restricted access due to the storm. He used his keycard to unlock the doors and walked through, locking them again when he got outside. The wind roared around his neck, biting his ears, and made it difficult to breathe. Thirty-foot waves splashed so high they were within a few feet of crashing over the deck. The ship tilted sharply, and a guest's forgotten sandal tumbled over the side. He was crazy to be out here on a night like this. It'd be all too easy to lose his footing and be washed overboard.

He stumbled forward, fully aware that his feelings toward Jesse had smashed through all the boundaries he'd so carefully constructed. In spite of, or maybe because of this, he had to know.

What happened out here?

The ship lurched under his feet, shaking his normally steady sea legs.

He should have followed her out here, made sure she was sober and safe. Then none of them would be in this situation. A wave splashed against the rail, and he slid a few feet toward the outer railing before the boat righted herself.

As he rounded the aft curve of the ship, the wind died to nothing, and though the ship still rolled, he was safer here, balanced in the center. He caught his breath and walked the scene.

After watching the video, it wasn't hard to imagine Jesse's tiny body being manhandled. It *was* hard to ignore the twist of jealousy in his stomach. When he'd seen her in Mr. Hart's arms, he'd been shocked—like he'd run into an ex-lover in the arms of a new lover. Completely irrational and inappropriate. She'd never been his. Not really. They were friends. He'd pushed her away too often to expect her to ever guess at his feelings. He'd killed his chances with her long ago.

The deck had been swabbed clean of blood. Raindrops hit the rail, and wind swirled around the corner. Not the most romantic scene. Why take a date out here and not to his cabin? Unless she didn't want to go to his cabin.

But what he'd seen in Jesse's eyes hadn't been hesitation. It'd been hostility. She hadn't looked comfortable, but she also hadn't wanted Gabriel to spoil the moment. Of course he wouldn't have, no matter how much he'd wanted to keep her from being in Mr. Hart's arms. It wasn't his place.

It *was* his place to make sure she was taken care of.

Another gust of wind escalated the storm and tilted the boat down a large swell. Gabriel braced his legs and rode it out. Just off the bow, the ocean roiled, dark and oily.

Gabriel reviewed the few bits of evidence they had. Delice Andre was way off base. Everything added up to Jesse being assaulted. He'd never seen an ounce of violence from her, and he'd looked *closely* over the years.

He'd have to find a way to rein Delice in before she caused complications where there didn't need to be any more complications.

The ship shuddered. He needed to get inside before the storm got too bad. And before it got too late to attempt *any* sleep tonight.

A small flash of light from the floorboards drew his attention. Gabriel bent down. Trapped between a wall and a tie-down anchor was Jesse's teardrop diamond. It caught the ship's fluorescent lighting and sparkled around a fleck of blood. Gabriel pinched the diamond between his fingers and polished the jewel on his sleeve until it shined, removing all trace of Mr. Hart. He clenched the jewel in his fist, hiding it from the camera, protecting it from the storm.

11

JESSE

SOMEHOW, I'M BACK IN MY STATEROOM. I REMEMBER Michael, I remember screaming, then I remember nothing. But here I am. Back in what should be a safe place.

Safety is an illusion.

Momma's snores rumble from behind her closed door in our dark stateroom, the sound a childhood relic. The ship plunges down the side of a large wave, and I stumble, the effects of whiskey and blood and unanswered lust throwing me off-center.

The lust most of all. It's that addictive electricity again. A temporary freedom from a permanent guilt. Not triggered by sex. Triggered instead by the caress of lips.

I hit the edge of the suite's bar, and the animal inside me strains against its fraying leash. I slam my hand against the wall. I can't, I won't be sucked back into the darkness and the quiet it promises. Not again.

Already it feels as if I'm pinwheeling in the air, and if I fall there will be no turning back. Blood always follows a kiss.

Memories of college meld with flashes of Michael, Daddy's face circling around me like a twisted *Phantom of the Opera* and *Fantasia* mash-up, the coppery tang of a bloody kiss fresh on my lips.

Outside, the storm reaches a new height, and my feet twist together in the crash and fall of the ship. I grip the bar, wait for the plunging to steady.

The odd, dreamlike state of adrenaline and exhaustion take over my mind, and a cold fist, hard and clammy, balls in my stomach.

What have I done?

A shadow creeps in my periphery in the form of my father. Tall and muscular, solid and full of gray death. A thought, a solution starts to take shape, not quite fully evolved. It's made of stardust, waiting to be born into something I can act on. There's peace and quiet in the blood, peace and quiet I crave, and now, there are answers. I touch my lips, the sticky blood on my chin.

A heady combination of fear and life fills up all the hole-punches in my soul. The sweet scent of rotting blood drifts up from my dress, my skin, my lips. Some of it mine. Some of it Michael's. I press my bottom lip into my teeth, and the taste of iron touches my tongue. All backdropped by Momma's snores.

She can't know that I've lost time again. That I've hurt someone else. She can't find out.

I fumble with the strap of my dress, and under my trembling fingers, it pools to the ground like liquid smoke. I unclasp my choker. The small diamond is missing from the chain. I hide the damaged necklace deep inside my work bag, pick up the dress, and slide open the balcony doors.

They squeal. A loud squeal I hadn't noticed during the sunlight.

Momma murmurs from under her door, and I freeze.

If she wakes, she'll kill me. She'll feel it's her responsibility to rid the world of an evil she's created. She will pick up her cane and beat my spine until my kidneys bleed and my bones crack.

A minute passes, two.

Silence.

Her soft snores start again, and the air rushes from my lungs.

My heart drums a percussive *rat-tat-tat* against my ribs. *Hurry.* I sneak onto the balcony, clad in nothing but a pair of silk panties and heels. The wind is a dominatrix whipping my body with flicks of ice. I drip the dress over the side of the balcony and the wind plays with the blood-specked material, tugging it from my grasp.

I let go, one finger at a time, and the dress slides out of my hands. The sharp air gives the dress new life, and they dance together in a sensuous routine, leading to a watery bed. The boat dips, the wind rages, the rain hits, as if they are affronted by having helped me destroy evidence.

I should feel relief at having the dress gone. I should feel safe. I should feel like I can forget it ever happened. Instead, a steady stab pricks my stomach, picking away at the last unbroken piece of me I have left. Michael was never anything more than a one-night stand, but he didn't deserve that. No one does.

The shadow falls over my eyes again, prickling the back of my neck with ghost-chills. I walk back inside, inch the balcony doors closed, and step into the shower to wash away the rest of the evidence.

Dried blood runs away, hitting the tiny shower stall in pink raindrops. I stay for a while under the hot water, steaming my skin clean. My tongue traces my lips. The spongy pressure of Michael's mouth is fresh in my sensory memory. Softly resistant, then compliant. So different from animals and fish. Is that what the creatures that feasted on Daddy's face experienced? Firm flesh and muscle, slippery and drink-flavored, bitter. Sweet. My mouth waters at the memory.

This will be the last time I think about this. I'm on dangerous ground. Like an alcoholic who lives in a bar, the fascination of mouths is enough to keep me awake at night. Always, *always* Daddy's lipless face is transposed on their faces. I can't get away from it. It haunts me. It is my ghost.

Water runs over my flesh, creating little rivers down my breasts, making my skin look like melting plastic. The rivers travel down, soak my panties, puddle around my shoes.

A numb laugh pops out of my mouth, and the depths of how not-in-my-head I am hits me again. I shimmy out of my water-soaked panties and likely-ruined shoes, finish washing, and step out of the shower. I wrap a towel around my body and walk into my makeshift bedroom. Guilt sends me dark thoughts, and I'm not sure I can live with myself.

I could throw myself overboard, like I did with the dress.

The thought hits me with a zing that electrifies my veins.

Control of a different sort. An end to my circular thoughts and lost answers. A solution for the pain. I take a step forward, and the whispers start.

My way, Jesse-girl. Not yours, mine.

It's him. He's here. At his favorite time of night, when I'm punch-drunk from exhaustion and too much whiskey, when the moon has set and it's the dark hour. This is when he's strongest.

Daddy's fingers grip my arm, sinking past my skin and wrapping around my bones. It's hot and cold, it makes me sick, it hurts. I gasp against his touch, shake my head. But we both know I don't have what it takes to fight him. Not in the dark, not now.

I can feel the tatters of his skin brush my ear. *Stick to our plan.*

What plan? Daddy doesn't lie, but my memory is broken. Tears burn at my eyes, and I take another step. Death would be easier than this.

You want to remember? Daddy's voice, deep and certain, growls in my ears. *You want peace? You'll listen to me. You'll follow what I tell you to do. And you will not question me again.*

I shake my head.

I can destroy you, Jesse-girl. And I will. I will take over. I will let the darkness rule. You'll never be free.

A sob breaks in my throat.

Unless you do what I say.

"No," I whisper, but it's weak.

Obey.

I stumble across the floor to the sofa bed, climb between the sheets, clothed in nothing but the towel, and keep my eye on the ghost in the corner until the storm passes, until the boat calms, until the dawn breaks, gray and purple deep in the horizon, over the wide and empty ocean.

12

JESSE

Our stateroom goes from dark to light in an instant, the overhead lights searing through my eyelids. "Momma, shh." I pull my pillow over my head and try to drown out Momma's morning noise.

"It's seven a.m., Jesse-girl. Get your lazy bones out of bed." Her shrill voice tenses my shoulders. I'm not even awake, and already I need a massage to relax.

"I've been asleep for an hour. Leave me alone." My words crack in exhaustion, my throat raw from the night of drinking and being half-strangled.

"You made the decision to be irresponsible, not me." Momma's know-it-all voice irritated me when I was twelve. It pissed me off when I was twenty. In my almost-thirties, it's nearly enough to make me commit matricide.

The covers rip off my bed, and cool air rushes over my naked body. Bright light shoots at my eyes, hitting a bullseye on my hangover. Momma stands at the foot of the sofa bed in a lime-green find, complete with the scent of *eau de toilette*. A sneer curls at her lip, disappearing into her poorly-bleached mustache.

"Momma! Do you mind?" I scramble for the sheet, but she holds the white fabric in her arms, wadded up and out of reach. It's been a long time since I was naked in front of her, and being so now feels like I'm on trial, like she's judging my body for not being as voluptuous as hers. My finger at last finds the sandpaper edge of my towel, still damp but I don't care. It's armor. I bring it up to my small breasts, covering myself as best I can.

Behind her, the door to the master bedroom stands ajar. The bed is unmade, and clothes are scattered around the floor in piles. Nothing hung up, nothing in drawers. The one benefit to Momma stealing my room is I don't have to look at her mess the entire trip. Not like at her house, where there's an ever-changing maze of clothes and trash to get to the kitchen.

Her gaze flicks over my body, rests on the hickey just below my collarbone, the bruise at my neck. "Explain."

My heart ticks faster, and I bring the towel up higher, but that exposes other parts of me. I push it back down. "I met a guy." I leave it at that. Any more details about last night, I'd have an encounter with her cane. Even if I got rid of the cane, it wouldn't matter. Momma is resourceful.

Her expression assumes the classic position—somewhere between disdain and pride. I never know which it is with her. "So you were out late playing the slut, hmmm?" Disdain. Definitely disdain.

"Weren't you the one who said I needed to get laid?" Sass attaches to my words before I can think to remove it. I cringe, never knowing exactly how much is too much. The line is a constantly moving entity.

She throws the sheets at my face. "I've ordered breakfast. It'll be here in five minutes. Best be decent." She walks into her bedroom.

"Where are you going?" I rub at my eyes, my shoulders finally relaxing with the extra steps she puts between us.

"To get dressed." She raises her eyebrows in challenge. When she receives none, she continues on her way, leaving me to scramble for clothes. The morning sun shines bright over the ocean, transforming the Northern Caribbean waters into a void of aqua-blue. No sooner than Momma's door shuts, there's a knock.

"Damn you," I mutter, very quietly, and wrap the damp towel around my body, tucking it in between my breasts. I hurry for the door, tripping over my still wet heels. I kick them out of the way, run my fingers through my hair—no help for it—and open the door.

Luxury Lines crew members are well trained. The server doesn't flinch. He acts as if it is totally normal to serve food to a barely clothed woman. He sets the steel-plated food on the table and leaves. Geysers of steam puff out of the metal lids like miniature volcanoes. I take the wrapped silverware off the tray and set the table. Our eggs are fresh. Typically, they'd be the shake-and-pour eggs. If I had to guess, Gabriel has struck again.

What does he think of me after last night?

I tug at my lip with my teeth. Can't be good.

Momma walks in as soon as the server goes, which convinces me she timed it all just to punish me for my night of debauchery. She tosses me a baby blue nightgown, one of hers. I catch it, start to pull it over my head, and stop.

I'm sick of it.

Her assuming that I'll wear this, I won't do that, I will go along with whatever she says. It grates against my bones. I drop the gown, let the rough cotton puddle to the floor, and sit at the breakfast table in just my towel without saying a word. She raises an eyebrow and starts in on breakfast.

It's a small win, but I'll take what I can get.

She takes a bite of her breakfast and tosses a copy of the Mainstay, the ship's daily newsletter, on my plate. "Care to explain?"

I want to crawl back under the covers. Those three words are a red warning flag that means Sharks in the Water. Get Out. But I don't know what I've done.

"It's a newsletter." I avoid her gaze, push the paper to the side, and spoon scrambled eggs onto my plate, careful to keep them steady, despite the shake in my hand. Careful to pace my breaths, despite the climbing pressure in my chest. "Shows the day's events and weather—"

"And lost dogs," Momma interrupts, her voice full of you're-in-trouble.

My hand clenches around the spoon. *What did I do?* I scoop some more of the eggs and carefully serve Momma before answering. "I didn't think they allowed dogs on cruises." My voice is fake-casual. She can tell.

"Says it's a service dog." Momma's eyes flash clear blue and pierce my skin. "Some poor passenger out there has had his dog *stolen*."

"You don't know it's been stolen. It could have fallen overboard." I shrug. My heart speeds to the edge of out-of-control. *Where's the cane?* "Why do you care so much?" I edge my chair away from her as I sit, moving out of arm's reach.

"Did you kill it?" She presses her lips together, hard enough that they turn white.

My heart stops so suddenly I'm not sure it'll start back up. Forget the cane. This mental game is what Momma enjoys best, and I'm her favorite piece to play with.

"I'm past all that." My face feels pinched, and my voice comes out hoarse. "You put my clean bill of health on the refrigerator, remember?" *And hung it with a banana magnet, front and center—a constant reminder to behave or back to the hospital.*

I shovel eggs into my mouth and butter my toast while chewing. After years of therapy, my past urges are well under control, but Momma still doesn't believe in me. All I have to do is think of Leo and know I'm cured. I'd *never* hurt my cat.

Last night flits into my head, and a rush of anxiety slams into my chest. I reach for my pocket, searching for my lip balm, before remembering I'm wearing a towel and my lip balm is buried in my purse.

My heart picks up speed again, the beats colliding into each other until it feels more like a hum than a beat. The room wavers, my vision narrows, my breaths shorten. I can't get air in.

"Good grief, Jesse. Can't we eat breakfast first before dealing with your issues?" Momma's voice hits me from a distance, the punch solid, but dull. A thud against a body that doesn't feel like my own.

I close my eyes and take tight, deep breaths. I have spare lip balm. I have a thousand spares. The panic recedes from high tide. I scoot away from the table, hurry to the nightstand by the sofa bed, and yank out the drawer. Grab a cherry-flavored tube and coat my lips. My breathing returns to normal. My heart thuds in time to my internal rhythm.

I keep my urges in control *most* of the time.

Momma takes a deep, double-D raising breath and lets it out slowly, as if I've been that big of a burden through the years. "Better?" she asks in between a bite of egg. I nod, return to the table, and she picks our conversation back up. "If you've done anything, I mean anything"—she taps her cane against my knee, a warning shot—"to draw attention to us, I'll never forgive you."

Definitely not telling her about last night.

"Momma, you should eat your eggs. They're getting cold." My voice trembles, but she doesn't notice.

She takes a bite of rubbery bacon to spite me, then scrunches her nose. The fat under her chin jiggles. "Is this real bacon?" She turns it in front of her face as if she could tell by looking at it from a different angle.

"Microwaved." I pop a grape off a vine, crunch it between my teeth, and leave the table, dropping the towel to the floor, daring her to judge me again.

"Where are you going?" She demands around mashed up food.

"To get dressed. Have to write an article. I have a job, remember?"

"Fat lot of good it's done you." Her viewpoint that *scribbling down some words is not real work* reverberates around every spit-laden syllable.

I grit my teeth, and my retort smashes between my back molars. My job is my escape hatch. It's the one safe place I have, and I'm not going to let her soil it with her negativity.

Knock, knock.

I look down my body-in-the-buff and dart behind the wall, blocking myself from view of the door. "Momma, can you get that?"

"I'm handicapped, remember?" She smiles a poison-sweet smile and casually takes another bite of her breakfast.

I attribute the irresistible urge to strangle her with the rubbery bacon to my hangover and wrap my discarded towel back around my breasts. I hurry to the door and swing it open wide, eyes down, expecting our tiny cabin steward.

Instead, my gaze confronts a uniformed crotch. I lift my head, my gaze trailing over a strong, muscular body and a gulping Adam's apple, and lock eyes with Gabe. His brown eyes are dull and tired, hiding shadows under his lashes. He raises his hand and dangles my lost diamond between his two fingers.

13

GABRIEL

Estoy al horno—con papas—she's naked.

Jesse stood in the opening of her suite, door propped open by her barely-covered hip. A towel. That's all she was wearing. A glorious, tiny, white towel. Gabriel could see every curve, the shadow in the dip of her cleavage, the slightly frayed end of the short, short, there-is-a-God-short towel brushing the tops of her thighs. Her pixie hair feathered around her face, rumpled and disheveled, like she'd been thoroughly used all night.

Words. Words would be good. But he couldn't complete a thought, much less form a word.

Instead, he dug out the lost diamond and presented it to her, hoping she could break the spelled silence.

"You found my diamond." Jesse batted her dark lashes.

He shouldn't be having these kinds of thoughts, but...that towel.

The edge of the material tucked in between her breasts moved. Would it fall?

It struck Gabriel that this was the second time in twenty-four hours he'd been confronted with a guest about to expose themselves. Only this time, it'd be a fantasy-come-true instead of a nightmare-turned-real.

"Gabe?" Jesse's voice snapped his gaze back to hers. He'd lost momentary consciousness in the small valley between her breasts.

"Yes, um, right. Here you go. Thought you might be looking for it." Good grief, he sounded like a virgin schoolboy talking to his first crush. Felt like one too.

"I was, thank you." Her eyes warmed to an exotic honey-green, and he had the urge to dive in to them, even knowing the shallow depths could kill his career.

He dropped the diamond into her outstretched hand, his fingers brushing her palm. The towel moved a little more. Gabriel stood there, unable to move his feet, unable to tell her goodbye, unable to keep any sort of professional mask plastered to his face.

"I wanted to check in, make sure you were all right." He checked her over, discreetly. Her neck was pink with a few broken blood vessels from Mr. Hart pulling her necklace. She had a suck mark at the base of her collarbone, but he doubted that was from the attack.

Something changed in her expression, like a muscle tic, or a flinch, or maybe just a quick flash of pain in her eyes, but it disappeared before he could diagnose it.

"You're sweet. I'm okay." The waver in her voice said she was anything but.

Physically, she seemed okay. But pain often went beyond the physical, and deeper than the limits of the body. Pain resided in the soul, deep in its dark pit. His was a pain he'd known for too long, pain he'd gotten far too accustomed to. A pain he wished he could forget.

And he'd just caught a glimpse of hers.

"I'm glad. I wish—" He stopped the lecture he had building at the back of his throat. That she shouldn't have been in a secluded area with a man she barely knew. That she shouldn't have drunk so much and left herself vulnerable. That she should've followed him back to the casino, so he could've kept her safe. "Next time, come find me, okay?" What did he mean by that? Come find him instead of another man? Let him be the guy on her arm? Come find him next time she felt in danger? All of the above?

"Find you? For what, Gabe?" Her pert lips, wet and glossy, moved around her words, and her tongue, pink and tiny, tagged the space between her teeth. But it was her eyes that drew him in, froze him to this awkward spot. They somehow darkened and lightened and danced and grew in intensity, all at once.

"Anything. Whatever you want, need, anything." He meant it. He'd be her friend, her protector, whoever she wanted him to be. He never wanted to see that look on her face again. Never again wanted to see her world ripped in two.

Her eyes dimmed, and the smile tugging at her lips faded. What did he say?

"So that's it. You're here to serve? Make sure the customer is happy?" Her tone went flat, air hissing out.

He grabbed her hand, his throat going dry. "You know that's not what I meant."

She wiggled out of his grasp. "It's okay, I get it. Don't worry. I'm not going to sue or write a bad review. Has Mr. Hart been removed from the ship yet?"

"I'm working on it."

"Please let me know as soon as he is. I'm not going to feel safe until I know he's gone." She crossed her arms, protecting herself, dramatizing that deep shadow that plunged between the twin set of perfect, rounded skin.

Gabriel swallowed. "Of course." He didn't move. He should leave, before he screwed this up even worse than he already had.

She stood back and studied him for a moment, that languid green gaze lazily tracing his body. "Why are you really here?"

His skin buzzed. *Tell her the truth, Che. Tell her you can't get her out of your head.* "Spend the day with me." His answer came out in a gust of air, surprising him.

Surprising her too from the shocked look on her face. "'Spend the day'? Doing what?"

"Whatever you wish."

The smile came back, and a little thrill sparked in Gabriel's chest. "I have an article to write, but—" She hesitated and that slight pause, the few micro-seconds she took to think over his suggestion—it felt like a day and a half had passed. "—that can wait until a little later. I've got a side project I'm working on, and I could use your help."

Gabriel felt himself melt into a goofy, not-suave-at-all grin. Didn't care. He whipped out his phone and began delegating his duties to other officers. "I'm clearing my schedule this very moment. Give me twenty minutes, and I'm all yours."

She smiled at him, and it was easy and sweet. The awkward tension between them gone. She softly clicked the door closed, and he got on the radio with his second-in-command, using the VIP excuse. His first duty was to running the ship smoothly, which included being the captain's right-hand man and ensuring the success of each voyage. Surely taking care of one of Luxury Lines's VIPs fell under that role. She was more than a VIP to him, of course, but this excuse got him exactly what he wanted. A Luxury Lines-sanctioned day with her—no need to hide behind the job. Today, she *was* his job.

Twenty minutes later, Jesse breezed into the library-themed lobby of her floor. Her loose-fitting pants and tribal-inspired tunic emphasized her delicate features. An embroidered silk bag was slung over her shoulder, and she had her typical notebook in hand.

He stepped close to her, needing to breathe her in. She smelled of lavender and melon, something sweet and fresh like the scent of dawn.

"So what's this project?"

She pulled out her notebook and turned to a flagged page. He caught a flash of a bulleted list, but she snapped it closed before he could decipher the words. She turned from him, looking around the small library, and took a deep breath before facing him. "When I was a little girl, I was on this ship."

Gabriel went very still, his breaths slowing, his heart barely pulsing.

"It was our first family vacation, the first time I'd ever been out of my little town. I imagined myself as some sort of explorer, and I was sure, I was so sure, that I'd find either buried treasure or true love on this ship. I was nine years old and straddling the line between wanting to play with dolls and wanting to kiss boys." She looked up at him then, and there was a sad smile that tugged at her cheeks. "But none of that happened. Instead, I lost—" She swallowed and started again. "My dad died here. Not on the ship, but on one of our shore excursions. And I've had a really hard time processing his death over the years." She rolled back her shoulders and straightened her spine. "So today, I'd like to visit some of the places on this ship that remind me of my dad. Kind of a farewell tour."

"I thought you were here to celebrate an anniversary with your mother."

"That's not why *I'm* here. The cabin I was originally booked in—can you open it for me? I just want to spend some time in there—see if it sparks any memories."

"Sure, no problem." He heard himself say, even though his heart had caught back up with the beats it had missed and then some. Because this *was* a problem. A big, big problem. If Jesse found out he was there that day, she'd never want to see him again. If she remembered and pieced together that *he* was the reason they called the search off, that *he* was the reason her dad was dead...he couldn't go there. Couldn't imagine the kind of devastation he'd have to witness her go through again. All because of him.

Gabriel searched her face, for what? He wasn't sure. But her eyes were clear, her expression resolute. She wasn't happy, but she *was* determined, and determination possessed its own kind of joy.

They took the stairs down to deck two, avoiding the crowded Promenade, the casino, and definitely Swig. No way in hell was he taking her anywhere near that bar.

"Is there anything else you'd like to do today? I could set you up at the spa, we could go to a trivia game, catch a show?" Surely she didn't intend to spend the entire day on her farewell tour.

She shook her head. "I do need to sign up for a shore excursion for our stop in Jamaica." She paled a little. "Snorkeling." Defeat resonated through those three syllables, as if snorkeling was the last thing in the world she wanted to do. Given how her father died, it was the last thing he wanted to let her do.

"Snorkeling? Are you sure? Most of the coral reefs in Jamaica are dead."

She wiggled her notepad at him. "I'm sure. It's on the list." And huffed out a breath of air.

Gabriel bit back a bubble of nervous laughter. "The list? You have a hit list of things to do this week?"

She scrunched her nose up and nodded. "Memories," she sang in an off-key Barbara Streisand impersonation.

Before he was ready, they stopped in front of the original cabin Jesse had booked. He stole a glance at her, wanted to ask her if she was certain, but she didn't know he understood what was at stake here. Facing her dad's death, trying to recover memories of that day...it was like a knight charging at a dragon blindfolded. She knew the dragon was there, just not where or how big or how hot his flames burned.

He unlocked the cabin.

Jesse walked in ahead of him and turned a small circle around the room.

It was a typical ocean view stateroom. Small footprint, little floorspace, and a tiny porthole window that looked over a swollen ocean. It was one of their smaller ocean views, sold at a discount because of the small window size. This room...it was Jesse's foundation. She'd crafted her life to building a skyscraper career that towered over this miserable room, and yet, she was back here, running her fingers over the laminate wood of the desk, touching the privacy curtains that could hide the bed from the rest of the room. She froze there, staring at the bed or out the window, he couldn't tell, one hand lingering on the curtain.

"Jesse? Would you like me to leave you alone?" His voice sounded too loud, as if he was shouting in a church.

She didn't answer, didn't move.

He cleared his throat and tried again. "Jesse?"

No answer.

Gabriel backed away to give her some space, bumping into the coffee table. Jesse whipped around and caught him in her gaze. She was a statue, carved out of marble, her mouth in a strict line, her eyes dull as stone.

"Yes, leave." She blinked twice, slow and calm. "Please," she added, as if forcing herself to be polite.

Gabriel dipped his head, sympathetic pain trickling through him. "I'll be waiting in the lobby if you need me." This was hard for her, being in this room. He'd seen it yesterday when they had first walked into the cabin, and today it was like she'd shut down.

Grief could transform or destroy a person. Gabriel could only hope that by opening this door, he hadn't given Jesse the keys to her own destruction.

———

GABRIEL WAITED IN THE LOBBY, ignoring his phone, the side-looks crew kept sliding him, and the urge to go back to the stateroom. It'd been an hour. But she said she'd meet him here when she was done, and he didn't want to interrupt. Grief, no matter how old, was always a lonely affair.

His phone buzzed again, another reminder for another task. He checked his mental list for anything he could do while waiting here. There were still announcements to be made, preparations for docking in Jamaica, restocking supplies, staff changes, and a million other little things that all combined to make up his job.

His phone buzzed with a new message. He curled his hands around the edge of the lobby's bar. He didn't want to check it, wanted to keep his mind focused on Jesse, but between not knowing how long she'd be and the itch of a well-developed habit that begged to be scratched, he opened the Luxury Lines app. Something on the screen jumpstarted his pulse. It took a few more seconds for his brain to activate and acknowledge the Code Red.

"Shit." The word fell from his mouth with the silence of a dropped bomb, followed by the sound of his heart exploding into his ribs.

He'd had exactly two other Code Reds in his entire nineteen years on the cruise ships. The first was a knife fight between two Columbians on deck one. The second involved an overboard passenger. Blood had been drawn in his first Code Red. A bodiless funeral had followed the second.

He left a message with the bartender in case Jesse came looking for him then forced his steps to a hurried, everything-is-just-fine pace, super-glued his professional smile to his face, and speed-walked to the bar on deck six, Fish. Not the most imaginative, but definitely the most upscale. A two-deck tall aquarium anchored the circular bar, becoming the feature piece and the main reason Fish was the most popular meeting spot on the ship. Romantic in the evenings, dance club at night, family-friendly during the day. Everyone loved Fish.

Delice ran through the aft door just as Gabriel entered through the forward. She still hadn't mastered the passenger mask and looked as if she'd just discovered a body. He'd have to talk to her about maintaining composure no matter what they were facing.

The bar had been cleared, so when Delice met his gaze there were no obstacles and no masks needed. Her anxiety matched his stress. They stepped into the bar at the same time.

The shades had been raised to allow light in. Tables covered in white linen with centerpieces of live betas swimming around daisies decked the floor. Sunlight hit the tables but didn't make it all the way to the center of the room to the aquarium. The only other light came from the aquarium itself. A blue, underwater glow that set off the fish as they swam in a cyclone formation, up and down the long, glass tube.

At least, that's what they normally did.

But part of the attraction of this aquarium was the more aggressive fish. And eels. Baby sharks. Things passengers did not want to be caught in the ocean with but didn't mind seeing contained in a cage of glass.

For the most part, the fish coexisted peacefully. Fed regularly, they had no need to attack.

Today though, they were in a frenzy.

Gabriel and Delice walked toward the spectacle, quietly, aware of each other but *not* aware of each other. Like observers of a cock fight. One slow step dragged after another after another. A flash of brown waved in between the flip of scale and fin. Playful bubbles danced above the feeding frenzy, disrupting a cloud of blackish-red liquid hovering about mid-tank.

"Oh good, you're both here." A take-no-crap voice startled a release of the stale breath in Gabriel's lungs. A bartender popped up behind the black marble and hefted a box of beer onto the counter, her blond ponytail swinging over her shoulder. "Tank will need to be cleaned, for sure." She thumbed over her shoulder. Completely unnecessarily. "'Course the fish'll take care of the mess if you let 'em. 'Cept for the fur."

"The fur?" Delice asked. Gabriel detected the slight hesitation, the note of *please, no* in her tone.

He sympathized.

The bartender stocked the fridge under the counter, going through her duties as if there wasn't a fiasco happening a mere two feet behind her. She paused, looked between the two of them. "Well? C'mon. The poor thing ain't gonna bite you. Not anymore." She lifted the counter and waited for them to pass.

Gabriel waited for Delice to take the first step. More her job than his, after all.

Delice was apparently thinking the same thing of him.

The bartender snorted, bounced her gaze from one to the other of them.

A wash of shame followed *Papá's* words *Be your best man.*

Gabriel led the way, ducked under the raised counter, and came face to face with the victim.

"Jelly." The name conjured up an image of a nudist he'd rather forget. The image in front of him was one he'd rather forget as well, but there was no hope of that, save a strong bash to the head followed by a case of amnesia.

Wads of fur floated around the tank, battered by blood-mad predators.

Gabriel distantly heard Delice on the phone, ordering the aquarium crew to immediately respond. He heard himself ask how many had noticed the body before they shut down the bar. He wrote down the info, but it was as if his voice was not his own and his fingers belonged to a puppeteer. His attention concentrated around the spin of fish, the flashes of fur, the glimpse of white bone.

He'd have to tell his passenger that Jelly was dead.

Not only dead, but dead in a horrific way.

How had the dog fallen into the tank?

Gabriel had dealt with worse. Gabriel would deal with worse, he was sure. But to deliver the news that they hadn't been able to protect one of their littlest passengers, that they'd have to steal back Delice's promise...it made his gut hurt.

Footsteps clanked against the metal scaffolding above, built to access the tank without disturbing passengers. A net appeared in the tank and prodded into the cluster of fish, gently moving them away from their unscheduled meal.

The fish darted away from the net, self-trained to avoid that intrusion of humanity.

Jelly floated into the net, his body stiff and unrecognizable as the crew retrieved it. Gabriel heard a thud, then retreating metal footsteps. Delice got on her radio. "Meeting in five in Control. Bring the dog." She flicked her gaze up to Gabriel's face. "That means you, too, Staff Captain."

"Right." His mind spun with all the tasks necessary to contain the situation and diminish the talk among the passengers. Was it best to speak with those who saw the dog personally or to let it go?

He didn't know. No one knew who or how many passengers noticed the dog. One family for sure. A little girl certainly. He'd meet with them next. The situation would be controlled. He'd do his duty. He'd be his best man for Jelly, for the dog's owner, and even for Delice.

Because the heat of not finding the dog was falling squarely on her.

Gabriel followed Delice into Skynet, the square of her shoulders getting sharper and more pinched by the second. Crew members buzzed like a kicked nest of hornets.

Jelly's body was rolled in on a human-sized metal table, fresh from the morgue.

"Unless you're on the investigating team, out," Delice called above the buzz. About two-thirds of the crew left, leaving a small handful of investigators to examine the matted fur that used to be a dog.

"CSO Andre," Gabriel started. "My priority should be our guest and—"

"I need you here. I saw something." Delice grabbed a scalpel and a Hagedorn needle and used the two tools to thread through Jelly's tangled mass of fur. "There you are," Delice murmured, talking to the corpse, a small smile softening her sharp features.

Gabriel shifted, crossed his arms. His phone beeped, reminding him of the thousands of other places he should be...and none of them were here. "Delice, you have thirty seconds."

"Aha! There we go." She dropped her tools to the table with a metal clatter, stood back, crossed her arms, and waited. A smirk resharpened her features and rubbed Gabriel raw.

He leaned over the tiny body. A small waft of death hit his senses and punched his gut. He backed away, took a deep gulp of fresh air, and returned, this time with his hand covering his mouth and nose.

Jelly had been eaten. His little white canines were exposed under torn lips, polished to a professional clean. Only the pads of his feet remained intact, from what Gabriel could see.

"Do you see it?" Delice was borderline excited, as if she had found the next clue in a treasure hunt.

"I see a dog that's been mutilated, and I have a guest I have to break the news to. You are wasting my time." Gabriel took a few steps away from the table, out of the cloud of death that was getting worse and worse the longer the dog lay there, warming under the examining light.

Delice picked up the scalpel. "Yes, mutilated. Exactly right." She began to pace and gesture like an enthusiastic college professor.

"The question is," Delice continued, "mutilated by whom?"

The rest of the team exchanged glances, and murmured confusion filled the air.

"Delice, we all saw the fish eating the dog. That poor animal should be in the morgue, not up here decomposing."

The crew nodded in agreement but stopped when Delice whipped her glare on them.

"Yes, it's been eaten by the fish. But not the lips. Those have been cut. Cut with something sharp." She adjusted the lamp, and everyone crowded around her. Gabriel took another deep breath, found a white polishing cloth in his pocket, and covered his mouth and nose again before joining the group.

She used the scalpel to point out the incisions. "See here, this is where it started. And see how jagged the slices are? I think the poor thing was alive when this was happening," she paused, letting that sink in. "She struggled and fought, but not against a fish. Against a person."

A wave of nausea pushed through his gut. "He," Gabriel said, as a cover to how her words affected him. She was right. Dammit, she was right.

"What?" Delice jerked her gaze up, eyes narrowing.

"The dog's name is Jelly, and it's a he, not a she."

"Doesn't matter," she waved away his correction. "What does matter is who." The smile returned to her face, sickly sweet this time, like something rotting in the walls. His stomach tightened into a knot. "Staff Cap, who do we know that likes to tear off lips?"

A surge of protectiveness, hot and heavy, roared through his blood. "You have got to be kidding."

"Someone did this to this poor dog. And right now, I've got one guest who fits the profile."

"Don't. You. Dare." His fists tightened, and he took a step toward Delice before he could stop himself.

"Officer Rollins," she gestured at her second-in-command. "Please bring guest Jesse David in for questioning."

"Rollins, stand down," Gabriel ordered. "Delice, you have absolutely no proof. I cannot allow you to question a guest based on supposition."

Delice ignored him entirely. "Go, Officer. I expect her here in less than an hour. Staff Captain Gutierrez has no authority inside this room. Or over the security of this ship." She paused and turned her hard gaze fully on him. "That, S.C. Gutierrez, falls solely on me."

Officer Rollins left the room, and the rest of the crew wisely busied themselves on other tasks.

"I'm going to the captain with this," Gabriel said as he messaged the captain. An immediate response came back, and Gabriel updated him on the situation.

I'll take care of it. The captain signed off, and Delice's phone immediately rang.

Gabriel stilled her hand from reaching for her phone and leaned forward over Jelly's dead body. "You're going to lose your job again, CSO Andre. This time, over a dog. And where do you go from here, huh?" Her face struggled to remain composed.

While she answered the captain's call, Gabriel reeled Officer Rollins back in, heading him off before he could harass Jesse. Then he straightened, took a good look at Delice, and, satisfied at the pale-ash color she had turned, adjusted his coat and left Skynet in the hands of its trembling CSO.

14

JESSE

"—AND WHY YOU HAVE TO LEAVE ME HERE, I DON'T know. You could have taken me with you. It's not the easiest thing gettin' around in this wheelchair I'll have you know." Momma's voice is as insistent as a parakeet wanting attention.

I shake my head, loosening up some of the sticky thread coating my mind. Sunlight fills the suite. Breakfast has been cleared from the table, and my bed has turned back into a sofa. How did I get back here?

"Glad to see you wearin' something girly at least." She flicks at the black bikini I'm wearing, with a sheer cover-up skirt tied at my hip.

Logic catches up with the sinkhole that's just opened in my stomach.

I was in the old cabin with Gabe, and now I'm here.

I lost time again.

"Momma, what time is it?" How much did I lose? What did I do?

"Two o'clock. Why? You leavin' me again? Maybe I want to go sunnin' too."

Two o'clock. I left with Gabe around ten this morning. Four hours. I've lost almost four hours.

I back away from her. In my hand, I already have my bag with my laptop, writing notebook, and sunscreen. I have to escape before she realizes what happened. "I've got to write my article. See you later, Momma."

"Don't you leave me—"

I close the door on her demands. I'll pay for it later.

Right now, I can't be around her and process what happened. That's twice in the past four days. That I know of. And if past anniversary effects are any indicator, my blackouts are just going to get longer and more frequent.

I'm running out of time. I've got to find my answers before I lose this entire week to the darkness.

I go by the deck two lobby on the off chance that Gabe is still there. Maybe he can tell me what I was doing. I'll have to be careful. He can't know either. He'd run screaming for the horizon if he knew.

The lobby is full of people, none over six feet tall. Gabe's not here. It's not until I am ogled by an old man wearing a beret that I fully connect the dots that I'm in a bikini. Stomach, breasts, legs, I'm all exposed. I push into a corner, unwrap the skirt from around my hips and rewrap it around my chest, my arms trembling, my mouth dry. The skirt is sheer gauze, but it's better than nothing.

I don't like this. My swim gear is a one-piece, complete-coverage swimsuit, not...this. I don't even know where I got it, don't remember packing it, don't recognize it.

I press my lips together. I can't go back to the stateroom to change. That'd mean facing Momma. Instead, I find a nearby ship phone and dial Gabe's extension.

"Staff Captain Gutierrez. How may I serve you?" His voice is enough to honey-coat my stomach, soothing the acid-eaten edges.

"It's Jesse."

He goes silent, then "Are you all right? I waited for you in the lobby, but you never came back." There's a hint of hurt wrapped up in the compassion in his voice. He wanted to spend the day with me, he cleared his schedule for me, and the day is half gone.

"I, um, fell asleep. Last night caught up with me, I guess." Guilt is a sour aftertaste at the back of my tongue, but I can't help it. If I could control the blackouts, I'd never have another one. "I'm heading up to the VIP pool to work on my article. Join me?" He's quiet. "I'll have apology nachos waiting."

There's a little chuckle on the other end of the line that warms my bones. I didn't even realize they were cold.

"Nachos, huh? How could I say no?" His voice wraps around me and brings me home.

"You can't. I'll see you soon." With Gabe, I've always felt like I belong. He's always accepted me for exactly who I am, no questions, no misgivings. Around him, I can just be Jesse. My steps lighten, and I hurry through the ship's crowds, wanting to beat him to the pool, have those nachos waiting as promised. I round the corner and almost run into the clear glass of a shop window, smack into a mannequin wearing my black bikini, my sheer cover-up.

My heart whirs, my throat pulses. I've been in that store. I've shopped for that bikini. I bought the whole damn outfit.

And I don't remember a second of it.

I hold my breath as I push through crowds, until I plow through the revolving doors to the lower pool and suck in deep gulps of the chilled air just outside. Fresh Caribbean salt, chlorine, and cabin fever scent the recycled air, and the sun makes a good attempt to warm me up, but the chills prickling my skin go deep. I take a few breaths, stay still until my heart slows down, until I can breathe naturally again. What else did I do during my blackout?

I tug my lip between my teeth, push the panic down, because...Gabe. I can't stand him up again.

On the deck, it's a warm eighty degrees. The sun shines, and the wind blows just enough to cool the heat. The scent of strawberry daiquiris and pool-side barbecue mix together, creating an immediate vacation-feel. Families play in the water with beach balls and pool noodles. Kids run screaming around the pool deck with the predictable "No running!" call from a parent following.

I climb the stairs to the next deck, a sunning-only deck with older women, skin the texture of brown paper sacks, lying on their stomachs, swimsuit straps undone. I keep climbing.

The third deck is sparse. With no elevators up to this level, other than a restricted, handicap-only elevator, it almost guarantees quiet and peace. Sweat rolls between my breasts and down my back. That's the one thing people never realize —unless they'd read my article in last year's Luxurious Cruises Around the World edition. You do so much walking on a cruise ship, you needn't worry about calories.

I catch my breath and hold onto the upper rail, the wood polished, smooth, and warmed from the sun. From here, the lower deck pool spreads out beneath me like a small pond. The deck I'm on is higher than the sides of the ship and the beautiful Caribbean stretches out from one side of the horizon to the other. Clouds disappear behind us, leaving behind the last of the storms. Despite my issues with this ocean, its beauty is undeniable.

I reach the gate to the upper deck VIP pool. A sign on the wooden entrance forbids anyone under the age of twenty-one from entering, and a keypad next to the gate allows access only to Luxury Lines' highest paying guests. As such, it's a quieter, older crowd with plenty of open spots under shaded cabanas. I go to the bar, order nachos and cocktails, claim a cabana close to the deep end, and take out my writing arsenal.

As my computer whirs to life, I grab my pen, notepad, and timer, and conduct an old writing exercise. A familiar routine guaranteed to clear my mind. After the first day of this so-called vacation, I feel like I need a full-out shamanic smudging ceremony.

I push Momma out of my mind. I shove Michael and that whole total disaster into a box and seal it shut. I push away the shadow of impending doom my blackouts cast. I breathe in, breathe out, focus on the present moment—the feel of the wind playing with my hair, the sensation of the sun warming my toes. I close my eyes and write for ten minutes solid, scribbling whatever comes to mind. It doesn't have to make sense—it just has to be written. Like taking out the garbage, this clears the mind-clutter. The timer goes off, my mind is wiped clean. A burden is lifted.

I glance at what I've written.

What I've drawn.

The scribbles start out as letters, letters that morph into lines, black smoke, the open sea, and a body, floating. I trace the letters and turn the paper around, finding words, names, random years, places I've been for work—Amsterdam, Sydney, Marrakech. Each name seems to tremble against my fingertips, as if they contain energy.

I slam the notepad shut before anyone can see. The black, beaten cover of the spiral notepad seems to grow ten times its size.

The picture is innocent. Disturbing, but innocent. Yet there's an iciness that frosts down my throat and pricks into my stomach. I shake my head. *Get it together, Jess.*

I don't know where the image or words came from, some deep recess of my brain, but obviously I needed to unload that image for the words to flow.

I flip the page and come up with a catchy title for my article within minutes, but the cold feeling in my stomach doesn't uncoil. Instead, it winds tighter, a cobra about to strike.

I rub at my temples and push my hair away from my face.

A crew member comes by with a large plate of nachos and two fruity cocktails served in pineapples, and my shoulders slowly relax at the distraction. The pineapple cocktails are a total tourist trap, but I couldn't resist the look on Gabe's face when he sees what I ordered.

The pool has grown slightly more crowded. At one end, three generations of women hang onto the edge and do leg exercises, while sharing an inside joke that leaves at least one of them in tears. Some European-styled men walk by in bikini bottoms smaller than my own. Everyone here seems to have someone else, someone to vacation with, someone they enjoy being with.

"Pineapples? Really, Jesse?" Gabe's teasing voice runs over my skin and fills my belly with fizz. I stretch out my legs, turn toward him, and drink him in, tension leaving me in one gigantic *whoosh*.

The sun warms his dark skin, making him look like an Egyptian god painted in gold. His brown eyes hold something reserved just for me. It makes me want to morph into a kitten and curl up on that sunlit patch of his skin and hoard all his warmth. I stand, slowly, my eyes trained to his gaze, and take a step closer to him before thinking.

I take another step after.

I'm within wrap-your-arms-around-me reach. We both know he won't. I'm not the kind of a girl that inspires men to risk careers. But...there's a *but* there. It's been budding since last night, growing since he showed up at my suite this morning. If I'm lucky, it might even bloom into a full-on exception to the rule.

"I thought you might like that." I look up at him from under my lashes, falling back on our harmless flirting. But when the black center of desire in his eyes widens, I'm not prepared to be sucked in. The fizz in my belly turns to a flurry of bubbles, and my doubts begin to pop them, one-by-one.

Momma convinced me long ago that the man of my dreams would remain safely in my dreams. I'm too broken.

What if Momma's wrong?

Besides my cat and my driver, Gabe's the only relationship I have that is kinda okay. What if I screwed things up when he saw me with Michael? But, he's here. He came looking for me. Surely, *surely* he knows that Michael was a fling, a distraction.

"Your apology nachos are getting cold. Sit down with me?" My mouth goes dry, and my heart pounds a series of fresh bruises against my ribs. I check the pool for any Luxury Lines crew, wait for the bartender to turn his back, and graze my finger against Gabe's fisted hand at his side. I press my lips together, my breath caught somewhere between my toes. This is a line we've never crossed, but here I am, leaping over it and probably plunging into the Sea of Rejection.

Gabe's whole face freezes for a moment that feels like a three-thousand-word article but, in reality, is probably only a ten-word headline. The black centers of his eyes widen even more and swallow all the brown. He keeps his body absolutely still, but I sense the war being fought inside. His hand unfolds and reaches for mine, kickstarting my lungs to draw the breath all the way back up and through my body. He returns my caress, the soft graze of our hands invisible to all the world but us and the sunlight.

"Apology nachos are my favorite kind." The way he says it makes me think there's a chance that I may be his favorite kind.

Small pulses of tingles shoot from the stroke of his finger against my wrist and plow straight into my heart.

"Staff Cap Gutierrez"—the bartender calls out from the pool bar—"do you have a moment?"

Gabe makes a small groan in his throat. "I'll be right back. Don't go anywhere." His gaze locks onto mine with a force I feel all the way to my toes.

"You better hurry, or I'm going to eat all your nachos." Somehow all the junior high jitters stay out of my voice. Gabe wants me. He wants *me*.

He backs away, a smirk curling his mouth, and reluctantly turns around. My lips spread into a soft smile. Momma was wrong.

And if she is wrong about this, she could be wrong about everything.

Gabe rejoins me, a grimace replacing his earlier smirk. "Duty calls. I've got to take care of a crew problem. I'll be back in a little bit, but if you need to take off, I understand."

"I think I can hang out here for a bit. Take your time, I'm not going anywhere."

He presses his lips together. "I'll be back soon." He takes another glance at my bikini and lets a groan come out of his voice. "Very soon. Don't drink my pineapple." He reaches for my hand, gives it a little squeeze, and hurries off, leaving me with a laugh bubbling in my throat.

Gabe's done the impossible. He's chased away my anxiety. And made me feel comfortable in a bikini.

The pool stretches out in front of me. I haven't been underwater in twenty years. Not in the ocean, not in a pool, not in the bathtub. Daddy's voice is louder there, but maybe, just maybe, I can do this. Conquering my fears, facing who I used to be—a girl unafraid of the water, of being herself—it may be enough to fight off the blackouts and *remember*. And if I can remember, I can fight Momma and her version of the truth. I can fight Daddy. The thought is enough to give me courage to walk to the deep end, crouch down, and dip my feet in.

My search for answers was always going to lead me back to the water. This water just happens to be much safer than the death water we're floating on—which I'll be in soon, thanks to my therapist's list of to-dos. Jumping in the pool isn't on the list, but it seems wise to do a trial run. Visit the old cabin, spend time in the Cigar Bar, go to the helipad at night, snorkel—these are all on the list. Each task has been carefully discussed, drilled down to the moments I could remember spending with Daddy leading up to his death.

There are answers under the water. Maybe enough of them to finally heal the brokenness growing inside me.

I peer through the pool, down, down, down to the aqua-blue bottom. I check the depth marker. Ten feet. I think they've forgotten a zero or two on the sign. And there are waves. There shouldn't be waves in a swimming pool. All the care-free people play, splashing should-be-illegal waves, oblivious to the danger. Drowning is the third leading cause of unintentional death worldwide. Why don't more people know that?

I shake off the thoughts. I can do this. Swimming. This is my way back to the beginning.

The concrete catches at my swimsuit, and the grate collects all the careless waves and pinches my thighs. A quick dip. Two seconds of my head being fully submerged, then if the memories don't come, I'll get out.

The water sucks at my calves, and my heart punches against my throat as if there's a miniature boxing champion hidden in my chest. The sky starts to dip and swirl, and my hands go numb. I breathe through my nose. *Stop it.*

The deep end glares at me. I glare back. Momma's voice is in my head, whispering *weakling, unlovable.*

I clench my fists. I am not weak.

I slide into the water. It creeps up my body, sucking at my breasts, stopping at my shoulders. It weighs a thousand and ten pounds. The roar in my head muffles all sound. Visions of the past put a film over everything, as if a movie projector is pointed the wrong direction and the actors and scenes are displayed over chairs and people. I press my lip into my teeth, taking comfort from the familiar pain. I can do this.

I edge down, the water creeps up my shoulders, and a pair of bare feet stops in front of my finger, gripping the edge.

"Look who it is." His words are slightly slurred, but his voice hits my memory-center and I'm flooded with images from last night.

Michael.

My heart trips. Oh. Shit.

My gaze flicks up to his. His swollen, stapled lip barely moves, but he winces, then hits the guy next to him.

Six other guys, big guys, dangerous guys, crowd around him, and the air crackles. As if all the molecules around us have charged and are about to explode.

Adrenaline hits my veins, but I have nowhere to run. I let go of the wall and tread water backwards. Michael follows, easing into the pool in his swim trunks and t-shirt, careful to keep his stitches above water. "I didn't do anything. I didn't force myself on you. Tell them." There's a plead in his voice, a frailness. Once it breaks, he'll break me.

His breath heats my cheek, and I swim backwards, but for every inch I gain, he gains two. He closes in, and fresh waves of panic crash over my head.

"I don't know what you're talking about." The words come out in halted breaths, forced between gulps of air. My vision goes fuzzy. My hands go numb. I'm losing the ability to stay afloat.

He grabs my wrist. "Yes. You. Do."

I lose my breath. My head dips halfway underwater. *I can't breathe.*

Michael jerks my wrist, making sure I'm paying attention. "I didn't do what you said I did. What you told them. You bit me." He touches his lip, winces, and something in his expression changes. I close my eyes, wait for it to be over. "Tell. Them."

"Michael, let her go, man. You don't need this."

My chin dips under, and I take in a mouthful of water. My heartbeats tumble against each other.

The water gnaws at my cheek, and Michael swims away at his friend's insistence. Fear slams into my blood, a giant tangle of tentacles and sea monsters. I'm alone in the middle of the deep end. The edges of the pool stretch further and further away, and the panic becomes a lead weight in my chest.

And down down deep, the little fishies swim...

I gasp in water. My lungs fill. I sink, and the sunlight dims. My scream erupts in a flurry of bubbles, muted by watery cotton. No one can hear me, and I'm not going to make it out of this pool alive.

Pressure builds in my head. I struggle harder and harder, claw for the surface.

My vision fades, but Daddy's whispers grow louder. *Give me blood, I'll give you rest. You owe me, Jesse-girl. You owe me.*

My toes scrape the bottom. Everything goes black.

15

GABRIEL

Gabriel barely made it to deck two before the radio on his phone beeped. Passenger incident at the VIP pool. The few sips he'd gotten of his pineapple drink curdled in his stomach.

Jesse.

He did an about-face and rushed back up the stairs. Passenger incidents took priority over crew issues.

By the time he reached the VIP pool, sweat was a river running down his spine. The scene before him was tense, crew members and gawkers looking over a woman sprawled on the deck, the bartender leaning over her administering CPR.

His heart thumped into his gut, one long *boom*, and then it froze. Seconds stretched into the sky, not just stopping time but disappearing it entirely. On the way here, he'd prayed it wasn't her, but it'd been a while since God had listened to his prayers.

He'd recognize that black bikini protecting her porcelain skin anywhere. He should never have left her.

A couple of crew members surrounded her and did crowd control.

The ship's medic ran onto the deck from the other side of the pool, heading straight toward Jesse. Gabriel rushed after him.

Just as he got to her, Jesse leaned over and coughed up water, the purple tint fading from her face as she sucked in air. Gabriel kneeled next to her and rubbed her back, taking over for the bartender, helping the medic get the rest of the water out of her lungs. Water seeped through the knees of his uniform, and a distant voice reminded him he'd have to change soon to keep up the appearance that all is well for the rest of the guests. But all was not well.

The medic pushed him out of the way, and he stepped back, let him do his job, and save Jesse. The medic checked her lungs, wrapped her in an aluminum blanket, rubbed her back, and spoke to her in soft, accented tones. Jesse visibly relaxed under his touch, nodding at his questions.

Gabriel walked next to one of the crew members. "What the hell happened?"

He nodded across the pool and crossed his arms. "He did."

Gabriel followed his nod and saw a group of guys held back by members of Delice's security team. Delice was nowhere to be seen.

Gabriel gave Jesse another glance—she was in good hands—and stalked over to the group.

A bunch of twenty-somethings surrounded one guy sitting on a chair. The guy looked up, and Gabriel found himself staring into the stitched-up face of Mr. Michael Hart.

His response was immediate, uncontrollable, primal, and if the captain had seen it, grounds for firing. He grabbed Michael by his damp shirt and pulled him to standing. "You did this?"

"Staff Captain Gutierrez, I'll take it from here." Delice's voice hit him in the spine, but he didn't let go.

"This man will be removed from this ship at once. Get him out of my sight." Gabriel's voice growled, threatened, promised violence. Only when he saw the threat reach Mr. Hart's eyes did he let him go.

Gabriel backed away, his arms and legs shaking from stifled rage. He needed to punch something. Hard. Repeatedly.

Delice turned toward him, and he saw the argument in her eyes. He also saw her recognize that now was not the time to argue with him or to plead Michael's not-so-innocent case. "S.C., I believe Miss David needs you."

Her words were an ice shower to his rage. He snapped around and saw Jesse sipping at a mug of something warm. He didn't remember traveling across the deck, but he was suddenly there, at her side, kneeling beside her and staring into her bloodshot eyes. "I just can't leave you alone, can I?"

She smiled, and in it she showed him how stretched thin and close to breaking she was.

He wanted to be closer to her, to wrap his arms around her and protect her from now until forever, but he remained a professional distance. Too many eyes were watching, and he couldn't help her if he got fired.

"Did he attack you again?" He was careful to phrase it in a way that she could nod *yes* or shake her head *no*.

She swallowed and looked up to the sky, biting and sucking on her bottom lip. She nodded.

"Did he push you in?" In all the years that he'd known Jesse, he'd only seen her in the water one time. The day her father drowned.

She shook her head.

"You were already in the water?"

She sucked on her bottom lip and stared into the depths of the pool.

"Part of your farewell tour?" he guessed. Because why else would she suddenly change up her habits.

Her gaze struck his like a green-white dart of lightning.

"I pay attention," he said to her silent question.

The medic edged in and checked Jesse's lungs again, giving her instructions to take it easy, drink lots of warm honeyed tea, and save her voice. Gabriel backed off to give him space to wrap things up. A small presence at his side made him look over.

"Delice." He nodded. "Have you taken Mr. Hart into custody?"

"I'm arranging to question him now." She gestured across the deck with her chin. Some of her security team were clearing out the pool lounge and ushering Michael and his university prep squad in. "He's pretty drunk. I think he was mixing liquor with his pain meds. He smells like a tequila tasting room."

"Not a valid excuse," he growled.

Delice nodded in agreement. "Is she okay?" She peered around Gabriel to gawk at Jesse.

"The bartender saw her and pulled her out in time," Gabriel said. "She coughed up a lot of water, but the doc says her lungs are clear. She needs rest." He heard the concern in his own voice, more concern than the typical passenger warranted. Did Delice pick up on it?

"Glad to hear that. I need to ask her a few questions." She tried to side-step him, but he matched her movements.

"Why?" He crossed his arms and widened his stance, becoming a very effective wall.

She huffed. "Because Mr. Hart was seen in the water with her shortly before she almost drowned."

"Yes, and you have them detained in the pool lounge. So why do you need to talk to Jess—Miss David?"

She sucked on the inside of her cheek. "Because those two have history, and I need to hear her side as well as Mr. Hart's side. Or would you rather her not be able to tell her side of the story?" Delice pursed her lips, her pose all *gotchya*. "Now if you'll excuse me, I'd like to do my job." She propped her hands on her hips and waited for him to surrender the battleground.

He took a breath, let it out noisily, and moved out of her way.

Delice pushed her way through the crew, and Gabriel matched her step for step. No way in heaven or hell would he let Delice talk to Jesse alone.

Delice did her best to ignore him. "Miss David, if you're up for it, I need to ask you a couple of questions."

Jesse's gaze flicked to Gabriel, and he subtlely shook his head. She didn't need to answer a damn thing.

"I'm sorry, but I'd really like to rest. Doctor's orders." Jesse shrugged and coughed, the effort shaking her thin shoulders. He couldn't tell if it was pretend or real, but it *was* effective.

Delice set her jaw. "I'll check on you in a few hours and get your statement then." She stepped to the side, and Gabriel took her place.

The ship's medic gave Jesse the all-clear, and Gabriel was finally able to wrap an arm around her, helping her stand. She stumbled a little, and he kept his arm around her, under pretense of carrying her bag and helping her walk inside. Her bare skin was chilled and smooth and prickled under his touch. He swallowed and tightened his grip, tried to focus on anything but the silky sensation of her skin under his.

Gabriel checked over his shoulder as he led Jesse onto the handicap elevator. Delice stared at them, her bulldog face on, and he knew, just as he'd known it was Jesse in trouble when he got the call earlier, that this wasn't over. Delice Andre would keep digging until she found something on Jesse, trusting her gut above evidence, circumstance, and common sense. Gabriel needed to find out why she wouldn't let this go and what made her tick, but most of all, he needed to stop her before she caused Jesse any more harm.

If she didn't, Gabriel was fairly certain that he'd be unable to control his rage.

Again.

16

JESSE

GABE WALKS ME BACK TO THE SUITE, SLOWLY, AS IF I'M easily breakable. My spine straightens, and I want to tell him that I'm not an invalid, but then he might take away his hand, and I'm starting to crave his touch.

He stops in front of the door. "Think you'll be okay from here?" The question is a tease, and a smirk tips his lips.

"I think I got it."

"So much for our fun day." He shrugs, and his expression is so disappointed-little-boy that I laugh—which hurts.

"Hey, the day's not over yet. I've still got items on my list, and I need your help to do them." My voice sounds like a horde of hornets, buzzy and harsh.

Gabe's gaze softens, and I lean into him, crossing that physical boundary once again, letting him know that it's okay that he does too. He picks up on my non-verbal and strokes my arm with the back of his finger. "Whatever you need, whenever you need. Just give me the word."

My lips spread into a smile, and I can tell they are dry, chapped, in major need of lip gloss, but under his gaze, it's not a crisis. "If I'd known all it took was almost drowning to get your attention, I would have arranged this years ago."

His eyes widen. "Jesse...you've always had my attention."

"Not like this." I find his hand, place my palm flat against his, and bring it up between us. His hand swallows mine, but it's not threatening. Not at all.

He pulls me in and wraps both his arms around me, kisses the top of my head. "Not like this," he echoes, and I'm not sure I want to decipher the sadness I hear in his voice. "Rest up and call me whenever you're ready." He squeezes my hand then leaves, his broad shoulders commanding the space in the narrow hallway.

The stateroom door barely closes before Momma jumps up and grabs me by the chin, eating away at the peace I found in Gabe's arms.

"I'm fine. Just took in some water." I back away from her prodding hand. She's not good at mothering, and I'm not good at accepting.

"Don't tell me you tried to kill yourself." She crosses her arms over her protruding belly, jiggling in a one-piece orange swimsuit that was stretched out ten years ago. It takes up all the visual energy in the room, like a construction barrel that's survived a ten-car pile-up.

"I didn't try to kill myself." I don't roll my eyes, but it's all there in my tone.

"Oh, my Jesse-girl. How sad your little life is. To think about killing yourself while on vacation—" She interrupts herself to have a dramatic moment. Her words drip with sticky, sugary lies. I used to lick them up and swallow them down as love and acceptance, but I've lost my taste for her sweets.

I turn my back, and this time, I roll my eyes. "We both know you couldn't care less about my well-being." I drop the bag I was about to fill with ice and clink two cubes in a whiskey glass instead.

"It's a little early to be drinking, don't you think?"

I hold my finger up. Pour my drink. Let it slide down my throat before I give her my full attention. She remains silent, tight-lipped, until I release her.

"The more attention you bring to yourself, the harder everything will be," she says, changing tactics. "They'll be watching us."

I slam my whiskey glass down on the counter. A crack runs through the glass, reaching the rim at the same moment my thoughts explode out my mouth. "Momma, what on earth are you talking about?"

Her gaze widens, her lips part, but she doesn't answer.

I try again. "Why are you really here?"

She's got a confused look on her face, but I'm too tired to try and decode it.

"Justice, Jesse," she finally says. "I'm here to get justice for your daddy." She says it as if I should have known, should have already understood.

"And just how do you plan to do that? Fake an injury to get a free cruise? Sue the cruise line? None of your crazy bullshit will bring Daddy back."

Once again, her lips form an O. She shakes her head and something clears in her gaze.

But I turn from her. I'm done. Between the chlorine in my lungs, the fresh hit of alcohol, Gabe—

There's a whuff of air, then a hard rap against my spine. My lungs collapse, my air leaves in one hard *omphf*. Another hard whack to my kidneys sends me to the floor.

"You have no idea who your father was."

I look up at her. She's holding the cane in two hands, her cheeks lightening two shades under her pink blush.

"He demanded justice above all else. Eye for an eye. Life for a life. Do you not remember..." She trails off, her gaze focusing on the past. "Of course you don't." Her voice softens, sinks into memory. "Your father begs for revenge. Do you not hear him at night? Feel him over your shoulder?" She reaches a hand toward me, the cane out of sight. Momma's most effective persuasion tool is not that cane, but her own twisted mind. The cane is her sidekick, but she's the real villain.

I jerk away, see the shadow in the corner of my eye. Daddy's back. Hands and feet missing from his mutilated body. His voice garbled and frothy, full of blood and seawater. His teeth bared from gum to bone in a torn, involuntary smile.

No little girl should ever have to see her daddy's corpse.

No grown woman should be haunted by her father's ghost.

"You do see him. He's there for you as he is for me. Jesse"—she grabs my hand, pushes it to her breasts, and holds it there, her manipulation silently wrapping around me, constricting my arms to my sides before I realize what she's doing—"he was a great man, and he won't rest until we punish those responsible."

He won't rest.

But he did rest. Last night, for a moment, a second, in the salty blood, Daddy rested.

Yes, Daddy demands justice.

But not Momma's way.

"Momma, whatever you're planning, it's not going to work." There's a silencer on my voice, keeping it low and soft. I grab lip balm out of my cover-up's pocket and roll it around my lips.

She narrows her eyes, her gaze penetrating my barriers. "Do you remember how often we had to move after your daddy died?" She changes the topic, classic manipulation. "Your little obsession with carving up the neighborhood pets ruined nearly every home—"

"You *know* I don't remember any of that. Let it go." My pleads don't stop her. She's a steamroller, an armored tank.

"But are you past all of it? Really? What about that poor man's dog? You did something. I. Know. You." She thrusts her finger at me with every word, her unforgiving eyes icy and inescapable.

My stomach twists, and the whiskey pushes into my throat. "I didn't. I'm cured." I turn from her, needing to convince her. Convince myself. "Doctor Miller gave me the all-clear nine years ago. You ignored it then. You're ignoring it now."

"Oh no, Jesse-girl." She keeps on coming, two feet away, one foot away.

"Stop calling me that." My voice begs, digs in my pocket for the white flag.

"You're who I say you are, Jesse-*girl*." Moisture from her tongue mists my face. "You will do as I say, or I'm turning you in." Her eyes are blue and black marbles, hard and unmoving. "You killed that dog. Carved him up just like you did the others."

"I didn't." I gasp, but my thoughts flicker to Michael.

"You. Did." She doesn't have to thrust her finger to pound in the accusation. My own doubts do that.

"You have no evidence." I sound hatefully weak.

"Don't I?" She rummages in her pocket, pulls out something wrapped in toilet paper, along with a picture, and slaps it onto the bar. "Found your trophy. Just like when you were younger."

I flip over the picture, and a long-haired terrier with brown eyes stares back at me. My heart tramples my ribs, my hand trembles, the picture flutters to the floor. I don't want to see what's wrapped up in that wad of paper. I don't want to, but I have to. I reach out and pinch the edge. It's wet and stained pink. I don't want to see. I want to see. My heart kicks up one, two, three.

The paper peels away. Flattened whiskers against blood-stained fur. Two long, perfect strips of furry flesh.

The floor falls away from my feet, bile rises in my scratched raw throat, and I can almost convince myself that I'm watching this scene from above, tethered by the thinnest thread of denial.

I don't remember doing this.

But I didn't back then either. The only evidence was the scratches on my arm and the black blood under my finger-nails that I would have to suck and gnaw at for hours to get clean.

An image flashes in my mind. The dog's exposed canines, stained with yellow and black. The hot pant of its breath. Its yelps. Its screams.

The blissful silence of Daddy's voice in my head once the smile had been captured.

"You'll do as I say, Jesse-girl." I distantly recognize the tremble in her voice as triumph. "You'll help me give Daddy justice, or you'll go back to behavioral treatment. And I'll make sure you stay there for the rest of your life."

DAY THREE

Down, down deep,
In the big ocean blue,
Swim three little fishies,
A Daddy and A Me and A You.

17

GABRIEL

GABRIEL SPREAD HIS BARE TOES AGAINST THE THIN carpet of his cabin, grounding himself to the ship as it rocked gently back and forth across the open Caribbean waters. Jesse had disappeared again yesterday. He wanted to attribute her distance to everything she was going through, but a throbbing in his lower gut wouldn't leave him alone. He pressed his hand to his side, the unexplainable worry about her making him nauseous.

She said she'd call him, that she needed him to help her on her so-called farewell tour. But she hadn't called, hadn't shown up for dinner. To his knowledge, she hadn't left her cabin after he took her back.

Not that he could blame her. If it were him and he'd gone through what she had, he'd sleep the rest of the day and through the night.

He stood and stretched out his bones, cracking his spine. He felt paper-thin as he went through his morning routine. Even his sister's coffee didn't provide its usual trip back home. The job was weighing on him even more, and he needed a change. He'd thought a promotion to captain was the answer, but even if that was on the table, he wasn't so sure. His pseudo-relationship with Jesse had plastered the sacrifices he'd made for this career over every reflective surface on the ship. Before, he'd thought the job worth the sacrifice.

But now that that meant sacrificing Jesse—any relationship for that matter—he couldn't do it. Not anymore.

He buttoned the last polished brass button of his uniform, tightening the collar around his neck, and grabbed his radio and phone on the way out. His phone rang before he could reach the door.

Couldn't his job wait for thirty more seconds? Was there ever a time he wasn't officially on the clock?

Gabriel pushed down the gruffness rising in his throat and answered, "Yes?" He left out his customary greeting. It wasn't even seven in the morning yet. He didn't have to be polite until *after* seven in the morning. New rule. His rule.

"Gabe?" Her voice was tentative and child-like, and it threw him back twenty years.

He shook his head, swallowed the knot that had formed in his throat, just under his uniform's top button. "Jesse." Her name was his breath. "Are you okay? I didn't hear from you yesterday and I was worried."

He could almost hear her smile. "You worry about me?"

He walked back into his stateroom, sat on his twin-size bed, and stretched out like a teenage boy talking to his crush at school. His feet wiggled back and forth, nervous energy vibrating through him. The clock on his nightstand flipped to seven oh one. For the first time in his life, he was officially late for his job. His shoulders relaxed, and he leaned his head back against the wall. It felt good.

"How could I not worry about you? You're a magnet for trouble." He was joking, but she seemed to take it too seriously.

"Seems like. I'm sorry I bailed on you...again. Momma was tiresome yesterday, and I needed to rest."

I bet she was.

"Understandable. But you're up early today. Would you like to have breakfast with me?" Another new rule—Gabriel could eat with guests at his choosing. His job required building good customer relationships, which put him above the cruise line's policy of not eating with guests.

Jesse breathed into the phone. "You read my mind. How about the Scullery?"

Gabriel's nose wrinkled. The Scullery was the all-you-can-eat buffet on deck seven and reminded him of the food court at a mall. The food wasn't bad, but it was loud and anything but private. He wasn't quite ready to put his new rules under the scrutiny of that many people. "What if I treat you to a sunrise breakfast in my favorite spot on the ship?"

"Sounds intriguing. And where might this spot be?" He definitely heard the smile in her voice that time.

"Meet me in the Sky Lounge. I'll show you."

Gabriel hung up and checked the clock. Ten after seven. A restless energy shot through him, adrenaline at visiting the other side of the line he'd constructed over the years taking him higher and higher. Who would have thought breaking the rules would feel so good. Would be so addictive.

He left his stateroom, leaving his coffee paraphernalia out in plain sight.

It wasn't until he was halfway to the Sky Lounge that he realized he'd forgotten *Papá's* pocket watch on the bed. He hesitated, shook his head, and kept walking. Today was a day of firsts. First day late on the job, first day to eat a meal with a passenger, first day to walk around without the weight of *Papá's* life mantra hanging at his heart.

He would be his best man tomorrow.

Today was a rule-breaking day. And he intended to break all of them.

———

GABRIEL WALKED into the empty Sky Lounge, his arms weighted down with a large picnic basket full of breakfast, champagne, and blankets. The lounge was dark. He'd purposefully left the lights off. It wouldn't be long before the bartender showed up to open the area, but for now, this was one of the few vacant places on the ship. So quiet he could hear the creaking of steel and almost imagine the clanking of the invisible sails of the ship's nautical ancestors.

The Sky Lounge sat high above the jogging deck and the three pools. This wasn't his favorite spot on the ship, but it was a close second. Bowed floor-to-ceiling windows showed off the deep turquoise of the Caribbean far below, bending toward the pink and yellow horizon. This high up, they were on top of a pendulum, and the gentle sway of the ship from down below transformed into a vigorous rock-a-bye at the top of the jeweled world.

Jesse walked into the lounge, wearing loose-fitting jeans and a cropped white t-shirt. The sun peeked over the horizon behind her, haloing around her head. He should have told her to dress warm, but that's what blankets were for. And body heat.

Take it slow. It was a warning shot, a voice that seemed to come from outside him, a jiminy cricket in his ear.

"*¿Qué haces?*" Jesse rolled Gabriel's native tongue around her mouth, and it sounded delicious and sinful and like coming home all in one bite. It made him smile from some place deep in his chest, a place covered in cobwebs and dust, one that had had the curtains drawn for far too long.

"*Bien, por suerte, cariño.*" *Cariño*, sweetheart. He didn't know why he kept calling her that except that it seemed to fit her. He crooked out his arm, and she fitted her hand around his bicep, stepping close enough that he could smell her lavender shampoo.

He led her to a half-hidden service door and used his keycard to unlock the keypad. To her credit, she didn't hesitate and didn't blink in shock at the narrow, steel bones of the ship. A white metal stairway wound its way around a pole in front of them. Jesse climbed ahead of him, and he acted as her failsafe. If she fell, he'd catch her. He'd soften her fall, every time.

At the top, Gabriel opened a thick steel door. It'd always seemed to him that this door was a portal to a new land, one where he was king in a kingdom of one. And now, he'd expanded his kingdom to two. He held the door open for Jesse, and they stumbled onto the roof of the Sky Lounge, into the shadow of the ship.

Above them, two of the ship's communication satellites turned inside their golf ball-shaped globes, sending GPS locations and status updates to the sky. The wind whipped around, and he could see her confusion even in the shadows. From this vantage point, the space was cold and steel and military.

He couldn't wait to surprise her.

"This way." Gabriel tugged her in the opposite direction, toward the sunrise. Hidden on the other side of the entrance, he'd bolted a few chairs to the roof, strung a hammock between two of the satellite towers, and planted some potted plants. He pulled a thick blanket out of the basket and weighed down the corner with the rest of the packed picnic, enjoying the look on Jesse's face.

It was like she was waking up after a long sleep.

The pink sun peeking over the rounded horizon hit her arms and bathed her in colored light. Her mouth opened in a small circle as she took it all in. His sanctuary, his sky, his sea. He draped a blanket around her shoulders. "This is my favorite spot on the ship. And if anyone knew about it, I'd be fired on the spot."

She wiggled her finger at his oasis. "I take it this is against code?"

Gabriel shrugged. "It's not like they said I *couldn't* bolt chairs to the top of the ship, but I don't think they'd like it." His phone buzzed at him, as if in agreement. By now, he was missing the morning staff meeting. He pushed the side button to ignore the buzz. If they really needed him, they'd call again.

Jesse snorted. "Understatement." She sank to the blanket and took a breath, the movement relaxing her shoulder, her limbs. "It's nice."

"That's it? Nice?" He was nervous, he realized. Jittery. Scared that she'd judge him, that she wouldn't find him cool. He felt like a teenager again, and he wasn't sure if he loved it or loathed it. He sat next to her, pulled out two lidded glasses of orange juice, and topped them off with champagne.

"Better than nice," she amended and pursed her lips. "It's delicious, maybe even more so since it's a secret. A risk."

Her words hit him right in the center of his chest. "Yes, exactly." It was the sweet taste of getting away with something, even if it was something as innocent as building a sanctuary in a war zone.

He set out a plate of cheese and salami, yogurt, and little breakfast sandwiches, hoping he'd found at least one thing she liked. "I raided the breakfast buffet on the way up here, but this"—he pulled out a French press already full of his secret coffee stash and added hot water—"is straight from my sister's kitchen in Argentina." He heard the longing in his voice, the knowing that it'd been far too long since he'd been home. From the look Jesse gave him, she heard it too.

"Your sister roasts her own coffee beans?" She sniffed at the steam. "I predict this is going to ruin me for the ship's coffee for the rest of the trip."

Gabriel smirked. "It will. She roasts and grows them. She has a boutique coffee plantation, mostly funded by online investors who get a coffee bean delivery each month as part of their investment. I help with the rest." He let the coffee steep for a couple of minutes, then poured them each a small serving into two travel mugs.

"That's sweet of you." She stared at him like he had the vestige of the Virgin Mary printed on his face. "To help fund your sister's business."

His thoughts flickered back to his sister's shaking voice over *Papá's* cold body. *What will we do now, Gabriel? How are we going to live?* Even now, he heard the unspoken words. Words his sister would never lay on him, but they were there just the same. *How could you do this to us?* Decades later, he didn't have the answer to that one. Nor the forgiveness within himself to let it go. "I owe her that much, at least." He broke his thousand-mile stare and did his best attempt at a no-cares smile. "Besides, what need do I have for all that money. My life is here, and everything is taken care of for me."

She didn't look like she'd let it go, but she nodded and stared into her coffee mug. He knew that Jesse understood the value of secrets...so much so that her brain had vaulted hers away from even her.

She took a sip of the coffee, and Gabriel found himself watching her, waiting to hear her judgment. Like a child who'd baked a cake for his *mamá*. "I can safely say that this is one of the best coffees I've ever had, and I've tasted a lot of coffee, from all over the world."

He slapped his knee. "I *knew* it! I've been telling her to enter her beans in one of those tasting challenges."

"That gives me an idea for an article. A *Best Coffees from Around the World* travel foray. I bet I can even get down to Argentina and visit your sister. Put her on the map."

Hope for his sister flared in his chest, followed immediately with guilt. "Jesse, I would never ask you to do—I never thought letting you taste—please don't think I'd ever use your position like that," he finally sputtered out.

She waved him off. "I wouldn't offer if I didn't want to do it. Besides, it'd be nice to delve more into the secret that is Gabriel Gutierrez."

His mouth dropped open. All this time he'd wanted her to open up to him, wanted to understand how much she actually remembered of him, and worried about her remembering what he did. He never once, not once, thought about what would happen if she found out what he'd done in his own life. Not just to her, but how he'd killed his own *papá*. He hadn't held the knife, but like his decisions with Jesse's father, he'd made choices. And his choices had killed the only father he'd ever known.

She rested her hand on his knee. "Gabe, I'm kidding. I would never pry into your life."

He covered her hand with his and stroked her knuckles, her hands cold and fragile. "You can pry, but you may not like what you find."

She sucked on her bottom lip and stared at him until he felt his soul exposed, until his secrets almost poured out. She squeezed his knee and looked away just in time.

They finished their breakfast in silence, the sun turning from pink to orange, breaking the dawn's spell. Jesse scooted closer to him, and he curled his legs around her, using his body to block some of the brisk breeze. Her hair brushed his lips, the lavender scent he was coming to associate with her filling his senses. He pulled her in close, hoping she couldn't hear the too-fast beat of his heart. Her body fit snugly into his, and it was like holding a patch of sun, tiny and warm. His phone buzzed him again, reminding him of the staff meeting he should be leading right now, the millions of other things that he was pushing to the side, all for this moment. Just one sunrise with the one girl who knew him beyond the uniform.

"Would you be up for helping me visit a couple of other places on the ship today?" Jesse asked, her voice tentative, like she wanted to cut her farewell tour short. She picked up his hand and began playing with his thumbnail, both a familiar touch and exploratory at the same time. Somehow, they'd reached this awkward state, where they'd both admitted to wanting to cross the friendship lines they'd drawn over the years, but too scared to take the steps. They were dancing in a loop, and he wanted to move to the next dance with her. Soon.

"Of course. I can't be available all day long, but I'm sure I can find time to let you in a few places. What did you have in mind?"

"The old dining room for one. I can't remember where it used to be." She pulled away from him, her restless mind jumping to the next item on her list. If only they could stay right here, in this moment, surrounded by the wind, far away from the day, far from her search for secrets.

"It's just the lower floor of main dining. I'd be happy to show you." He started cleaning up the leftovers, giving him an excuse to hide the effects of his adrenaline-punched heart. The more she saw, the more she remembered, the closer he got to being cut out of her life.

"Great. And I need you to let me into the Cigar Bar. I noticed it was closed."

He jerked his gaze to hers. "You went to the Cigar Bar when you were nine?"

"My dad took me everywhere with him." She looked as if there were more to that story, but if she wasn't going to press him, he wasn't going to press her. Not yet.

He shrugged. "We're renovating it, but of course I can let you in. Is that all?"

She shot him a smile. "For now."

He paused in his packing, risking a glance at her expression. "So, is it helping? Your farewell tour?"

There was a glint in her eye, too dark to be called mischievous. "Oh yes, it's helping. I think my therapist would be proud."

His heart pumped a bit harder, *thunking* against his bones. *It's helping.* But how much did she remember? What if she already remembered it all?

18

JESSE

Gabe leads me back into the warmth of the ship. I am chilled through, but it's as if being around him has given me a nuclear core and I can't feel the cold. The Sky Lounge has come to life in our absence, and other cruise guests sip on cappuccinos paired with over-sized croissants. As a travel writer, I've always felt like I'm something other than a normal vacationer, and now, being with Gabe and seeing things through his eyes, I feel even more alone. Except when I'm with him.

We step into an empty elevator car. The doors close, and I place a hand on Gabe's arm. I'm not ready to give him up just yet. "Thank you for this morning. I know it can't have been easy to get away."

A surprised beam of sunshine blasts from his smile. He covers my hand with his. "You're worth it, Jesse."

The elevator dings on the next floor, and we stop to take on more passengers. Gabe scoots to the back of the elevator to make room, looking as uncomfortable as a giant in Munchkinland, and...

I'm worth it.

I've never been worth it.

I steal a glance at him. I've caught that sunbeam from his smile, and it's held captive in my chest, warming me up from within. Other passengers crane their necks to look up at him. He's impressive, standing a head above all other men, buttoned-tight in his navy-blue uniform. It makes me proud to be around him, proud to maybe call him mine.

A breakfast buffet occupies the middle of the main dining room, and the tables are sparsely filled with casually dressed guests. There's a relaxed, sleepy feel to the room, but once Gabe enters, the servers stand a little straighter, the clink of fork against plate resounds a little sharper. He can't help but be noticed.

Gabe maneuvers through the tables and chairs, following a zig-zagging path through the dining room to the far corner, sectioned off by a wall and a column that once held up a balcony. "This is the start of the old dining room. From this pole, you can draw the old walls."

I step past him and let my memory fill in the hazy details. "It was maroon and gold back then, wasn't it?"

Gabe sucks in a breath. "You remember that?"

I shrug. "I remember insignificant details. Nothing that really matters." Then, the way he answered my question hits me. "Wait, were you here when I was here?"

Gabe's pale, his muscles gone completely stiff. "I was." His words are clipped, brittle.

Sometimes when interviewing a hostile subject, I've found that they have all these smooth sides. My questions slide off and I can't get to the true story underneath. Until I hit a snag in their surface, a hangnail that if I tug hard enough, I can make them bleed out all their secrets. This feels the same. I've hit a hangnail, and I didn't even realize that Gabe had a smooth surface.

What is he hiding?

"Do you remember me?" What else could it be? This is a long shot, but if he remembered anything, *anything*, it may be enough to jump start a memory.

He licks his lips and glances behind him. "It's a really big ship, Jesse. Even back then. Chances of us meeting..." He sighs.

"Yeah. You're right." Disappointment floods through my system, a better downer than a depressant. Not because we didn't meet, but because now I'm sure we did. He's lying. But why?

"S.C. Gutierrez?" The ship's CSO stands behind Gabe, hands propped on her hips. Her gaze flicks from me to Gabe, and something crosses her face. "We missed you at this morning's staff meeting." Her tone is not conversational but accusatory.

Who is this woman to question him?

His jaw tightens, but he simply *hmms* at her, as if hoping his non-response serves to shut off the topic.

The CSO's gaze slides over to me again. "What kept you from the meeting?" The challenge is for him, but the judge-and-jury look is all for me.

Gabe steps forward. "Ms. Andre, what I do with my time and how I choose to spend it is none of your concern."

Reluctantly, she peels her stare away from me, clears her throat, and returns her attention to him.

"Unless there's something urgent," Gabe continues, "I'm in the middle of something important."

A spark of electricity zaps my heart. I'm the something important? A smile tugs at my lips, but I don't let it show.

The CSO looks like she wants to argue, but she presses her lips together and walks off.

"Will you get in trouble for this morning?"

He flips his hands over. "Not a lot they can do when I claim our most important VIP needed my services."

I purse my lips to the side. "That I do."

Gabe finishes showing me where things used to be in the dining room just as a server rushes up to him. "Staff Cap, we've got a Code Green in the kitchen."

"You got to be kidding me," Gabe mutters under his breath. "I'll be right there."

The server rushes to the back while Gabe turns to me. "I'm so sorry, Jesse. Duty calls."

"Of course." I wave him off. "What's a Code Green?"

He shakes his head. "You really don't want to know." He gives me a little bow and rushes off to the kitchen.

I spend a few more minutes in the dining room, but there's nothing here. It's been recarpeted, repainted, redecorated. There's nothing left of the old dining room, nothing but this one pillar and this one wall and a vacant space full of tumbleweed memories.

———

I HEAD BACK to our stateroom, my feet sinking further into the carpet with each step. I've avoided Momma since yesterday. I've done everything I can to stay out of her way, stay far away from her accusations.

The tissue paper clinging to the...*proof*...I don't remember doing that. I can't have done that. There's nothing in me that wants that.

We tell the truth in this house, girlie.

His voice is so near it gobsmacks me, sends me tripping across the floor. I look around, but no one else can hear him. He's loud and bassy, he echoes from the deep, he sets the hairs on the back of my neck on fire. My hands wrench into fists, my biceps bulge, I'm ready to fight, but he's nowhere. He's everywhere.

If it weren't for him, I'd believe me.

But since he *is* here, there's no telling what I am capable of in the darkness.

An envelope is tucked into the box outside our stateroom. I grab the envelope, unlock our door, and walk into the living room. Momma is sprawled out on my bed, reading an 80s-style bodice ripper.

She sits up, the back of her hair mussed, the front in a perfect curl. "Where you been, Jesse-girl?"

I don't bother answering her or remind her how much I hate being called Jesse-girl. I open the envelope, slide out two tickets for a Jamaican catamaran snorkeling excursion, and toss them onto the nightstand next to her. She reaches for them, pinches them between her fingers.

"Snorkeling, Jesse?" In those two words, I hear that broken-ness again. That pure animalistic pain that makes no sense to me. To have that level of hurt would mean my mother was, at some point, human. Not this shriveled, bitter crone she's shown herself to be. "You can't. *We* can't." The tickets tremble in her hand, and I snatch them away from her before she does something stupid like rip them up.

"We are. You wanted to be here with me. This is what I'm doing. If you want to join, great. I think it'd be good for you. But if not, stay here. Sulk. Wallow. I don't care." I drop my bag to the ground.

"But Jesse. He's there. You know he is." Her voice wobbles like old sagging skin.

"I thought you wanted to say goodbye to him. Wasn't that part of our plan? So yes, snorkeling, and whatever else we have to do to say goodbye to Daddy once and for all." I kneel in front of her. "We need this, Momma. We need to be free."

She meets my gaze, hers unfocused and watery, mine determined and unwavering.

"I'm scared too." It kills me to admit this, especially to her. She can use my words against me for all time, but in this, we're the same. We're both scared of facing Daddy. Scared of what it'll do to us. Scared if we'll come out the other side in one piece. Scared that if we do, we won't have anything left of him. He'll be gone, and we won't have any excuses left for why we are the way we are.

I place my hand over hers, and she grasps it, squeezes tight.

"You always were so much like him." She holds my gaze, looking deep into my eyes, as if she's studying me, searching for him. "He loved you more than me, you know." Her grip on my hand tightens. "He'd take you out for the nice dinners whenever we got a coupon, to the movies. You were his little girlfriend." She pulls me close, and this isn't loving, this isn't solidarity anymore. This is something else. This is the thing that has always haunted our relationship. "Me? I was his maid. His cook. His nanny. Nothing more."

I yank away from her and scoot backwards. She stands, towering over me, and we both know how easy it'd be for her to lift her booted foot and kick me across the room.

"I was his daughter," I remind her, try to talk some sense into her.

"You were more." Her teeth clench around the word. "You got his love. I got his dirty dishes."

It's like a veil has been lifted, and I'm seeing Momma for the first time. Seeing her hurt, seeing her pain, and though I'm not forgiving her for the years of abuse, I can almost get it.

She takes a breath, takes a step back from me, and rolls back her shoulders. "Snorkeling then. I guess my foot will need to get miraculously better before tomorrow." She goes for a smile, and there's a softening in her, almost as if we've found a common enemy to unite against. Or she's given up.

"There's no need for you to get in the water." I force my words through the tight squeeze in my chest and stand. "*You* don't need to remember what happened. *I* do."

"Yes, pumpkin, you do." She sucks on the inside of her cheek. "We need to know what you did. What did you do to your daddy, Jesse?"

And there it is again. That question. What did I do?

Did I kill him?

This is what I'm really here to find out. This is why I search. This is why I must remember. I'm betting it all on the slim chance that the answer is 'no.'

19

JESSE

There's a soft knock at the door. CSO Delice Andre stands on the other side, chest puffed out, hand resting casually on her radio.

The ship lurches, shifting into a new gear, and we adjust our footing.

"Can I help you?" I cross my arms and fill up as much of the space in the door as I'm able.

Andre hooks her thumbs in her belt, nudging her Taser gun. "I need you to come with me."

I look her up and down, letting her see that I don't care what she needs. Gabe warned me about her.

"This isn't an option, Miss David." She swallows, and it looks like she's trying to hold tight to her composure.

"Oh, but it is." I smile, showing her I'm not worried about her options. "Unless you are making an arrest, I don't have to agree to any questioning." I prop my hands on my hips, mimicking her. "Are you arresting me?"

Her brown eyes dart back and forth. Normally this was a signal for an interviewee looking for an exit. But she was the one who had me cornered, so—

Her eyes stilled, drilled in on mine. "We have you on video."

Video? My heart thuds. Once. Twice. Not good. I know of exactly two times I've had a blackout on this ship. What if there were more? What did I do?

Delice's grin spreads through her lips, slow, unhurried, showing teeth. "Meet me in fifteen minutes in the Cigar Bar, deck ten. That is, if you want a chance to clear your name."

I click the door closed as she turns away, my breakfast churning.

"Who was that?" Momma's picked her book back up, holding it close to her nose.

"No one," I mutter. She doesn't really care anyway. "I'll be back later." I grab my bag and head toward the Cigar Bar. It's on my list of places to visit, but I don't think this is what my therapist had in mind. What does the CSO have on me?

The Cigar Bar has a crooked "Closed—Under Construction" sign. Gabe said it was undergoing remodeling, but once I open the door, it looks more like a gut and replace.

Delice waits for me by the windows.

I dodge a stack of pipes and the dismantled bar on my way to her. Dotted around the lounge are bolted-to-the-floor leather swivel chairs. I remember the deep, velvet red carpet, the dark wood walls, the replica paintings of classic stars. Singers like Frank Sinatra, Elvis, and Etta James and sports heroes like Arnold Palmer and Joe DiMaggio command little alcoves in the walls, complete with rounded bench seating around polished tables. Ready for a game of poker and cigars. The tangy smell of expensive cigars lingers, fills in the sensory details in my mind.

My eyes stung while we were here, and I begged Daddy to take me somewhere else. He told me to quit whining and pulled me close while he finished his poker game.

I trail my fingers along a wooden rail, the varnish catching at my fingertips, and I walk to where CSO Andre stands in front of the bank of windows.

She gestures to a pair of swivel chairs by the window and waits for me to sit. I do so and lean forward on my knees. Andre sits in the opposite chair and keeps her gaze focused on me. I wait for her to speak, but she's silent, tapping her lips, one, two, three. I lick my own and swipe lip balm over them. Still, she's silent.

I stand. "Well, that was enlightening. Thank you for wasting my time."

"We haven't started. Please. Sit." Andre drums her fingertips on the edge of the leather armrest.

I press at my lip and take a seat. Whatever this is, might as well get it over with.

"Did you hear about the passenger who lost his dog the other day?" She's small-talk casual.

I shift in my seat, press harder against my top lip. Can she see my pulse pound in my neck? Can she hear it? "I read the Mainstay. I thought we were here to watch a video." I cross my arms and tap my toe against the cocktail table that separates us.

"We're getting there." She waves, like it's a matter of no consequence, when all of this is only a matter of consequences. "That dog? Sad deal. His owner has seizures. Poor little Jelly was his service dog. Saved his life more than a dozen times."

I can feel the blood drain from my cheeks, my fingertips. "That is sad. Hope they find the dog soon." My voice sounds rusty and eaten through.

"Oh, we did. Not common knowledge though. Can you keep a secret?" She leans forward and drops her voice to a whisper as if we are kiss-and-tell girlfriends, instead of hunter and hunted. "Dog's dead. Found him floating in the aquarium."

My world tilts to the side, and I hook one ankle around the other, holding myself close. "Poor puppy. How did he get up there?" The aquarium glows blue in my mind's eye, fish bubbling in a silent circulation. I feel the metal grate beneath my knees.

"He had help," she snaps, her words clipped short. "Miss David, have you ever—"

My hand tightens into a fist. "Call me Jesse. Mrs. David is my mother."

"Alright, Jesse. Have you ever seen a dead dog?" The CSO thumbs through photos on her phone.

"It's been a while." The words spring off my lips, dry, humorless, and full of guilt.

"Let me refresh your memory." Andre turns the phone around, and a close-up of the dog's face punches at me. Sucked out eyes, stiff skin, empty smile.

I clench the hem of my shirt, knotting the fabric in my fingers. I don't want to see the pictures. They're gruesome, full of maybes.

"See the edges of where his lips used to be?" Andre keeps the phone in my face, no matter how much I back away, no matter how much I try to look away. "The fish didn't do that. Someone else did. Those sharp slices? Definitely a knife."

"I'm going to be sick." I'm not, but I can't be here any longer. The memory of Momma's voice strikes against my skull. *What did you do?*

I didn't do this. I can't have done this.

I stand, move to leave.

Andre kicks a construction bucket towards me. "Here you go. I can wait."

I study her. She doesn't want a confession, she wants a fight. And I'm not going to give it to her. "It passed." I grab a tube of lip balm out of my bag and spread it over my lips.

"You know the interesting thing about all this?" The CSO thumbs through some more photos, making sure I see each and every one. "It all leads back to you." She thins her lips and waits for my response.

"Really? And how did you come to that conclusion?" My voice weakens. Does she have evidence? What did I do? Part of me wants to see me in my unconscious state. The other part wants to run for the Sahara and dig a giant hole to stick my head in.

"A hunch. Observation. And this." She pulls up a security video. "Day we boarded the ship, you went for a walk, didn't you?"

"I've been on lots of walks. Kind of required to get from place to place." I flutter my hand in the air, another of Momma's moves, but where Momma is flippant, I feel careless and rough around the edges.

"Sure, but you see, this hallway only leads to more staterooms. The dog's owner's stateroom, to be exact. Did you have someone you were going to visit?" The CSO cocks her head, as if she is really interested.

"I don't remember everywhere I've been." I glance toward the windows, before I realize I've just signaled my own need to escape.

"But surely you'd remember visiting someone's stateroom?" She presses.

"You would think," I mutter and glance toward the door. Another escape. Can't help it.

"You have a thing for lips, don't you?" She asks it so matter-of-factly that it throws me back in my chair.

"What?"

"You know. Some people have a foot fetish, others collect dirty panties. But you...it's lips." She traces her own, and I can't help it. I follow every minuscule movement.

"Are you insane?" But my fingers are dancing toward the lip balm in my bag, and I'm nervous-swiveling in the leather chair.

"*I'm* not." She smiles, but it doesn't reach her eyes. It doesn't even reach her cheeks. "Did you know you put on lip balm about once every ten minutes?"

"You've been watching me?" This is a violation, and it bristles the hair along my spine, makes me want to hiss and spit.

The CSO continues as if she didn't hear me. "And you almost bit off Mr.—"

"I was attacked." I propel out of my chair and loom over Delice before I realize what I'm doing. "I didn't realize Luxury Lines condoned stalking and harassing guests."

"We don't." A deep, male voice echoes through the room, and it immediately sets my world right. Tension rolls off my spine, splinters to the ground.

Gabe.

He stands by the dismantled bar, half covered in shadow, looking like the hero of an action film. He takes a few steps closer, and sunlight covers him from head to toe.

"A Code Green? Really, Delice?" He doesn't wait for her to answer, just watches her shrivel in front of him. "Get out, CSO Andre." His jaw is tight. His muscles quiver. His nostrils flare. Oh, she is so fired.

She stands. "I know you killed that dog, Jesse," she hisses, hands shaking as she puts her phone away. "You ripped its lips off just like you tried to rip off Michael's lip. I know what you are. I've *known* what you are."

"CSO, now." Gabe's voice booms against the wood paneled walls.

She stiffens her spine and faces him. "This is *my* job. You're blocking my every effort and forcing me to find other ways to get what I need."

"Report to the captain. Immediately," Gabe says, leaning in and invading her space. "I'll let him know you're on your way. And why."

"Good. I've been meaning to talk to the captain about some trouble I'm having with another officer." She stares up at him, and it's like watching a Chihuahua try to stand up to a Great Dane. The door closes behind her, and Gabe rushes to me.

This time, there's no trace of the job that seems to cling to him like a red wine stain. It's gone. It's just him.

It's just me.

And Daddy. Always Daddy.

I sink to the nearest chair and raise a hand to my head. Gabe's footsteps stop just short of a beam of light that has a tinge of rainbow on the edges.

"Are you alright?"

I don't answer. How can I? A dangerous woman has video footage of me going to a cabin I don't remember. There's a dead dog that has my M.O. all over it. My mother has me ensnared in a trap I never saw coming.

I rub my forehead, massaging away a blossoming headache.

And Gabe. Gabe is perfect.

Except for what he's hiding from me.

"I apologize for Delice's behavior. Again. She's new and hasn't quite learned the difference between murder suspects and guests. She stepped over the line and will be dealt with." Gabe tries filling the air with reassurances, explanations. He's trying to find the cause to my effect. He's trying to fix it.

There's no fixing this. Any of it.

Outside, a cloud scuttles across the sun and a chill falls over the lounge.

"Mr. Hart will be sent home once we dock tomorrow in Jamaica. I'll make sure of it. He won't bother you again." Gabe kneels in front of me and grips the arms of my chair, barricading me in. I'm not sure if it makes me feel safe or trapped. "Jesse, I'm so sorry about all you've been through on this trip."

My fingers pause, and I finally know what I want from him. Not the truth he's hiding, not reassurances, not promises.

"Why do you care?" I sound so weak and fragile, it hurts to listen to.

"Excuse me?"

I move my hand from my face and take a good look at him. Past the uniform, past this mask he wears, cutting away the layers until I see him. Just him.

"You know about my blackouts, I'm sure you've guessed about my mother, you know what I am and yet, you still care. Why?" I trail a finger across my upper lip, CSO Andre's words stuck in my head. *Lip fetish.*

His eyebrows raise as he realizes what I'm talking about.

"It's part of my job to—"

An inferno blazes inside me. "Don't do that. You're hiding behind your job, and it doesn't work with me. Not anymore." I press my lips together and shift my legs. The cloud blanketing the sun moves on, and a beam of light centers on Gabe's neck, like a laser.

He huffs out a heavy breath, leans forward, and clasps his hands.

"I feel for you." His words come out quiet and thick. Slightly strangled.

I wait.

Gabe licks his lips and clears his throat. "You...intrigue me. Since the first day I met you, you've captivated me."

"Because I'm different." My head drops, but I have to know. Am I an experiment to him? A bit of intrigue? Or something more?

"Because of who you are." Gabe's hand caresses my cheek, and it's warm and rough and intoxicating. "Over the years, you've become my constant. There's no one else—" His throat tightens around the words. "You *see* me. When I'm with you, I'm more than this." He pulls at his uniform, and his eyes are shiny, intense.

My heart squeezes, twists. His vulnerability, his need to be loved and *seen* is as great as mine.

"So we're the same." My voice breaks down, and my body trembles. Why am I trembling?

Gabe tucks a piece of hair behind my ear and lifts my chin. I'm lost in his eyes, and they are earnest, genuine.

So how could he be lying to me?

"I guess we are." He traces my cheek, my eyebrow with his thumb. It seems as if he's thrown the rulebook he's kept between us all these years right into the ocean.

And I want it to be gone. I want to close this gap between us, finally, after all these years.

"Every single cruise, I check the roster for your name. I watch the boarding ramp for your face."

The beats in my chest are slow, but hard, pounding out an ancient beat.

"But you know about my blackouts. How could you—" I start to wave him away, but he catches my fingers, turns my hand over, and traces the bluish vein crossing my wrist.

"You deal with memory loss after a tragic event in your life. That isn't who you are." He circles a green bruise left on my arm from Michael's attack, and his eyes turn to fire. He bends down and presses his lips to the mark. "You're messy and complicated." He raises his gaze to meet mine, and I am trapped in his eyes. "But so is everyone. We just get to hide it better than you do."

I lean toward him. He is making this so easy and so very hard at the same time. How can I close this distance, knowing that he's lying? He's keeping something from me, he has answers and he knows I need them.

I want him. I want him more than I've wanted anything in a very, very long time.

I shift closer.

And stop.

I want him. I want genuine, authentic, not-lying-to-me him.

I pull away from him. "Gabe?" I keep my gaze locked on his. I want to watch his facial expressions for any sort of lie indicators. I want to be sure I'm right, before I throw away the only chance at a relationship I may ever have.

He's breathing heavy, his brown eyes are dark with desire, and he's close. So close.

I bite my lip, take courage from the bite of pain, and dive in. "I know we've met before."

He freezes. Every muscle in his face goes tight. I can almost see the barrier between us being flung back together, brick after brick after brick, sloppy mortar dripping down.

And there's my answer.

The door clicks, and we fly apart.

Captain Knight steps through the doorway, his dimples drawn deep in his cheeks. The smile on his face isn't friendly, but forced, distasteful.

"Mr. Gutierrez, Miss David. CSO Andre suggested I find you here." He walks across the room, stopping far enough away to demonstrate proper boundaries. Gabe's close enough to me to need the reminder. "Am I interrupting something?" His tone is far from inquisitive. He doesn't need to inquire; he already knows enough to make an educated guess. Gabe and I? We're more.

Or at least, we had the potential to be more. Before I stuck a knife in potential's back.

Gabe leaps to his feet, stands at attention. "No, sir. Miss David and I were just discussing the—uh—" Gabe sounds like a little boy in trouble for eating dessert before dinner.

I jump in. "He was making sure I understood how out of line your CSO was. He didn't want her actions to reflect poorly on my perception of Luxury Lines. You know how easily swayed my readers are." I tack on the reminder. Even though Gabe may have crossed a few lines, it's nothing compared to what I can do to this cruise line's reputation, and stock price, with a few well-timed articles.

"Of course, Miss David." Captain Knight's posture changes. His dimples deepen, he beams goodwill. "I simply wanted to come up here and apologize for all your troubles. You have my word that our CSO will not bother you again."

I pick up my hat. "I appreciate that." I touch the bruise on my neck, a subtle reminder that the CSO has not been my only trouble while on board.

Captain Knight is quick to pick up on it, as I knew he would. "And I hope you'll join me at my table sometime this week. It'd be my honor to host you and your mother."

"How kind, but I think I'll let my mother have the honor of dining with the captain." I press my lips together and hope that Gabe gets the message. Our conversation is not over. "She'd appreciate a night out without me, and I'll take advantage of her being gone to have a quiet dinner. All to myself." I keep my focus directed at the captain, but my words are all for Gabe. "Tomorrow's not good, but the next evening works for us. Shall I send my mother to you then? Around five-thirty?"

Captain Knight's smile has transformed from genuine to plastered-on. "That would be wonderful." His tone remains friendly, but it's stretched tight, it's plastic.

"And she'd love a private tour of the ship after dinner." I step closer to the captain, passing over his imaginary boundary.

The captain leans away. "I understand. I wish I could, but I have other obligations."

I take another small step, crossing fully into the captain's personal territory. "It'd mean so much to me to have the evening off from taking care of her. After all, my time with Luxury Lines hasn't exactly been restful."

The captain tightens his jaw, his dimples all but disappearing, his smile unwavering. "It'd be my pleasure."

"Wonderful. Thank you, Captain." I pat his arm and scoot out the door, dodging pipes and four-by-fours on the way, adding a little sass to my sway, and hope it's enough to take the heat off Gabe.

To give us some extra time. To give Gabe the chance to make things right.

DAY FOUR

"Swim," says Daddy,
So I wiggle my tail,
And we all do the boogie woogie,
Until we're joined by a whale.

20

JESSE

THE SUN IS STILL HIDING BELOW THE HORIZON WHEN my alarm buzzes the next morning. I shut it off and hold my breath. If I've timed this right, both Momma and Daddy will be asleep.

No sound coming from Momma's room. No whispers from Daddy's shadows.

When I was little, I got very good at sneaking around in the dark.

I peel back the sheets and slink out from under them without making a rustle. I have to find the proof she's holding. The blackmail. I do a quick search of my sleeping area, and everywhere else but Momma's room, even though I already know it won't be in the main cabin. She's probably sleeping with it tucked under her pillow.

It's been a few years, but I still have that catch in my throat as I ease her door open and take the first step inside her room.

Outside her bedroom window, the sky lightens to a deep purple. The ship slows, getting ready to enter Jamaican waters. We'll be docked in less than an hour, which means I only have a few minutes before the changing gears of the ship wake Momma up.

I ease to her closet and pull the doors open. There, at the bottom, is a blue duffel bag with black handles. Turned inside out and wadded into a tight ball. Empty.

What did she have in the bag?

I pat down the few dresses she's hung on hangers, but they aren't hiding any secrets. I put things back in place and turn around.

My heart stops. Momma's sitting straight up in bed, watching.

Darkness creeps toward me, reaching over my vision with oil-slick fingers, for the first time showing the progression of me losing time. It's a blackout, coming at me like the inevitable dawn, and nothing I can do will stop it.

"You ain't gonna find it, pumpkin."

The darkness crowds out my vision—

———

I'M ROLLING Momma off the ship onto the solid pier at the Port of Falmouth when I come back to myself. It's a blue-sky morning edged with darkening clouds and a warm, searching breeze. The ocean brushes against the pier, seagulls screech overhead, and on the other side of the gate, the port is bustling. I stop, tripping the person behind me. I'm wearing a one-piece swimsuit, a pair of cargo shorts, and an unbuttoned, white beach shirt.

I'm thankful I'm not in a bikini this time, but what I've done, I don't know.

Momma cranes her head up to look at me. "You're back, aren't you?" She huffs a short sigh as the crowd flows around us. We're rocks in the stream, a minor annoyance.

"What happened?" My voice feels hoarse, as if I've been yelling.

Momma shrugs and looks straight ahead. "I like the other you better."

"The other me?"

The other me during my blackouts. The one who buys a skimpy swimsuit, the one who visits staterooms, the one who may have done the unthinkable. I push her wheelchair again, sparing a hand to check my pockets for our excursion tickets. They're there, tucked into my cargo shorts. At least the other me is somewhat responsible.

"Momma, what happened?" I try again, but it's a no-win battle, lost before it even starts. In stubbornness, she outranks me.

She stares straight ahead. "Nothing."

But something did. I have a cut on my thumb, just a small slice, but it's new. And she's too smug for my comfort.

Whatever happened, it's in direct opposition to what the me of now wants. I tighten my grip on her wheelchair handles and clench down on my teeth. I can do so many impossible things. Speak dozens of languages, connect with people in tribes who've never seen an outsider, climb ancient ruins in dangerous jungles, kayak the world's most treacherous rivers, but this. This, I can't do. Because how do I fight myself?

In the distance, the Jamaican Blue Mountains rise and give a sense of lushness to an otherwise impoverished nation. I'd rather be climbing those mountains barefoot and without an escort than getting on board a booze cruise and playing in the ocean. But I have a mission and a ticking time bomb in the shape of my blackouts.

Steel drums interrupt my thoughts, and the chaos of the port seeps in. Vendor booths line the walkway. On one side, pop-up tents are filled with wood art, carved skulls, and toys. On the other side of the walkway, a permanent structure houses a Dairy Queen and a Quiznos. Such a shame. A jerk chicken restaurant, an artisan shop, or even a Bob Marley shrine would be better.

A disturbance at the port security entrance grabs my attention. Michael, with his damaged face, shoulders a preppy duffel bag as two Jamaican officers lead him through the security gates and into a waiting van. Somehow, his gaze searches out mine, and he doesn't break his I-see-through-you glare until the van door shuts and drives him away.

My spine releases a small bite of tension, and I'm finally able to take a deep breath. Gabe held true to his word.

Momma and I find our place in the shore excursion line and, thirty minutes later, walk onto another pier. The waves suck at the sides, like fish feeding on a carcass. My hands are pale, and the bones of my knuckles press against my skin as I stranglehold Momma's chair.

The wooden slats bounce under my feet. The last time I stood on a pier with the waves hammering underneath, my feet were quite a bit smaller and they skipped, happy, but not quite free. The past wavers my vision, and the toe of my grown-up sandal catches on a rotten piece of wood. I don't want to be here.

"Welcome to Jamaica, *mon.*" The captain of the platform boat waits for us on the pier. Arms wide and accent thickened.

Please don't let the boat start. Please don't let the boat start. I begin making deals with every deity I can think of.

On cue, the engine rumbles, and the boat vibrates, creating little man-made waves that clash with the ocean's rhythm. Proving either a higher-power doesn't exist or he—maybe she —doesn't care.

"So glad you could join us." The captain is still talking. Not to me, but to Momma. She waves him away and responds, but the roar of the ocean, the cry of the seagulls, the snapping of fishes' fins are deafening. "Help this young lady aboard." He directs some crew members to carry her wheelchair on board, but my fingers have frozen to the handles.

"We'll take good care of your momma, yeah-*mon*?" They play up the Jamaican accent for tourists and tips.

I nod, but don't let go. They exchange a look, then shrug, peel my fingers off, and take Momma away. I'm left alone on the pier. My cargo shorts blow against my legs. The wind picks up, and in the distance gray clouds build.

I could run away. The thought is all kinds of déjà vu. Momma can't stop me. I could run and run and...go where?

I'm on an island. Surrounded by water.

I can't breathe. It's as if someone has wrapped an iron hand around the base of my neck, fingers pressing into my throat, cutting off my air supply one finger at a time.

"Ready, *ooman*?"

It's not his use of *ooman*—woman—that makes me narrow a glare. It's his use of *ready*—a Jamaican catcall. "I'm not your *ready*. Show some *reespek*." I push past him and let my anger carry me onto the boat.

His laughter bounces off the waves. "Careful-*mon*," he says to his crewmates. "She speaks Jamaican."

The crew joins in with hyena laughter while someone starts up the music and Boombastic pours out of crackly speakers. The rest of the excursion crowd flows onto the boat, all dancing before their feet touch our impermanent aluminum island, one big blur of color. They give Momma a pitying look, sometimes a what's-up-with-grandma look, and dismiss her.

I sneak in a glance. She's the last person on this boat they should dismiss. She sits under a canopy erected over the center of the boat. Her hands are folded in her lap, her right pinkie finger playing with her wedding band. She looks innocent. Just sitting there enjoying the sun at her back. But behind her blue-blue eyes, I can see the calculations and the manipulations.

I find a place under the canopy and wrap my arms around one of the supporting poles. The boat jerks, and we push off from the pier. Land gets...not smaller, but more unreachable.

Where are the damn life vests?

A family of two-point-five sits next to Momma. A girl, about nine years old, with blond hair tied back in a ponytail, her daddy, and her momma with one on the way. My momma flicks her gaze at the dad, and her eyes widen. I follow her gaze, and my air cuts off completely. I hold on tighter to the supporting pole, my arms the only things holding me up, and darkness creeps in on the edges. Strong shoulders, square chin, sandy blond hair. Full lips. Looks a lot like Daddy.

Seems to smile more, though.

One of the hyena crew pushes a cup of rum punch into my hand. I can't drink. I don't want to give the ocean an edge, and besides, Daddy wouldn't like it.

The water is blue-blue like Momma's eyes. The gray clouds move closer. Maybe we'll get rained out.

A spark of hope singes my heart. *Careful, Jesse. You might get scorched.*

The engine shuts off, and the music turns down. The waves push against the boat and roll us around, tasting us like one tastes wine. The crew hops into high gear and starts shoving life vests, fins, and masks into everyone's hands. I hide in the shadows.

"Don't forget my daughter!" Momma's shrill voice drowns out even the sound of the ocean. Of course *she* can be brave right now. She's not going into the water.

The captain walks over with the snorkeling gear. He takes in my death-grip on the pole and seems to see past my dark sunglasses. "You do not have to go, miss. You can stay here, get first dibs at lunch."

Yes. Yes, yes, yes. I start to nod my agreement, but past his shoulder, Momma tightens her grip around the cane in her lap. The silver glints in the sun. She brought her cane? I blink, and the cane disappears. I shake my head. I'm imagining things. But I'm not imagining her tightened fists or the promising curl of her lips, the one that says *told you so* and *you can't do it, just like I thought.*

"I can—" My mouth is dry. I grab my previously abandoned plastic cup and drain the rum punch. Who am I kidding? The ocean already has all the edge it needs. "I'm okay. I'll go."

The captain looks me over again. "You can swim?" Doubt laces through his tone, and I don't blame him. I'm not exactly the picture of reassurance.

I nod. I can swim, I think. At least, I used to be able. The captain presses his lips together. I trace my own, fumble for my lip balm, hidden in one of my short's many pockets, and smear it over my lips. He nods. "Okay then. Sammy," he yells over his shoulder. "Get over here." He hands my gear over to the head hyena. "Help her get suited up, then escort her to the group."

I pull off my shorts, and then Sammy helps me fasten my life vest and mask. He holds my arms as I slip my feet into the swimming fins, adjusts the snorkeling tube, and makes me demonstrate I can breathe out of it.

It's like breathing through a straw. My chest tightens, and my breaths quicken. The air pushes around me, squeezing my ribs together.

"Let's go, *baby*."

Right.

I ease down the stairs to the ocean. Seven steps until the lapping tongue of the water reaches my toes. Now, six. Five. *No turning back now.*

The waves creep up the metal stairs, but it's not the splashing or the sucking or the deep throb of the ocean I hear. It's Daddy. His strangled laugh gurgles as he's drowning. As if he knows how much dying is going to screw me and Momma over. As if he knows that no matter what, I'm coming to him. He may have died in Cozumel, but this is the same water, the same fish. This is his grave.

The ocean pulls at my stomach. I don't remember walking the last five steps, and I don't remember the liquid silk of the water running over my calves and thighs. My panic subsides. I'm caught in the dead's warm embrace, and the dead do not panic. They do not feel. They just do.

I let go.

My body sinks into the water, held afloat only by the restraints on my vest. The waves bob me up and down and far off in the distance, lightning flashes in the clouds—confirmation of unanswered prayers. I take a deep breath, and even as my mind reminds me that I can breathe through the straw, my body refuses to listen. I roll onto my stomach and, for the first time in two decades, put my face in the ocean.

The ocean throbs. Daddy's laughter is louder. He's down here somewhere, among the biggest cluster of fish. I kick, the swimming fins tugging at my hamstrings. A crab scuttles around dead coral. They like the dead. My skin crawls and my breaths grow even more strangled. I suck in deep gulps of air, but I can only suck them down in time to the rhythm of Daddy's giggling gurgles. I don't remember Daddy ever giggling, except once. He only lost control once.

The cane was his, first.

The thought slams into me, rips me open. I drag my face out of the ocean, yank the snorkeling tube out of my mouth. Sprays of saltwater hit my tongue, and I drag in a gasping, choking breath.

"You okay, *baby?*" My keeper's shout rings out from somewhere behind me.

"I'm fine." I shout back, drowning out the little girl's voice inside my head. The one that screams for Daddy to save her. To not leave.

The little girl who still feels guilty that she's relieved he's gone. But Daddy's not gone, is he?

Salt stings my tongue, and I'm not sure if it's ocean or tears.

I shove the breathing tube back in my mouth, shift my weight, and plunge my face in.

He's calling me. In between the ocean's heartbeat and the flutter of fish, I can hear him.

You know how to give me peace, Jesse-girl.

A flash of red in the water. Fish are swarming. Blood. It's blood.

Screaming. The screaming is getting so loud. My feet kick me toward the red, even though my mind is stuck on *don't.*

I'm over the swarm. The fish are going crazy, a feeding frenzy.

They part.

And there he is.

Daddy's pasty white flesh dances away from his body in elegant ribbons of death. His feet and hands have been chewed off, and his hair floats around his face as if he's been turned into a nightmarish merman. Sun and shadow tiptoe across his skin as I swim nearer. Somehow, I've lost my life vest. The ocean's cold fingers penetrate, take advantage, but I've stopped fighting.

Maybe this has been my destiny all along. To die on Daddy's death bed.

My lungs burn, and my brain shouts for oxygen, but all that is distant. Not a part of me anymore.

Daddy opens his eyes. They're empty. Two black holes that shouldn't see me, but they do. He jerks his head, and I swim closer. I'm close enough to smell his decay, to touch his torn flesh floating like seaweed.

Do you forgive me, Daddy?

He smiles, and for a moment, I think I am forgiven. I can die, and we can both rest in peace.

His lips disintegrate, and the roots of his teeth begin to protrude. His jaw opens with a click, and his tongue wags out, black and purple and gray.

Avenge me.

It's as loud as the ocean's deep hunger.

I shake my head.

Avenge me.

I back away. I can't.

Oh, but you can, Jesse-girl.

He's right. I can. I have.

You will become my instrument. Death is in you. I am in you.

My lungs are exploding.

Daddy tilts his head, and I look where he indicates.

There's a little girl curled in the coral. Blond ponytail waving in the ocean's current.

I burst to the surface and find the screaming wasn't in my head.

At least, not all of it.

21

GABRIEL

THE STEADY HUM OF THE SHIP'S ENGINE AND THE warmth of Control's many computers wrapped around Gabriel. It would be comforting, if it weren't for the five-foot-two nuisance standing in front of him. He'd wanted to deliver the news to his Chief Security Officer in person.

"Jesse David is a hero," Gabriel repeated himself. "She saved a little girl from drowning."

"She what?" Delice's voice cracked and bounced around Control, silencing conversations and jokes. Crew jerked their attention from their screens to them, then buried themselves in their work.

"I said, she rescued—"

"No, I heard you." Delice shook her head. "How could she rescue that little girl?"

"You mean, because she's guilty in your eyes? And the guilty can't be good. Right?" A flash-flame of anger burned up his tone.

"No. I mean because she almost drowned yesterday." Delice fidgeted, side-stepping what he knew to be true about her. She was petty, and she'd sunk her teeth into the wrong suspect and couldn't let go.

From what he read about her last job—that she was fired from—this was a pattern with her.

"I'd think getting back in the water less than twenty-four hours after almost drowning would be a little too soon." Delice patted her bun, making sure all the pieces were in place, and took in a deep breath. "How's the girl?"

Delice turned from Gabriel and headed for the coffeepot. She poured coffee into her chipped mug and reached for the cream and sugar packets, overly nonchalant—as if she were playacting.

"She's okay," Gabriel said, choosing to pretend that Delice actually cared. "Shaken up, no apparent long-term damage. She's on her community's swim team back home—you'd think if any kid would be safe in the water, it'd be a kid like that."

"You'd think. But how was Miss David the one to find her? Where were her parents? The excursion crew? Why was Miss David the only one to see her?" Delice flipped the powdered cream packet back and forth.

"She told her parents she wanted to go back to the boat. They say they watched her climb up the ladder." Gabriel shook his head. Such a shame. And it could have been so much worse, if not for Jesse. "She must have jumped in for a quick swim after taking off her life vest. There was a knot on her head—doctor thinks she hit her head on something as she went in."

Delice stirred the powder into her coffee, the clumps collecting on the sides of the mug.

"So Miss David is either the hero or the cause," Delice muttered, so quietly that Gabriel almost didn't hear her.

"Excuse me?"

Delice leaned against the table and took a sip of her doctored coffee. She went on, as if he hadn't spoken. "I feel as though you and I got on the wrong foot. I'd like a chance to rectify that."

Gabriel narrowed his eyes and slid his jaw back and forth.

"I think we could make a good team," Delice continued, forced sincerity filling her words. "Let me prove to you I know what I'm doing. If I could just talk with Miss David, I could get to the bottom of things. Both with the dog and with Mr. Hart."

Gabriel felt his gaze turn predatory. He leaned forward, towering over Delice. "You talked to her yesterday, against orders. If you didn't get what you needed then, perhaps you aren't as good at your job as you think." He straightened and left Control without another word, a threat lingering in his wake. If he stayed, he'd say or do something there would be no coming back from. Delice was a problem, one that needed to be fixed. He'd write his recommendation to the captain to let her go at the end of this sailing and present all the evidence he'd gathered. Delice simply wasn't Luxury Lines material.

He leaned against the stark white ship's interior and pulled *Papá's* watch out of his breast pocket. Tomorrow, he'd spend the evening with Jesse.

Tomorrow, he'd come clean.

He let out a sharp breath, a hiss of pressure that didn't do a damned thing to alleviate the compacting pressure on his chest.

Tomorrow, he'd see if they could survive the truth.

DAY FIVE

Down, down deep,
In the big ocean blue,
Swim four little fishies,
A Whale and A Daddy and A Me and A You.

22

JESSE

It's a bright, sunny morning when the ship shudders to a stop in the middle of the ocean. Georgetown's port is too shallow for big cruise liners, so I'll take a small tender into the port. I walk to our balcony, wrapping my robe around me, waiting until the last possible moment to get dressed. Down below, the first tender docks on our ship, and it is impossibly small. I feel like I'm on board a toy boat in the middle of a giant pond.

My heart creeps into my throat, and I plunge my hand into my robe's pocket, gripping tight onto my lip balm.

You have a thing for lips, don't you?

The CSO's words have caught in my brain, and I don't want them to be true. My lips are dry this morning, but I keep my hand in my pocket, wrapped tightly around my security blanket. I'm shaking, but I won't let her be right.

"Ain't you gonna get dressed? We're gonna miss our boat." Momma's voice is more piercing than a flock of seagulls.

I slowly turn around. "We?" I blink at her.

She's wearing her one-piece construction barrel bathing suit under a knitted black swimsuit cover-up. No pants. Fanny pack wrapped around her waist. And tennis shoes. Not stylish ones, or even fancy-tacky ones, but the tennis shoes she wears when she clears the weeds out from around her double-wide.

They're still caked in mud.

"I'm done being left behind." She crosses her arms and juts out her chin. "I'm going."

"Momma, this one's a tour for work. I have research to do. And the tour guide was paid for one person, not two." Not you.

"ATM's on the way off the ship. Let's go, lazy bones." She thuds her cane onto the floor, tapping it twice.

The guests below must hate us, with all the cane thumping she does. It's the punctuation mark to most of her points.

I rub the bridge of my nose and let go a breath as I sidle past her. *Pick your battles.* Good advice from my therapist. Difficult to put into practice.

Thirty minutes later, Momma and I board a tender to Grand Cayman. She shuffles over the ramp, holding onto the muscled Luxury Lines crew. She's left the wheelchair behind but kept the boot, keeping up the pretense.

The two-decked tender has backless bench seating that takes up all the floor space. I slide into a spot near the middle, far from the edges, while the crew help Momma to a handicap seat near the exit. She gestures for me to join her, but I can't. My muscles have all locked in place. In some ways, the tenders are worse than the little catamaran we took snorkeling yesterday. We sit higher in the water, and the tiny boat sways with every wave—it'd take just one big one to push us over. Varying shades of blue stretch from ship to eternity. I close my eyes for the duration of the trip and pretend I'm floating on a water bed, not an overfull boat balancing on the ocean. It's only a fifteen-minute jaunt to the pier from here, but Daddy's voice is always louder on the water.

We dock at the port, and the crew usher us off with maximum efficiency before turning the boat around and speeding back to the ship. They're a study in hard work ethic, one of the reasons I love these islands. Every islander I've met over the years works harder than anyone I've encountered in the corporate world, but they play harder too. They live life at the extremes, and it works well for them.

Momma and I walk past dressed-up pirates panhandling pictures, through the security checkpoint, and into Georgetown's tourist zone. We wander past a coconut stand—Momma is somehow swayed to spend three quarters on a coconut water—before I lead the way through the cruise-guest-only gates.

We walk past high-end jewelry windows and art shops, Momma going slow in her walking boot. A mottled-brown chicken crosses our path, then struts onto the road as if it owns the place. It must, since all the cars stop for an impromptu chicken crossing.

I quicken my pace. My tour guide is meeting us away from the port and tourist traps, and we're already ten minutes late. The last thing I need to do is miss the tour, which will tank my article, ruin my deadline, and piss off my so-easily-pissed-off editor. I don't need his impending heart-attack on my shoulders.

"C'mon, Momma, we need to speed this up."

She walks slower.

Ahead, our tour guide waits in a powder-blue convertible Cadillac, top down. He's overly tanned, skin like leather, with wind-blown, sun-bleached hair. An ex-pat who's now making a killing off cruise-tourists who want a taste of island life.

Momma slides into the front seat, and I let her jabberjaw his ear off, while I get to work on my article, making voice notes into my phone and written notes in my notebook, holding the pages tight, keeping them safe from the wind. The scribbles and picture of the body is still there, but I can't bring myself to tear it loose and throw it away. It's a piece of my puzzle.

The tour guide pulls to a stop on the side of the road. We make our way down a few crumbling steps, and I take the lead, letting our guide ease Momma down the stairs. The sea breeze plays with my hair, and not ten feet away, the ocean explodes.

I lift my face to the sky as a girlish bubble of laughter fizzes from the bottom of my stomach and pops into the air. Water droplets from the sudden geyser falls around us in a soft mist.

I always make this stop, every time I come to Grand Cayman.

"This is my favorite thing about the ocean." I stand next to Momma and snap a few photos of Grand Cayman's blow hole. Our tour guide takes a stroll down the rocks, picking up shells and tossing them back into the ocean.

"A hole in a rock is your favorite thing? Figures." She crosses her arms and props up her breasts.

I turn to her, but she's staring off into the distance. "What do you mean by that?"

"You always did like a fixer-upper. Like your captain-buddy on the ship." She waves across the ocean, back toward the port. From here, the three cruise liners docked outside of Georgetown look like yachts, not 3,000-passenger ships.

"Staff captain, Momma. Not *the* captain." I have told her this before.

"You owe me a favor for going along with this captain-tour-thing tonight, you know this, right?"

"Yes, Momma." From the sideways glance he gives me, even our tour guide picks up on the annoyance in my tone.

"You do him yet?" Now she looks at me, her sea glass eyes piercing my skin, and licks her lips, slowly, seductively, disgustingly. It turns my stomach, makes me feel coated in grime.

"Gabe? None of your business." I look away and take some more photos of the geyser, just as it shoots into the air again.

"You're going to tonight, aren't ya?" She shakes her head, full of sass.

I don't answer. There's no point. No matter what I say, she'll twist it, turn it ugly.

"You know he was there, don't you?"

My camera slips from my fingers, the strap tightening around my wrist as the camera bungee jumps near my knee. "What?" I don't have to ask where. It comes together like the final twist of a Rubik's cube. Gabe was there, when Daddy drowned.

"Yup. Wasn't sure at first, but I saw his picture in your apartment and thought I recognized him. Then he meets us on the ship, and I knew. Kinda sick, if you ask me." She spreads her mouth into the kind of grin that cracks lips, her hot pink lipstick smudging in the corners, and she walks off, makes her way back to the car.

Things are going dizzy. Momma's a lot of things, and a liar when it suits her. She'll also tell the truth at the right moment to completely destroy my happy moments.

The geyser shoots up again, and I fumble for a seat on the sharp rocks. My center of gravity shifts, and I'm about to fall into a panic attack.

There's a reason he kept this from me.

I get up and follow Momma to the car. Our tour guide jogs ahead of us and gets the engine running. I grab Momma's arm before she can climb in. "How was he there? In what capacity?"

She shakes me off. "You'll have to ask him, but your boy? He ain't following you around like a lovesick puppy dog for your personality, girlie. It's guilt, and the sooner you realize that, the better off you'll be. Fuck him, but for god's sake, don't fall for him."

"Since when do you care about my broken heart?" I narrow my eyes at her and know I'm wearing an expression she'd like to slap off.

"Since your broken heart will interfere with our plans. This little quest of yours? It stops tonight." Her lips tighten. "Get your answers from your man, then let him go. Let all of this go."

She pats my cheek hard enough to make it sting and climbs into the car.

As much as I want to, I can't take her advice.

I've already fallen.

———

MOMMA DISAPPEARS into her room as soon as we get back from the tour. I finish making my notes, sketch a rough outline of my article, and do another search for the evidence of my misdeeds while she's in the shower. Her room is a masterpiece of chaos, clothes covering the floor, makeup spilled over the desk, food left on the bedside table. I think housekeeping has given up. There's a towel monkey hanging above her bed, but the rest of the room has been left untouched.

Behind the trashcan, a few wire casings glint on the floor like glitter. I pick one up and rub my finger over the still tender cut on my thumb. The perfect size for a sliver of wire. My stomach sinks, throbs against a new ulcer that burns. I don't remember wire. What would I have done with wire?

Her shower turns off. I hurry out of her room and slip into my own bathroom, my head pounding, guilt nipping at my heels.

What. Did. I. Do?

I lock the door behind me and grip the small vanity. The person staring back at me is tired, scared, bags under her eyes, pale lips, eyes wide. Why can't I see who I am on the dark side? Why can't I break through?

Why can't I be in control?

I step away from my reflection and start the process of covering her up. I hide the dark spots under my eyes, mask the fear with contouring and shimmer. I paint on a smiling seduction with a strong, warrior purple.

I create a picture of a woman in control, confident, and strong and slip into a slinky jumpsuit, covering me enough to be comfortable, and get ready for Gabe. He'll be here soon, and if he can shine a light in some of the dark areas, maybe other answers will skitter into view.

But first, I need him to believe the picture I've painted. Control, confidence, strength...they only become real if someone else sees them. If Gabe believes my paint strokes, maybe I'll be strong enough.

Strong enough to hear Gabe's truth.

Strong enough to face the secrets I've buried.

Strong enough to fight my way through the darkness, and whatever monsters lurk in my shadows.

23

GABRIEL

A CREW MEMBER JOGGED PAST GABRIEL ON THE Promenade, brushing against his shoulder. Gabriel cringed and ducked his head, his heart stress-ball squeezing. He hadn't felt like this since sneaking out of the house to visit his teenage girlfriend. Every other day of his career, he held his head high and—there was no other word for it—strutted through his ship, tending to his passengers and crew. But tonight, he skulked. Not just skulked, but hid his identity under a black, drawstring hoodie he only wore on his shore days to the gym. Under the hoodie, he was dressed in a dress shirt and tie.

He caught his image in one of the Promenade's shop windows. In a store full of high-end designer resort wear, his reflection made him look like the thug he used to be. He turned away and continued along the polished marble, dodging crew and guests. Each step strengthened an emotion that had been growing since the first initial spark of attraction to Jesse. It had grown slowly, silently, so unobtrusively that he hadn't been able to recognize it until now.

Bitterness.

It flavored his tongue, his stomach, his gut. It was the most dangerous of all emotions. Bitterness could destroy a man's career.

Bitterness could destroy a man.

He'd had to cover his evening duties with three other members of his senior staff, claiming a stomach bug had confined him to his room. Even his VIP excuse wouldn't work on visiting a guest inside their stateroom. That was a strict, fireable offense, no quarter, no talking out of it. His stomach bug lie would crumble under a second glance, but he was betting on everyone being too busy for second glances. Besides, hadn't he stored up enough goodwill over the past two decades to take a night off? Without making excuses? He deserved a night off.

And Jesse deserved the truth from him. No more lying, no more making her guess. He could only hope that she'd forgive him and not cut him out entirely.

Gabriel rolled back his shoulders, attempted to let go of the destructive emotion, and sidled onto the main deck. A blast of warm Caribbean air hit his face and made him regret the need for the heavy sweatshirt. The ocean rolled around the ship, gentle and calm, the watery horizon grazing the sunset sky. He turned his back to a security camera and double-checked the time on his pocket watch. What would his *Papá* say now? Was he being his best man?

Or was he just being a man?

Gabriel shoved the watch back into his dress pants. He couldn't very well be his best man if he didn't *act* like a man once in a while. And Jesse made him feel like a man. He could only hope his best for her, and the truth, was enough.

He ducked inside on the opposite end of the ship and headed for the elevator. The cool, dry air was a drastic change from the humidity outside. Tomorrow, they'd be in Cozumel. He'd be back to his staff captain role by morning, God willing.

The elevator dinged and announced floor eleven. Gabriel took a breath, hunched his shoulders in, and stepped into the lobby of the eleventh floor. His attempts to be invisible, so far, had succeeded.

"Yes, ma'am," a man's voice said from around the corner. Gabriel's heart reacted before he did, going into full stop. They turned the corner, and the man revealed himself as the captain, wheeling Jesse's mother toward the elevators. *Perfect timing.* In his eagerness to see Jesse, he'd forgotten the captain's arranged date with her mother.

"And I'd like the whole tour, mind you. Not some customer-friendly look-see, but the whole thing. Including the morgue," Jesse's mother commanded.

Gabriel couldn't see the captain's face, but he could imagine it. A strung smile wound so tight it was about to pop. If the captain recognized him, Gabriel's career would be over.

He adjusted his hoodie over his face, stepped into the library across the lobby, and crouched down, looking at the bottom row of books. Sweat tickled his spine, clung his shirt to his skin. His heart slapped his ribs.

The elevator dinged, and the captain wheeled Mrs. David onto the glass-enclosed carriage. The motors whirred, and they sank out of sight.

Gabriel took a deep breath and waited for his heart to slow down from almost-caught speed. He didn't like the familiar feeling. It was too close a reminder of his misspent teenage years. Too close a reminder of what he'd done. A flash of *Papá*, lying in bed, blood seeping through a head wound that would never heal, a death that would never leave him alone, *Papá's* forgiveness that he could never accept.

Gabriel stood, wiped his palms on his pants. He'd spent years atoning for that particular sin. He would not do so tonight.

Another deep breath, and he was ready. He walked out of the library and down the corridor to suite 1101, strategically avoiding the security cameras. If Delice happened to be looking, she'd sniff him out.

A woman dressed to win a bikini contest passed by, the scent of coconut oil trailing behind her, and any other man would have turned to watch her walk away.

Not him. No, he'd picked the most complicated woman he'd ever come across to be attracted to, intrigued by, consumed with. But it was that very complication that made him want, need, to know her better. To find out what made her tick, to be the one who understood her, even in her blackouts.

The few glimpses he'd had of her inner self had been a swirling mix of dark and light, tragic and beautiful.

Simply put, she had become his addiction.

Gabriel sent up another prayer that he wouldn't be caught, that Jesse would understand, that she could forgive him, and knocked on her door.

The moments could be counted by the thud of his heart. The space between each beat seemed to spin out in a place where time was fluid and unpredictable. The distant *ding* of the elevator interrupted the rattle of a serving cart. The cry of a child, the baritone of a man, and very distant, the lilt of a piano. All surreal. Belonging to an alien world he once called home.

The door swung open, and his heart stopped for a completely different reason. He wasn't sure it would ever start again. And he was totally, one-hundred-percent okay with that.

"You're early," she purred. And yes, *purr* was the right description. She poised in front of him like a domesticated cat who still had all her claws. One who knew when she was being admired. She shifted slightly, and all her curves went on display. The top of the black jumpsuit she was wearing was more like a vest, and a shimmery, milky-white *V* gaped open from her neck to her bellybutton. Next thing he knew, he was inside her room, door shut and locked, and hands on her waist. With nothing to say.

Didn't need anything to say.

Jesse wrapped her arms around his neck and pulled him down to her. He didn't hesitate. Years of cultivating the barrier between passenger and job, between Gabriel the staff captain and plain Gabriel, even the friendzone he'd forced upon them, fled at the sight of her plump lips. His addiction called. He needed a taste to get him through dinner. A small hit.

Her lips parted, shimmering under the cabin's low lighting. His tongue wanted to capture those teeth, that pink temptress in her mouth. He wanted to captain her pleasure.

His fingers grazed her bare stomach, and a little moan escaped Jesse's mouth. He dipped down, needing to seal that moan with his kiss.

She turned her head, dodging him, and pulled him into a hug that pressed all her small curves into his.

Rejection churned his stomach and kickstarted his doubts. His addiction would have to wait. She wanted things slow? He could give her slow.

For a little while.

Her hands massaged up his chest, trailed up his neck, his face, a light touch that melted him.

"Hi," she said, eyes closed and a soft sweetness on her mouth.

"Sorry," he said, apologizing for...what? Crossing the line? Not being a professional? He wasn't sorry. It was just a word with no feeling. His addiction wasn't in the least bit sated. It was fueled, his blood on fire.

"I'm not. I haven't been on a date in—" She traced her lips with one of her nails. A look, maybe sadness, raced across her features, but she blinked it away. And he wanted to understand that look. He wanted to know the depths behind her sadness. "I ordered dinner. It should be on its way. You can get more comfortable in the bedroom while they're setting it up." She gave him a pointed look at his outfit. Sweaty, wearing a hoodie, over dress pants.

"I couldn't risk anyone seeing me come up here. I hope you don't mind." He pushed his hood back from his head, grateful for his dark skin that hid the blush. Jesse deserved so much more than sneaking around and sweaty men.

She pulled him down to her again, this time kissing his neck as she pressed her body into his. Deepening the contact while keeping her lips light on his throat, a delicious contradiction. "I don't mind a single bit."

A knock sounded on the door, and his body pulsed in frustration. Jesse gave him a little push into the bedroom, whispered, "Take your time," and closed the door behind him.

He heard her open the door and let the waitstaff in. A sharp sprig of jealousy hit his chest. He didn't want anyone else to see her in that revealing getup. He knew exactly what kind of thoughts raced through men's minds at any show of unexpected skin.

He turned to face the room. Dresses of various hideous colors were flung about. All three sizes bigger than one-size-fits-all. A smell permeated the room. A lingering scent of mothballs, cleaning chemicals, and something slightly rotten. Looked like Jesse had given her mother the bedroom, which meant she slept on the pull-out couch. Anyone else, he would've thought it a selfless, respectful act. But knowing what he knew about Jesse and her mother, he doubted it was a choice.

For some reason, understanding that made his jaw clench.

He peeled the hoodie off his back and caught himself in the mirror. His once-ironed shirt now looked, and smelled, like it'd been sitting in the laundry for a week. He took a hard look at himself. Couldn't be helped. He needed a shower. He listened at the door, heard the clinking of the waitstaff still setting up in the suite. He peeled off the rest of his clothes and stepped into Jesse's mother's shower. He took a fast wash, one even the military would be proud of, found some fabric spray left by the cleaning staff, and freshened his clothes. Five minutes later, he was dressed, refreshed, and the waitstaff had gone.

He stepped into the suite. The lights were turned low. Pull-down service had made up Jesse's bed, turning the couch into a distraction. Had she asked them to do that? He stiffened at the thought. Dinner had been set up on the balcony, and he caught a glimpse of Jesse's slender leg through a split in her slinky jumpsuit that went all the way to her hips. No panties.

Me estás jodiendo.

The woman was commando.

How was he going to get through this dinner without bending her over the balcony and—

Ave María purísima.

Blood throbbed down low. It'd been too long.

He adjusted himself, cursed his disobedient member, and tried to walk without limping onto the balcony.

Jesse leaned forward and crossed her legs, emphasizing her endless bare skin, and tapped her finger on a whiskey glass.

"Hmm, that's better." She smiled appreciatively at his showered self.

He sank into his chair, drained his drink in one gulp, and set it down with a clink. "I wanted to look as nice as you do for our date." Lame, lame, lame. He was disoriented. He thought for sure she'd confront him about what happened twenty years ago, but this...this wasn't a confrontation. This was a seduction.

"You always look nice," she said and leaned forward, her shirt gaping open with only shadows covering her. His mouth went dry and all his conversational skills abandoned him as she came closer and slid onto his lap.

His hand went straight to that long slit exposing her thighs, and he caressed her smooth skin.

She shifted, turned toward him all the way, one smooth thigh on either side of his hips, and kissed the side of his neck.

Was she trying to avoid kissing him? Their unfinished conversation tried to shove into his mind. Was that the reason for her hesitation? Did they need to talk first?

She pushed her crotch against his pants, harder and harder, her actions an attack dog for his doubt. *She wanted him.* A quick surge of thrill rolled through him. It made him feel... *male.* Caveman-male. Powerful.

"Dinner can wait, don't you think?" she breathed and moved from his throat to his jaw to his ear.

Rhetorical question. He pressed her into him, burying himself in her breasts, picked her up, and carried her inside. He tossed her onto the couch-bed. She didn't seem to need foreplay, but damned if he wasn't going to take his time enjoying her.

He traced the curve of her breasts, dipping beneath the silk. Her skin prickled at his touch, and he replaced his fingers with his mouth, warming her skin. She grinded against him, breathing his name over and over. This woman...he could not get enough of this woman.

"I need to see you. Every. Inch," he whispered into her neck, then trailed his lips between her breasts, down to her belly-button. He found the zipper at her back and pushed her jumpsuit off her shoulders, down her waist. Exposing every inch. He paused, washed in her beauty. She was perfect. Absolutely perfect. Her round breasts, the soft curve of her waist, the nubs of her hips. "You are so gorgeous," he whispered.

"Gabe, please," she panted, her voice strained.

Her fingers went to work, shedding his clothes faster than he thought possible.

She kicked off his pants and flipped him on his back. Her eyes sparkled in the dark, catching flecks of moonlight.

His mind flicked to the protection he'd brought. As if reading his thoughts, she leaned down and whispered, "I need you bare and raw."

He nodded his agreement. He may have gulped, didn't care. She sank onto him, and his world exploded in a firework show. *Claro*, she felt even better than she tasted. He grasped her hips, and they moved to a matching rhythm.

Then his mind went blank, and there was only Jesse and her warmth and her taste.

24

JESSE

G<small>ABE PULLS ME CLOSER, CRADLING ME AGAINST HIS</small> chest. The bed creaks under our weight, the support bars digging into our sides. It's lumpy and uncomfortable, and I'd stay here forever if I could. Gabe is more than sex, and I haven't felt this way about a man since college. But we're limited on time, truth, and trust.

The smell of sex, a complicated tango of citrus and musk, permeates the sheets. The moonlight makes a fantastical path along the floor, and my body softens against his. I cuddle into him, pulling his strong arms around me, not wanting to break this moment, but there's no other way.

Gabe's soft breathing warms my spine. Did he fall asleep? I turn in his arms, and he nuzzles closer to me. A smile tugs at his lips, and I wish I could kiss his mouth. Such perfect lips. I trace the air above the slant of his upper Cupid's bow, the curve of the lower *labium inferius oris*. His lips are a perfect, tempting color of a dark reddish-brown. They make me want to nibble and kiss and bite.

"I have to go soon," he murmurs and pulls me in tighter, his fingers making lazy circles around my back. "I wish there was some way for me to stay." His eyelids fly open. "That is, if you wanted me to stay."

His worry that I may not want him makes me happier than I've been in years. Has it really been so long since I smiled because I wanted to, not because it was expected?

"I want you to stay. More than I probably should." I trace the contours of his face, his thick eyebrows, the crinkles around his eyes, all the features of a man well-lived. Of a life well-enjoyed. "But I also don't want you to lose your job." I kiss his nose and wrap my legs around his, my body a constant contradiction to my thoughts.

He pulls away a little bit and props his head on his hand, his bicep flexed. Moonlight catches on his skin, as if even the moon must pause and drink him in. He is beautiful. Whatever happens next, I've had a beautiful man in my bed tonight, and I'll have tonight's memories to help fight the future loneliness I've been granted.

"You'd be worth it, Jesse." He traces the curve of my cleavage, makes a circle around my heart.

I blink back tears, my heart full. He shifts, pulls me so I'm resting against his chest, and strokes my arm, so lightly it almost feels as if there's a ghost caressing my skin. I check the room for Daddy, under the breakfast table, in the wall mirror, hiding by the bar. He's invisible, but he's near.

We're almost out of time.

I pull from him, and my heart slows, stutters. "We need to talk." I wrap the sheet around me and tuck it under my arms.

Gabe takes in a deep breath and holds it, like he's getting ready to free dive.

My spine straightens, and I slip into interview mode, a safe space, a way to remain unattached to Gabe's words. "We knew each other back when my daddy died. Momma remembers you."

His tongue plays with the inside of his cheek. He sits straight and takes my hand between his. He's breaking through my interviewer's composure. I shake my hand loose, and a brief flash of pain lights his eyes, but I can't have him making me vulnerable. Already, I can feel Daddy's cold breaths on the back of my neck. He's waiting to pounce. My hands are trembling, so bad that I shove them under my thighs just to make them hold still.

"I never intended to keep this from you. Any of it." Gabe scoots to the edge of the bed with me, a corner of the sheet covering his lap. He leans on his knees and interlocks his hands. "I wanted to tell you, so many times, but the years passed and"—he shrugs and shakes his head—"it became easier to not say anything at all."

My tongue travels to my canine tooth and plays with the point, and I realize I'm not breathing. My heart pounds thickly in my ears, and everything muffles, sounds sticky, and the world goes a bit wavy.

Panic attack. I'm anticipating the worst news possible, but how bad could this be?

I force myself to take a breath.

"I was on the search and rescue team for your father. I was only nineteen but already on the officer track. My superiors wanted to give me some firsthand emergency experience, and they gave me more authority at the time than they probably should have. But—" He sucks in air, rubs his hands over his face, as if he's trying to wash away the secrets he's holding so tight. "I saw you, Jesse." And he looks at me, his eyes blazing through the dark. "I saw you on that pier, hands wrapped around your little knees. All sharp angles and barely holding it together, like you were afraid to cry. You were only nine, and if I'd seen you before, maybe I'd have made a different decision. Better decisions."

"What did you do?" My voice scrapes out, all sliced up.

"I convinced them to call the search off." He drops his head, swallows. "They shouldn't have listened to me, but they did. It'd been two hours, and there was no sign of your father."

My heart starts beating again. "Gabe, that's not unreasonable. I mean, I wish you would have told me, but—"

He shakes his head, reaches out, and takes my hand, and he's holding on as if I'm his life-preserver, not the other way around. "No, cariño." He stops. He's gone pale, he's barely breathing, his thumb strokes over my hand, and I want to make him stop. I don't want to know. I want to live with my head buried and my hand held by his.

"Your father was alive. For a good four hours after we called the search off. If we'd kept searching..." He meets my gaze now, but I can't—

The room gets swallowed up, the edges go fuzzy, and I'm falling. I tighten my grip on his hand, holding on, scrabbling for the edge, and Gabe is saying something, my name I think, but he's talking at me from across a ravine, a giant bottomless hole that has opened up all around me.

I'm alone.

I close my eyes and my breath slows until I'm not even sure I'm breathing. "Daddy was alive?" The words thicken in my throat, swell up, choke out my air, and suddenly, the world comes roaring back, everything snaps into place, and Gabe's hand is in mine. It's a stranger's hand, too big, too dry, too cold. I rip from his grasp. "And you, you left him? You're the reason my daddy is dead?" I stand, tearing the sheets off the bed. I want to scrub myself clean from the inside out, starting with the pieces of my heart that I so stupidly gave him.

"Sorry isn't enough, I know, Jesse, but—"

"You destroyed my life." I'm whispering now, and I can't look at him and I may be crying but I'm too far gone to tell. "My mother—she was never the same after he died. And I got the brunt of it all. She. Blamed. Me. And all this time, all this time." I'm losing it, I don't care. "You killed my daddy." My voice slams out of me and punches into Gabe with such force that he jerks back. "You. Killed. Him." The darkness starts to come over me, but this time red veins run through the blackness, making it glow, making it storm, and I don't care. "Go. Leave."

I turn from him and grip the table so hard the bones in my hands crack. Behind me, he rustles in the sheets, pulling his clothes on. I can feel him close to me, and then he leaves, without another word.

We were so close to perfect that we missed it by a thousand miles.

The door clicks behind him, and I sink to the carpet, tears clogging my throat, I can't breathe.

The one man I had a chance with—killed the one man who could have given me a normal life.

And Gabe, he saw me, at nine years old. He saw the gaps in my memory.

He's the reason for them.

I don't know how much time has passed, but Momma comes back at some point, wheeled in by an exhausted captain. I scoot into the shadows, so they can't see me, huddled in a fetal position, wrapped in dirty sheets.

"Thank you for an enlightening evening, Mrs. David." The captain bows and he exits, all gentlemanly manner, but his voice is pulled taut. He pushes Momma in far enough to clear the swing of the door and lets the door slam shut.

Momma sits in the dark, in silence, until the door clicks closed, and only then, only after we are assured to be just her, just me, does she take a deep breath. "I take it you've had a sweaty evening?" She doesn't wait for an answer. "Had to boink your boy toy, huh?" She flips on the light in time for me to catch her leer. It disappears as soon as she sees me. "He told you the truth, didn't he?" And the expression that flits across her face is one part pity, three parts something else. Something nasty.

I raise my head, and it feels like it weighs a thousand pounds. "Why didn't you tell me?" I want to be angry at her, but I'm empty, hollow. I've got nothing but the darkness writhing around. And Daddy, always Daddy, in the corner of my mind. I can feel him excited. I'm so close to the core of where I've hidden my lost memories, and he knows it. I know it.

Momma pushes out of her wheelchair and walks closer. "I didn't know until I saw that picture of you two in your apartment. Didn't want to hurt you, baby."

I want to believe her, but Momma never has my best interests at heart. And the tight line of her lips says it's not true. She's holding back a smile. She's enjoying my pain.

"It was all his fault." She has to forgive me now.

She steps closer, towering over me. "You'd like to think that, wouldn't you?" She strokes my cheek.

My heart cracks, her refusal to forgive me whipping my spine. I gather the sheets around my body and hug them to my chest, as if I'm still that little girl Gabe saw, holding my blankie while they bury my Daddy and Momma yells that it's my fault. Because I insisted we go snorkeling. I didn't listen to the instructions. I fell in without my life jacket while the boat was speeding across the ocean, and Daddy jumped in after me. They found me. Not him. Not until later.

Momma doesn't know I jumped in on purpose.

The answer slams into me from out of nowhere and freezes my muscles. I jumped in on purpose. Why? Why would I do that?

"Now, did you do what we talked about?"

I fight to catch up with her, to push my grief, my confusion, the all-encompassing pain down. To hang on just a little bit longer before the darkness takes over. I don't know what she's talking about, but my body seems to understand.

"Do what, Momma?" I wipe at my nose, but even as I'm questioning what she's talking about, my body is working against me, doing things I didn't command it to do. My hand goes straight to the crevice between the mattress and the back of the couch, and then drops Gabe's keycard into Momma's waiting hand, and the implications slam into me.

I lost time with Gabe tonight. Just enough time for the other me to do Momma a favor.

25

JESSE

I'T'S CLOSING IN ON MIDNIGHT WHEN I SNEAK OUT OF
our stateroom. I'm not any closer to finding the answers I
need, and Daddy's closing in, the darkness is getting
stronger. I don't have much more time to fix this. Daddy's
plan is there, throbbing in my neck, my fingertips.

He wants me to collect people's smiles.

Like the dog. Like Michael.

It satisfies Daddy's greed, and it's my way to make things
right.

I push through the sliding glass doors leading to the walking
deck, and a rush of warm Caribbean air wraps around my
skin.

I've got to tell him no.

I head for the helipad, the last place on the list my therapist
and I crafted. I know what I'm supposed to do. Deep breaths

on the way there, focus on the things I know are real. The stars, the breeze, the rolling ship under my feet.

People roam around, smokers lighting up on the darkened deck, the tips of their cigarettes like little lightning bugs flaring to life. A couple shares a bottle of wine. A mother walks her fussing baby. All of us are from different places and backgrounds, we speak different languages, love different music, and we're all united by one thing.

The waves.

For them, it's music, a lullaby, peace.

Their interpretation and mine are very different.

The stairs to the helipad at the front of the ship are unlit. I feel my way up them, stumble through a dark corridor, and emerge on an open, circular deck with a giant H painted in white. The lights are turned off, but above us, stars freckle the sky. Low on the horizon, two shooting stars arc, one after another, playing a celestial game of tag.

Daddy brought me here one night, long after Momma went to bed. Back then, we were the only two here, everyone else deterred by the chains blocking access to the helipad. Now, the ship has opened the space to stargazers, an unadvertised nightly show of stars.

Daddy walks ahead of me, a faded recording, staticky and pixelated. He's holding me at nine years old on his hip. I'm wearing ratty pajamas, Strawberry Shortcake pink, and I'm shivering. It was cold that night, and I didn't have a coat. My legs are wrapped tight around his waist, but I'm not cuddled in close. I'm arching back, and looking up, up, up. The sky is the same sky I walk under now, but back then it seemed so big, so magical.

Daddy had sat with me on his lap on a park bench, one bolted to the deck that looked out over the bow of the ship. I remember feeling nauseous, wishing I could enjoy the stars, instead of asking why Daddy wanted me there with him. Why did he want me there—here? I head to the bench now, holding my breath, watching stars fall down, down, down.

Down, down deep in the big ocean blue, swim two little fishies, a me and a you.

The song whispers in my ear as I step over the few other passengers stretched out on the deck, as I sit down on the bench, the ghost of Daddy's lap under my thighs. My mind gets stuck on the same refrain, a loop of the same words over and over again. If I could just get to the end of that damn song, I know my mind would unlock.

The ship slices through the ocean wind and is rewarded with a blasting breeze. Far below, the spray of the water arches up and splashes down. Across the ocean, other cruise liners follow, pinpoints of civilization. You'd think with this many people and this many boats, *someone* would have seen a man floating in the water and rescued him.

What were his last moments like? Had he given up hope? Or did he stare at the horizon until the very end, when his muscles tired and he faltered, when his mouth, then his nose, slipped beneath one wave, then another, then another? Did he forgive me for jumping in?

There's a breath of cold air at my neck. A short huff of *no*.

The couple nearest to me gets up and disappears into the background. I'm left alone.

"I won't do it, Daddy," I whisper into the night. "I'm sorry for what I did, I'm sorry if I'm the reason you're gone, but I can't do what you want." There's no answer, but I can feel him near, his presence billowing closer. "I need you to leave me alone. Please, this has to be goodbye."

"Jesse?" The voice is deep, too smooth, and too full of regret to be Daddy's.

I start, jerk around. Gabe stands to the side of the bench. Had he heard me? "I told you to leave me alone." Any scrap of Daddy and the answers he hides float away in Gabe's presence.

"I know. I saw you up here and wanted to make sure you were all right." He rubs the back of his neck and waits, as if he expects me to invite him to sit next to me.

"Why on earth would I be all right?" I shove my hands under my legs and stare over the ocean.

He hovers, not wanting to leave, but he has to. "If I could go back, change everything, I would." His words are ragged, ripped apart in the spaces.

Maybe in time, I can understand. Maybe, I can forgive.

But forget? Even with my track record, I don't think forgetting what he's done is something I can do.

"Jesse, I hate to even ask this, but"—he clears his throat, and I'm on edge, balancing on the tip of a sharpened blade, waiting to see which side will slice me up next—"did I leave my keycard in your room earlier?"

The words echo around my head, so hollow, so petty, so—*I can't even.* I stare at him, blinking.

"There's a GPS locator on it, and if I report it missing and it's in your room..." He trails off, muttering under his breath, "Not her problem, *Che.*"

GPS locator? A slam of panic I don't understand hits my gut. Momma has his keycard, and no amount of questioning her revealed why.

Gabe takes out his phone and waves it, showing me four digits on the screen. "If you do happen to find it, would you text me at this number?"

I nod, slowly, and Gabe's phone beeps with an alert. A text that says Code Black scrolls across the screen.

"What's Code Black?" My investigator's curiosity won't shut off, even around a man I want nothing to do with.

Gabe sucks in a short breath and flips his phone around. "Passenger death."

26

GABRIEL

Gabriel shouldn't have followed Jesse here. He should have concentrated on his job, stayed out of her way, respected her wishes. But his soul had seen hers, and in it he saw his match. He was bound to her, and she couldn't saw through the rope. If she wanted distance, he'd give her distance. But he'd remain in sight, protecting her, ready to step in should she ever change her mind. That's what he'd decided when he stepped out of her stateroom earlier, when he'd had a moment to breathe, to process.

And then he'd seen her, flitting through the dark walkway like a fairy on a secret mission. And all that had flown right out of his head.

His mind spun. A message from CSO Delice Andre read: "Passenger Death: At 11:52 P.M., Guest Evan Reese was found DOA in his cabin. Investigation proceeding. No foul play suspected. At this time, it appears the guest died from natural causes. Previous medical conditions included seizures. My office will keep all apprised of any further developments."

Gabriel's stomach burned, and inappropriate images of Mr. Reese wavered in front of his vision. "Oh, shit." He took two steps toward the exit, but that rope tying him to Jesse yanked him back.

She stood, her hands clasped at her heart. "What happened?"

"It's..." He couldn't tell her. She was done with him, and his burdens were his to bear alone. He finished with "Nothing for you to worry about."

"I've never heard you swear in all the time I've known you. What happened?" She stepped closer, and starlight danced in her jungle-cat eyes. She cared. She was pissed beyond belief at him, but she still cared.

"The passenger had a history of seizures. Lost his service dog first day of the cruise, and the poor animal turned up dead. Mutilated, really. Lips torn off, and the dog discarded into the aquarium on the—" He stopped. She'd gone an alarming shade of pale-white. "I'm sorry, you don't need all the details."

She sank to her knees, hitting the deck with a sharp knock.

"Are you all right?" Gabriel reached out to touch her.

She clutched her hands to her chest and rocked back and forth, muttering...something. He leaned closer.

"No, Daddy. No, no, no, Daddy. And down down deep, the little fishies swim, the little fishies swim, all the little fishies swim."

It was a song, but barely a whisper. He wasn't even sure she knew she'd spoken out loud. He watched her for a moment, wrapped up in this...trance. Frailness descended on her like moonlight, and even though he was frozen in place and had no clue what to do or how to help her, even though he knew this wasn't normal or natural and should disturb him, he leaned even closer. Savored her delicate lavender scent.

He reached out and patted her back, and his touch broke her trance. She looked up at him, face composed, and reached up a hand for him to help her up. "Thanks. Must've got light-headed. I'm so sorry to hear about your passenger."

He blinked. "Jesse, what song were you singing just now?"

She turned her face to the ocean and clenched her fists. "I was singing?"

He nodded, though she couldn't see him. He needed to leave, to see to Mr. Reese, to walk through the events with Delice, but he couldn't leave Jesse here. Not now.

"You remember I told you I was trying to recall what happened when Daddy died?" She continued to stare out into the ocean, as if she were trying to scout the dawn.

He stepped beside her and faced the ocean with her, so she knew he was there, listening. "I do."

"Ever since, I've had these blackouts. They're worse around the anniversary of his death." She shrugged. "I guess I sing in them." Her laugh was self-deprecating, and she choked it off short, as if remembering that they weren't supposed to be talking, that she'd banned him from her life. "You should go."

He stayed a moment longer, hoping she'd look at him, forgive him. But her profile sharpened against the night sky, her silence deepened.

"I'm here for you, Jesse. No matter what." He backed away when she still didn't respond and walked down the steps and through the dark corridor.

It wasn't until he was halfway to Skynet that his stomach twisted against his gut.

Jesse didn't know what she did in her blackouts.

Throw in a controlling mother, and it'd be enough to make anyone go mad. He could understand that, except...

His heart thumped against his ribs, a sledgehammer to his beliefs, Delice's voice gnawing on his thoughts. An image of Jesse came to his mind, of her stroking her mouth with her nail and pressing it so hard against her upper lip that her finger turned white.

DAY SIX

"Hungry," says the Whale,
So we do a flip and a flop and a sideways
*   spin,*
Until it's just A You and A Me,
Alone again.

27

JESSE

It's well after midnight when I walk into our stateroom and face Momma's bedroom door. I'm not holding back anymore, not waiting to see what she does. I've said no to Daddy, now I'm saying no to her.

There's something else, something that's my fault, and it's big, it's making me sick, but I can't remember. I'm forgetting something.

I go over what happened this evening, searching for the missing time. Moonlight slants across the floor, and the open sea slips by. I find it. Somewhere between seeing Gabe tonight and walking back to the stateroom, I have a stretch of time missing. My mind is a chalkboard, and that segment of my evening has been blotted out with a dirty eraser. The chalk is smeared, and dust floats around the room, but there is no hint of what happened or what I did other than a thickening in my throat. A knowing that this has to be the last time.

I open her door. At the sight of Momma in bed, covers kicked off and her nightgown hiked up around her thighs, I stop. Brace myself against the door frame as the world whiplashes around.

The cane is propped against her nightstand, within easy reach. The other single moms in our trailer park kept baseball bats under their beds or guns under their pillows. Not Momma. That cane is all she's ever needed. If she has this in hand when I wake her up, I'll be wearing the bruises for a month.

I creep closer, hold my breath, and reach for it. The shaft is cool in my palm, slick and hard. I pull it away from the nightstand, but it holds fast.

I raise my gaze, slowly traveling up the cane and into Momma's tripped-alarm stare. She yanks the cane back, so hard I'm pulled with it and I land in her lap, the danger zone.

"You think you're old enough to wield this now, huh?" She raps the end against the base of my skull, and I roll away, just missing being hit a second time. The cane thumps onto the mattress with a dull thud, inches from my shoulder. "Just what the hell do you think you're doing?"

I fall off the edge of the bed and scramble backward. "Why do you need Gabe's keycard, Momma? Why did I find wire casings in your room?" I back against the wall, flex my biceps. I'm ready to fight her for this, ready to wear those bruises if that's what it takes.

She stares at me, all wide-eyed, then throws her head back and laughs. "Oh honey, really?" She puts her feet on the ground and shoves them into her pink, fuzzy slippers.

My heart has stopped beating. Why is she laughing?

"You're so pathetic, it's sad." She shakes her head and takes a step toward me, the cane thumping against the floor. "Do you remember visiting me the day you got back from that Moroccan trip?"

"The day I got back..." Flashes of my slightly disturbed apartment flare around my vision, Leo limping... "I didn't visit you. I took Leo to the vet." Proof I didn't have another blackout.

"And then?" She presses.

Then...I reach for it. Leo's appointment took maybe an hour. I left the vet's office, carried Leo out in his carrier, buckled it in, climbed in the driver's seat. Started the car.

Then, nothing. Just whispers of leftover emotions, blurry and fleeting.

My heart starts back up, speeding fast, too fast, explosion-fast.

"I don't remember," I whisper, and the words are shards, splinters of glass that cut my throat on their way out.

Momma puts the cane down, reaches across the bed, and pats my hand. "You called me, Jesse. Then you showed up on my front step with the wheelchair, the duffel bag, and the plan."

I shake my head. "I couldn't— What plan, Momma?"

She goes on as if she hasn't heard me. "It's the first time in a long time that you've made me proud. You're finally listening to your father. We're going to give him what he wants. He needs to rest in peace. *We* need peace, Jesse." She lets me go. "He haunts me too."

"What plan, Momma?" I say again, more forceful this time.

She cocks her head. "When the other you wants you to know, you'll know. Go to bed, it's late." She waves her phone at me, brandishing the time like a sword.

I bite my tongue.

The sight of the phone triggers something in my memory. A spark falls into the dark place. "A man died today." The words fall from my dry lips before I can evaluate the consequences. My head explodes in pain with the recovered memory.

Momma stops all her frenetic motions. "What?"

"A man...the owner of the dog...he died today. Of a seizure." I sink back as the explanation spills from my memory. That's what I lost. My relief at recovering my memory is shorter lived than a news headline. What did I do? How did I respond? Did Gabe see anything other than me singing a song?

Momma grabs a handful of my hair, waiting to distribute a caress or abuse. The coin is still up in the air.

She yanks back so hard my spine bounces off the floor. "So you're a murderer again, aren't ya?" She kicks my ribs, and the world explodes in familiar stars. "What is wrong with you?" Her calloused heel drives into my breast, my lower rib, my belly. She stops, out of breath, and hovers over me panting, while I writhe around my new wounds, trying to protect myself and escape from the pain at the same time. "If you hadn't killed that dog, that man would be alive. And you know it."

But I hear what she's really saying. If I hadn't jumped from the boat, Daddy would still be alive.

She disappears from my limited periphery and rustles in the far corner of the suite. A few seconds later, she's tying something around my wrists, cinching them together.

"Momma, stop!"

"You ain't going nowhere, girl. You're a danger to yourself. To everyone around you. To me." She drags me by my wrists into the living room, drops me by the bar and zip-ties my wrists to the cabinet handle. "This is for your own good, pumpkin." Her breath is shaking, she's trembling, and she runs her hand over her face, through her hair. "I never thought in all my years I'd see this day."

I slump back against the cabinet, my gaze darting around the room, looking for something, anything, to cut me loose. "What day is that, Momma?"

"The day I didn't feel safe around my own flesh and blood." A tear glistens in her eye as she shakes her head, turns away.

She drops a pillow and a blanket next to me. "Get comfy. Tomorrow, we put all this to rest."

She goes into her bedroom, shuts the door behind her, and clicks over the lock.

Her words spin in my mind, a whirly gig in a hurricane, as I try to loosen the zip ties around my wrists.

What plan? Put what to rest? What did the other me do?

I want to believe that she's lying. But given my childhood, my blackouts, the things I used to do in the times I couldn't remember...anything is possible.

Including hiding some plan from myself and conspiring with a mother I can't trust.

28

JESSE

I don't sleep. I can't. Not when my wrists are tied at chest level and there's some *plan* locked in my own brain. The moonlight traces my skin, outlining me in shadow and light, until the haze disappears and in the very darkest of the night, Daddy whispers. Incessant and endless. Whispers of things he wants me to do, how he wants me to do them. Bloody things. Tantalizing things.

"Never again, Daddy," I whisper, again and again, until something deep inside me starts to believe the words. A tingle runs through my hairline, somewhere between a caress and a pull. I don't know what plan Momma and I concocted, but I will do everything in my power to undo whatever it is I've done.

The sun rises, and it grates against my skin. My mouth has been clenched shut, and my tongue has taken on the impression of my teeth. I open my mouth and stretch out my jaw, flex my toes. I'm ready.

Momma stomps out of her room with her nail clippers. "You'd think on a ship as nice as this one, they'd leave some scissors lying around." She places the sharp edge of the clippers against my wrist and pops open the zip ties holding me hostage.

I shake out my wrists, electric fire zinging against my fingertips as the blood comes rushing into my hands.

"You've got thirty minutes before you need to leave. Get dressed." She goes back into her bedroom, but leaves the door open behind her as if she needs to keep an eye on me.

"Go where?" I ask, my mouth dry, in desperate need of water.

Again, she gives me that look. "On shore. Cozumel. You'll know what to do when you get there, I suppose. And if you don't...well, it won't matter too much." Her voice is little-girl giddy, and it makes me sick.

I slowly get to my feet and slide open the doors of the balcony. The blue water of Cozumel speeds by, the ship slowing with every nautical mile. Fresh, Caribbean air rushes around my body, ruffling the slinky jumpsuit I still wear. Clangs and shouts and the gear shifts of the ship fill the air, and the pier at Cozumel floats into view.

I push away from the rail and go back inside. Dress in a pair of loose drawstring beach pants and a flowing top. Today, I don't want to be touched.

Momma exits her bedroom, dressed in a pale pink suit with a flower she stole from somewhere in the lapel. "You're still here? You're on a time crunch, Jesse-girl."

I look at her, widen my eyes. "I have zero idea what you're talking about." But once again, my hands have acted without my permission and grabbed my bag, and there's a tick-ticking pressure building in my chest.

She tilts her chin, something in her face softens as she slowly shakes her head, and I get a rare glimpse at the mom she could have been, at the mom I could have had. She pulls me in close, kisses my forehead, and buries my frame into her body. Her scent floods my senses. Caress soap, with a hint of sour fruit.

"Momma?" I whisper, because for some reason, this feels like a goodbye.

Then she opens the door, shoves me into the hallway, and slams the door closed without another word.

No one roams the hallways, and all the sounds from the rest of the ship are muffled. The silence throbs in my ear. I walk down the beige row of staterooms, and deep inside, something snaps. I'm untethered, floating aimlessly in rough waters, as if my limbs have no bones and I'm caught between two currents.

I join the small crowd of late-to-leave cruisers, and we migrate toward the aft of the ship. The shore excursioners have already left, so now it's just us stragglers, heading into Cozumel to eat, drink, shop, and fight the end-of-vacation depression.

I take the stairs, knowing somehow that I have no time to wait on the elevator. Every tick of the second hand builds pressure around my spine. By the time I reach deck one, my bruised ribs are eating into my stomach. Another gift from my mother.

"Jesse?" His voice stills my blood. His deep baritone bounces around my chest cavity, making me at once happy and sick. I tighten my fists and keep moving forward, not looking, not looking, do not look.

If I look, I'll forgive him of everything.

"Jesse, wait, please." My arm jerks back, I spin around, my vision going dark and sprinkled with bright bursts of pain, and I think I scream. I keep my eyes closed and wrap my arms around my battered ribs, holding together all my pieces.

"*¿Qué carajo?* What happened to you?" His hands are on me, and we're walking away from the security line. We can't... No. Time.

"Stop manhandling me." I yank away from him and grind my teeth against the pain. I don't have time for his guilty conscience. I have to get away from him, now.

"You need a doctor." He wraps a big, strong hand around my arm, his fingers overlapping as they circle my bicep, and he pulls me down the corridor. My need to get off this ship wars with my need for him. I push that traitorous emotion down and tie it with a string. Crew members walk by, carefully looking at their feet. Gabe's jaw is set and flecked with morning stubble. Bags line his eyes, and I wonder if he slept at all last night. If I'm the reason he couldn't sleep.

Don't care.

"I don't need a doctor. I need you to stop assaulting me. I have an appointment on shore I cannot miss." I shove all the impersonality I can manage into my tone, making sure he hears the *don't care.*

He stops, heaves a breath, and gently pushes me into a small, unoccupied storage room. He imprisons me against the closed door with his arms, muscles taut on either side, and I'm embraced by his scent, by his nearness, by my own despicable reaction to it all. He's the reason Daddy is dead.

He leans close. "I'll let you go when you tell me what happened to you."

I force my hand away from my abdomen and shake my head. "I'm fine. I really must go."

He slaps his open hand into the wall next to my head, and I jump. "Dammit, Jesse. You look like you've been cranked through a meat grinder."

About what it feels like too. But I can't give him the satisfaction of knowing my pain.

"I am no longer your concern. You made that decision when you lied to me for years about Daddy's death. And *you knew* I was looking for answers. You. Knew." My words hiss out of my mouth, their venom surprising even me.

His head jerks back as if I'd physically slapped him. He hangs his head and takes a deep, ragged breath. "I will never stop being sorry for that. I should have been honest with you. Especially after all that's passed between us." His eyes meet mine, and in them, I see unmet longing and remembered lust. And maybe, just maybe, a missed opportunity for something more. "I am so very sorry."

I press my lips together and duck out from under his arms. Dry skin sandpapers against dry skin, and I fumble for my lip balm and smooth it on before turning to face him, one last time. Because even if I'm not sure of anything else, I am sure of this. This is goodbye.

"I need to go now...and you need to let me." I wait for him to move.

He closes his eyes, lets out a breath, and moves out of the way. I wrap my hand around the cool handle, and he grabs my arm and pulls me to him. He crushes his mouth to mine, teeth grazing against my lips and fingers running through my hair. *I'm going to be sick.* His lips are wrapped around mine, he's forcing himself into a place no one belongs, and Daddy whispers in my ear. But the screaming in my head is all me. Gabe pulls me in closer, and a shotgun of pain roars through me.

The room wavers, and the darkness crowds in. It's as if he senses it, breaking the kiss off just as my teeth snap closed. The urges inside are too much, too strong, too... I have to get away from him. I gnaw on my own lip and fumble for the door handle. "Goodbye, Gabe." The words come out breathless, a normal response to a passionate kiss.

What I'm feeling is anything but normal.

I walk out the door, through security, and into the safety of sunlight, where Gabe cannot follow.

———

THE CRUISE SHIP pier is a funnel straight into the heart of tourism traps. It feels like flea market day in *El Rastro*, but cleaner. I've been here often enough that I know which stores give the best deals—though they're still a rip-off—the locations of the cleanest bathrooms and the best bars.

I still don't know where I'm headed, or why, but my feet move me forward. I hold my head high and dodge the crowds to avoid anyone touching my battered body.

Colors blur in the crowded Cozumel market. Everything is too bright, too loud. The smells, the sounds, they seem to compact my skull. Daddy is in every face that passes. Sometimes just his eyes, filled with darkened disappointment. Sometimes his smile, sometimes full, sometimes rotting, but every face is pulled into an expression of loathing.

In refusing him, have I sacrificed my answers? He'll never forgive me. He'll never give me what I need.

The cruise ship looms over the port, floating on the big ocean blue...*little fishies jump and little fishies fin...all alone...again.* Pieces of that incessant song flake away from my memory and stick to the walls of my brain. Daddy used to sing it to me, make me sing with him, then he'd chase me around the house...chase me and...and...

My mind refuses to grasp for the ending. But the sick, full-of-acid emotion is there, and vomit burns the back of my throat.

Daddy did something at the end of that song...what's the end of the song? Why did I jump from the boat to run away?

My desperate stretch for lost memories pauses. My brain calms and quiets, and in that quiet, the real question I've been asking myself all these years comes through.

Why was I so relieved when he died?

Inside, all the whirling chaos slows and stops. The question echoes through my chest, my soul, my past, re-shaping every memory, every moment.

Daddy's faces close in, blocking the sun, and the smiles rot away and the eyes shrivel up and are whipped by the wind, and they crowd in and crowd in and crowd in and I can't escape. His dead breath stings the back of my neck and melts away my hair and burns a hole into my mind.

I sink to the ground. The trash-littered concrete burns my knees, my ribs cut into my lungs, and I hide. A hundred copies of his exposed jaw click together, louder and louder, and they won't stop and they deafen, the *click, click, click* and his whisper in my brain is all I can hear. All I can see. All I can taste.

A small, cool hand strokes my arm. "Miss Jesse?" A young voice says, innocence and purity staining the insides of my ears.

I look up, and Daddy is gone. The little girl I pulled from the water pats my arm while a crowd of adults stand around doing nothing. Her soft blonde ponytail is half-undone by a day of play, and her hair frizzes in a gauzy halo.

"Why are you sad?" Her sweet, youth-high words are enough to brighten shadows.

I follow the line of her bones, from wrist to shoulder, connecting my body to her heart. Her skin is slightly reddened from the sun, but it doesn't mask the fingerprints on the underside of her arms. I recognize those bruises, and I recognize the purple shading under her eyes and I recognize how she holds herself, all her limbs pressed together to protect what she cannot. I recognize her bruises from my past.

I flick my gaze to her daddy, who stands in a predator's pounce, ready to attack those who threaten his prey.

And now I know what to do. I know how to satisfy Daddy and quiet his whispers and save my soul.

I know what the key is to unlocking all my answers.

I pat her hand and stand. "I'm okay, sweetie. I just got dizzy."

The crowd looses a sigh and walks away, probably relieved they don't have to help. Her daddy steps forward. His likeness to my daddy flips my stomach and creates a reaction I'm not sure how to begin to analyze. His large, square shoulders fill the frame of my vision, and the small cleft in his chin rivets my attention. "Can we get you some water or food? Do you need anything?" He carefully arranges his face in kindness. I recognize that too.

"I'm fine." I wave away his request and refocus on the little girl. "How are you feeling? Not going swimming by yourself again, I hope?" She ducks her head and smiles, but shakes *no*.

"We never got a chance to thank you for saving our little girl. We owe you, more than we'll ever be able to repay." Tears glisten in his eyes, making his words seem all the more authentic. I don't believe them.

"Repay me by making sure she grows up safe and happy." I don't blink when I say the words. I use my stare and my strong tone to convey what I can't say. That I'm on to him. For what, I'm not quite sure. But something. Something terrible and inhuman and wrong. Wrong, wrong, wrong.

He nods, smiles, says *thank you* again, and walks away, hand wrapped tight around his daughter's arm, and this time, *this time*, I feel the blackout approach. A physical presence, humid and weighted like a storm.

Not this time, I urge my brain. *Let me stay.*

My feet take over, lead me past a tiki bar, and turn into a back alley. I feel detached, as if I'm floating just above my own head, yet still connected to every nerve ending in my body. The broken concrete of the alleyway shifts under my thin shoes, the sour scent of piss on sidewalks makes my lip curl, but I am not in control.

For the very first time, I'm observing from the sidelines of the other me.

I walk half a block, turn right, and find a Telmex booth. I feed coins into the payphone and dial a number.

29

GABRIEL

Gabriel entered Skynet for the port's debriefing, peeling off the daily sticky note that covered up the word Control. Delice sat in her office, clicking away at her keyboard, making everyone wait on her before starting the debrief. It was only a matter of time until she was out of here. Gabriel picked up a piece of trash, balled it up, and *swooshed* it into a nearby bin. The crew member nearest to him smirked and gave him a nice-shot nod.

Once Captain read his report, Delice was a goner.

Delice walked into the room, her phone ringing over the low volume of the waiting crew. She looked at the screen, and her forehead wrinkled. "Hold on a sec." She held up a hand to the rest of the room. "This is Delice Andre."

She waited a second, then her body fell slightly to the side, like she'd lost her center of gravity. Gabriel was there in an instant. That kind of reaction? Bad news.

"What?" Her voice was full of no, and her hand dropped away from her ear. She'd gone ash-colored, her gaze frozen at her phone.

Gabriel grabbed the phone from her limp fingers and got it to his ear just in time to hear a husky, familiar voice. "There's a bomb on the ship. You have thirty minutes to find it," the voice said, monotone and unemotional.

His center of gravity went the way of Delice's, listing to the left. Throbbing filled his ears, and the world narrowed to a small tunnel surrounded by darkness. "Jesse?"

The click echoed off his ear drum.

A bomb? Jesse had planted a bomb? His body caught up with his thoughts, adrenaline punching through his gut, crash-landing in his chest. No time for thinking. There was a bomb.

"That was Miss David?" Delice's hands were on her hips, eyes wide and color back in her cheeks. She shook her head. "We don't have time for this." She checked her watch and leapt on top of a chair. "People, we have a situation." She waited a split-second for everyone to focus on her. Split-seconds were all they had now. "We have a bomb threat. Somewhere in the engine room. Initiate Code Dark Knight, now."

Skynet halted, froze, held its collective breath. Everyone in the room seemed to hang on the cliff of silence, fingers growing sweaty, slipping from the edge. Falling.

That couldn't have been Jesse.

Bam.

The crew hit the ground and rushed into high-stress mode, moving at a fast-forward pace, high-stakes sweat pouring into the air. Gabriel shook off the fog, his blood blazing. That wasn't Jesse. And if it was, he couldn't deal with it now. They had a ship full of people to evacuate. The ship blasted off seven short horns, then a series of pre-recorded announcements in every language directed passengers to evacuate the ship.

"Twenty-eight minutes, people," Delice shouted.

Gabriel's heart beat *pit-pop-pit* like a machine gun. "Where's Alpha Team?" His voice boomed through the chaos, cutting through the panic. Things freeze-framed. His vision blurred at the edges as an overdose of adrenaline hit every inch of his body.

Delice radioed the Port of Cozumel, asked for backup, for a bomb squad. Her radio squawked to life. "Remove your ship from this harbor, NOW."

She raced to the security monitor, pleas and begs for help falling off her lips into the dark void of the radio. The video feed showed tiny green boats launching into the harbor and zooming toward them. The *Armada de México*. Within seconds, gunned ships surrounded them.

Delice's phone buzzed with the captain's call. Gabriel shoved the phone at her, already knowing the captain needed to follow security protocol, talk to his CSO. Delice's gaze jerked to Gabriel's. She didn't acknowledge him, just yanked the phone from his hand to her ear.

"Code Dark Knight?" The captain's voice was a roar so loud Gabriel could hear it above the panic. The ship shuddered in a quick start-up, against all engine recommendations. "Tell me you've found the bomb."

"The team is in the engine room now," Delice said. "We've got twenty-six minutes left. Deploy the lifeboats, Captain." She hung up and darted her gaze at Gabriel. He nodded once, grabbed his phone, and ran from the room. He made for the nearest exit and plowed onto a narrow, crew-only deck.

Cozumel sailed away as the ship made it to open water. The gunned boats dropped back, providing a barricade, staying out of explosion range. A thought injected another two doses of fear into Gabriel. How were they supposed to disable the bomb if they were inaccessible to a bomb team?

He got on the radio, checked the phone app, and headed to the main deck to help get passengers off the ship. The Luxe app showed security teams making for the engine room, sweeping the other levels, little dots of lights that moved along decks, all too slow.

They weren't going to be able to do any more than a first pass. Unless the bomb was in plain sight, they'd be too late.

Gabriel ran down the stairs, his phone buzzing in his hand.

He took a split-second to glance at the screen and came to a hard stop.

A message scrolled across his phone. *I know where the bomb is. Play a game with me, and no one will get hurt.*

He went still, and the world went white around the edges, encasing him in a bubble.

Who is this? he typed back.

Wrong question. Time to play. Tick-tock. The person sent an icon of a cartoon bomb. How much time was left? He checked the nearest clock. Twenty minutes. His phone buzzed again.

Rule 1: Tell no one you are speaking with me.

Rule 2: Tell no one what you are doing or where you are going.

Rule 3: No questions.

Follow the rules of our game, get to the end, save the ship. Would you like to play?

Gabriel's fingers trembled over the keys of his phone. *Yes.*

30

JESSE

I hang up the Telmex phone, palms sweaty, and slam back into my body. The atmosphere clears, and I'm alone in my brain. My heart feels like the pinwheel-fast heartbeat of a mouse. Animals know when their last moments are upon them. Even baby animals. I press against my chest, trying to make it stop, and make my way through the back streets of Cozumel, winding into the busy marketplace.

There's a bomb.

A bomb I knew about, planned, helped Momma plant.

Fragments of memory spin back to me, as if I've unlocked a blocked pressure valve and debris is hitting me from all directions.

Momma's bag is on the floor of our suite, not yet unpacked. I'm on the floor, wiggling at the connecting parts of Momma's wheelchair.

"Careful!" She screeches, high-pitched and off-key. I slow my movements and work at the snaps on the cushions. They come apart with little force, but I strive for gentleness, remembering her warning.

My fingers hit something warm, solid, and rectangle-shaped, hidden under the seat cushion. My nail finds the edge of the tape holding something to the chair and I pull.

Two, four-pound blocks of C-4 drop into my hands, and my fingers tighten around the white clay.

Shouts float on the breeze, whipping me back to present. Armed boats zoom across the water, flanking the Luxury Lines ship on port-side. Two minutes later, the ship groans to life and coasts away, toward the open water. Lifeboats are being launched, getting passengers off the ship.

The cut on my thumb, the leftover wire casings, the lost time.

How could I do this? I don't know how to make a bomb, let alone know where to find the materials to make one and give them to Momma. But I knew what that C4 was. Not modeling clay. That would have been the normal reaction. Because that's exactly what it looks like, feels like.

No, I'd known exactly what it was and what it was for.

And the only way I could have known that is if things went down exactly how Momma described.

This was my idea.

The knowing makes my fingers buzz, turn numb, my breaths shorten. I hold my breath deep in my chest and wait for the buzzing to stop.

It doesn't.

My journalist brain whirs, looking for answers, for the plot, for the conclusion. Why would I have called in a bomb threat after planting a bomb? If I'd just wanted to destroy, I wouldn't have cared about any sort of alert.

What was my plan? What did I do?

31

GABRIEL

Gabriel's fingers trembled over his phone.

Good boy. To play this game, you'll need a scalpel, a defibrillator, and two pounds of salt. Get those items and get to deck 8. You have 7 minutes.

A scalpel? Where would he get a scalpel? Ship doctor's office. Deck two. There was also a portable defibrillator there. Gabriel turned around, swung open the crew door, and ran for the stairs. His steps pounded on the painted metal as he flew down the inside of the ship. But the salt? Sometimes there was rock salt in the crew supplies, for their northern sailings to salt the ice off the decks. If he was lucky, there would be some left over.

He rounded a bend in the stairs and clattered onto deck two. Crew scurried past him, everyone mission-focused on evacuating the ship. He needed to tell someone he had a line open with the bomber. How would the bomber know? He slowed and flagged down one of the crew. "You there. I need you to—"

His phone buzzed. *Did I mention I can see you?*

He gritted his teeth. "Carry on." The crew gave him a look, then ran off. Did the bomber have access to the cameras? How? Gabriel shook his head and ran down the hall, skidding into the empty office. He grabbed the scalpel and the defibrillator and ran out the door. Down the hall was the crew supply closet he'd ducked into with Jesse earlier. He ran through the door and went to the back of the shelves. If it wasn't here, he'd have to go to the kitchen—and there was no time for that. He dropped to his knees, pushed aside buckets and rope, and there, at the back on the bottom shelf, sat a large bag of rock salt. More than he needed. More than he could carry.

He grabbed a bucket, scooped as much as it could hold, and spun out of the supply closet.

Deck eight. He had three minutes left. There was no way he was going to make it in time. Had to try. He eyed the stairs, then the crew elevator. The crew elevator would be faster, if it was empty. Had to take the chance. He slid down the hall, punched the button, and the doors yawned open. He slammed down the button for deck eight, and the elevator shuddered, then moved.

The doors slid open just as his phone buzzed. He fumbled for his phone. It was quiet, vacant. This level had already been evacuated.

That was close. Just think. If you hadn't stopped to talk to the crew, you would have made it.

His stomach twisted. *I made it. Ship's clocks are fast.*

He heard voices and looked around. A young mother struggled with her toddler, and Gabriel's stomach dropped.

"Sir? Sir?" Her words were heavily accented. "Where go?" she asked in broken English.

His phone buzzed. He held a finger up to the woman and looked at the message. A laughing smiley face waited for him. *I like you. Too bad.*

Gabriel's breath caught in his lungs and his spine tingled, waiting for the explosion. He stared into the woman's eyes. He'd failed her. Everyone. His phone buzzed again, and instinct took over. He tackled the woman and her kid, hit the deck, covered them with his body. She screamed. The toddler wailed. He let his breath out, his head dizzy. Not an explosion. "I'm sorry. *Lo siento mucho.*" He climbed off her, then held up three fingers. "*Cubierta tres.*" He helped her up, put her child in her arms, and sent them away on the elevator.

There was another laughing face waiting on his phone. *My hero! I'll give you one more chance. Pick everything up and go to the President's Suite. You have two minutes.*

He frowned at his phone but followed the instructions. The President's Suite was under construction and locked. Only accessible with a ship officer's keycard. Two minutes to get there. Ten minutes until the bomb went off.

Gabriel ran. He skidded to a stop in front of the President's Suite, swiped his replacement keycard, and plowed through the door.

He got a whiff of mothballs and citrus, then pain exploded across the back of his head and everything went dark.

32

JESSE

I LEAN OVER THE RAILING NEAR THE PIER'S EDGE AND watch our ship grow smaller and smaller on the horizon. The party music from a nearby bar is a stark contradiction to what's transpiring on the water. From when I placed the call to now, there are twelve minutes left on the countdown. The ocean laps at the rocky barrier, just a few feet below the ground. Panic ripples across the port as Luxury Lines passengers realize their ship has left without them. They rush toward the pier, only to be stopped by guards accessorized with assault rifles.

I glance at my watch. Five minutes left. Have they found the bomb? Have they disabled it? My emotions are mixed. I don't want the ship to explode, but if it doesn't, will they know it was me? Will Momma tell them?

I suck in air as a new thought resounds through my skull. Momma would never go to her death peacefully. She's fought her way through life, and she wouldn't stop now. Whatever she's planning, it's not dying on that ship.

The second hand moves past the ten hour. I cringe and suck in my breath, and my ribs poke against my lungs, but there's no explosion. I check my watch again and close my eyes. My ribs shoot sharp electric pains through my chest as I let go a deep breath. There's no explosion. They disabled the bomb.

This was too easy.

Momma doesn't make things easy. And if we had planned this together...

The laughter and loud conversations, the party music, even the blue sky and the bluer water, it all fades. I'm sucked back to the past, to a long-ago memory, to little-girl me.

Momma had a collection of beautiful dolls. Some made of porcelain, some with real hair, others that felt like a real baby when I held them, their bodies soft and heavy in my arms. They were old, as old as Momma. I was maybe six or seven years old when Momma left me at home all alone. Before she left, she told me that we'd play a game. If I followed her rules exactly, I'd get to play with the dolls when she got home. The rules were don't make a mess, don't go in her room, don't touch her dolls.

She was gone all day long. We didn't have television. Momma claimed the devil could infect your mind from the images. We didn't have books. And my one Barbie doll had lost her hair and the paint had faded from her eyes. I didn't want to play Momma's game, and she'd never know if I touched the dolls. I crept into her room and took down one doll. My favorite. I'd named her Emily. Her eyes closed when I tilted her back, and she looked so peaceful, so serene.

I put Emily back where she belonged, even remembering to cross her legs at the ankles and smooth the wrinkles out of her pink dress.

When Momma came home, it took less than five minutes for her to realize I'd played with Emily. I don't have any memories from the rest of that day or the next. Just waking up in my bed, my arm in a homemade sling, Emily torn to pieces at the foot of my blanket.

Something hard *thunks* in my gut. Momma loves to play games...head games. They're the only type of game she's certain to win.

Is this one of her games? If it is, I'm losing.

So why— Snippets of Momma's words cut through my memory, chase me down. The broken picture frame in my apartment, Momma recognizing Gabe, the feel of the C4 in my hands, just like modeling clay. Momma needing Gabe's keycard. Momma keeping from me who Gabe really is.

The world comes back into focus, everything in my stomach turns into a hard knot, and I'm impaled on a solid spike of truth. It drives all the way through me.

There is no bomb.

But that doesn't mean Momma's not here to kill.

I have to get on that boat.

33

GABRIEL

Gabriel woke to the sound of running water, an explosion of pain at the base of his skull, and off-key humming. His eyesight was bleary, unfocused, and he was freezing. He tried to get up, but he slipped, his hands tied tightly behind his back. Water sloshed around him. He blinked again, clearing the fuzziness out of his head. He was in a bathtub, stripped down to his bare chest. A mosaic of tile surrounded him, the lights in the bathroom dimmed to candlelight low.

Jesse's mother stood over him, pouring the bucket of rock salt into the water with him.

"Mrs. David?" he croaked, his thoughts still muddled, unable to process what was going on.

"Ah, good. Your memory's intact. You'll need it." She smiled, and it wasn't kind or full of humor or even savagery. It was manic, a smidgen shy of totally insane.

"You're the bomber?" He looked around for her wheelchair, but it was gone, as well as the boot on her foot. "How did you get access to the cameras?"

She waved his missing keycard at him. "Jesse's not as innocent as you'd think. That girl has always doubted her sanity just enough to do anything I say, given the right circumstances."

His mind spun. He didn't know what Jesse's *mamá* was talking about, but she sounded crazy. "I did what you said. I played your game. You have to stop the bomb."

She stilled, then broke out into a cackle of laughter. "Oh, you precious boy. You think I brought a bomb big enough to blow up this ship on board? Don't you think security would have spied that on the way in?"

A small amount of pressure let off his chest. "There's no bomb. It was a trick. To get me here."

"Oh, I didn't say there wasn't a bomb. But that's not your business. This, however"—she picked up the defibrillator he'd brought—"this is our unfinished business. You think I wouldn't recognize you? That I wouldn't remember *exactly* who you are and what you did?" She stuck the adhesive pads to his chest, then set about removing the safety wiring with the scalpel.

She'd had him bring all the devices she needed to torture him.

His stomach sank even as his heartbeats sped up. He struggled against his bonds, the zip ties digging into his wrists, the water sloshing up his neck.

She saw his reaction and bit down on her smile.

"I told Jesse everything. I told her the truth." His breath was coming shorter, faster, shallower and shallower.

She leaned close. "You think I want a confession from you? I don't need a confession. Unlike Jesse, I *remember*. I've remembered every day of the past twenty years how you and Jesse killed my husband."

She flipped the green switch on the defibrillator. The machine buzzed and beeped, and she pressed down the orange shock button. Gabriel had no time to prepare, to react. Electricity coursed through him, bending his body backwards and raising him up, the shocks amplified by the water, the salt. Jesse's *mamá* watched, her shoulders relaxing as every muscle in his body cramped, exploded into fire and pain.

The shocks receded, and he fell back into the water, his body flipping from limp and exhausted to charged and on fire.

Mrs. David hovered her thumb over the orange button again, waiting for the machine to recharge. "What I want from you, Gabriel, is for you to suffer. And then I want you to die, knowing that help is within reach, but outside your grasp. You'll die with the same suffering that you caused in my husband."

An acidic terror filled his chest. It was no more than he deserved. The suffering he'd caused from making rash decisions, from being impatient with other people's lives, from destroying two families. His own, with his decision to run with the wrong crowd, making *Papá* step in and put himself in the sights of the gang Gabriel had joined as a teen, and Jesse's family, back when it was more important to him to advance his career than to protect and save a life.

"And Jesse?" Gabriel rasped out, his throat clenched, his muscles screaming behind him, cramping through his arms, his legs, up his spine. He could take all this as his own punishment, if it weren't for Jesse.

"Jesse will know *my* suffering."

Panic filled his veins, a jittering that had nothing to do with the electricity coursing through his muscles. Jesse didn't deserve this. Jesse had suffered with her mother twice over. Jesse had been her mother's punching bag for the better part of her life.

And she was the reason he'd fight now. He'd fight to save her, he'd fight to stay alive, he'd fight to keep her from suffering.

The light blinked under the orange button, and Jesse's *mamá* mashed it down.

Gabriel tensed his body, trying to fight off the electric charge, but he felt each of his muscles seize one by one.

He felt his own heart stop.

34

JESSE

I⊤'s hours later before the boat returns to the port. The sun sets over the horizon, and chatter from the other passengers fills the air. I skip the guest line. Gabe recognized my voice. If he told Delice or turned me in, security will never let me get on the ship.

At the other end of the port is the crew line. I flash my press pass at one of them. "I'm writing an article for *Travel the World*, and I'd like to interview you. Do you have a few seconds for me?" Interviews were one of my main weapons to get into places other people weren't allowed. Interviews appeal to egos, and egos stroked the right way are the key to most locked doors. I lead us inside the ship, to the side of the crew security check-in. Even here, there is security to get past, but it's lax enough to give me a chance.

As I interview the crew member about his job, his home, and his background, I take baby steps past the security desk, and he follows without realizing it. By the time the five-minute interview is over, I have a new fan, and I'm past security. "You don't mind if I go through here to get back to my room, do you? That line is so long." I nod at the back of the ship where the rest of the passengers are boarding.

"Sure, just don't tell my crew leader." He winks at me as we share our secret. I hand him my card, tell him the article could take another year to come out due to our publishing schedule, and let him get back to his work. I hurry through an empty crew hall and duck out on the other side, behind passenger security and in the clear. I rush up the stairs, avoiding the packed elevators, and by the time I'm on mine and Momma's floor, I'm out of breath. I still haven't caught it by the time I reach our stateroom.

I take a breath, try to steady my lungs, and unlock the door. The door clicks shut behind me. The stateroom is as quiet and as dark as my body is numb. I listen for Momma's breathing, for the fall of her foot, for the swish of the cane. Nothing.

But she's here.

Shadows creep along the floor, and the ship sways to an ignorant beat. There's a killer on board.

And now, I'm sure. It's not me.

"You figure it out yet, girlie?" the darkness asks, around the curve of the main living area, to a place I cannot see. She could be anywhere. The cane *tap-taps*, beating out a dirge.

Adrenaline pumps in my stomach. An old feeling. Old and familiar and reminiscent of all my childhood memories. Like the scent of cut grass or the chirrup of crickets or the iron taste of blood.

"Where's Gabe?" My voice is low, strong. But she can see through it, to my weakness, my frailness. She can travel the maze of my soul and douse the light at its center faster than anyone on earth. Even faster than ghosts.

Daddy isn't here. He's hiding somewhere safe, waiting to see who wins. Who is most deserving of his whispers.

"Gabriel is paying his price. You know what he did." The cane *tap-taps* again. "Now it's time for you to remember." Her voice moves, creeps closer. "You killed your daddy." She appears around the corner, her suit white in the dark, floating toward me as if she's already joined Daddy in the afterlife. "You betrayed him, Jesse-girl." The cane catches a hint of moonlight and smacks against her leg with a fleshy *thump*.

And with that *thump*, I've finally had enough. Enough rejection, enough betrayal, enough believing that someday, she might love me. I tighten my fists and crunch all those hopes into tiny crumbs, then open my hands and let them all fall to the ground.

Darkness doesn't serve me anymore.

I flip the switch, ready for the sudden blindness. Momma's not. I crouch down and spring toward her. I hit her stomach, my shoulder sinks into her side. The cane drops to the ground. She stumbles backward. Her mouth flails open, and she sucks in empty air.

I pick up the cane. Emotions flood through me, connecting to the bites of pain at every single nerve ending. I push it away and gnaw at my lip, my heart faltering with every beat.

"No more, Momma." There's a strength to my wavering voice, and it shines through all my broken pieces. I've finally found my rock-hard center.

"Jesse," she heaves, finally finding her breath. "Give me the cane."

"I said, no more, Momma." I balance the cane in my hands. The cool metal warms at my touch, as if it is the lover I've always needed. "I was nine years old. I did *not* kill my father. I jumped in the water to run away, and he followed me."

"Of course he followed you, you selfish brat. You were the love of his life. He wasn't going to let you get away."

Love of his life? It makes me sick.

"Where's Gabe?" I tap the cane against my leg, mimicking her threats.

"He's taking a long soak." She backs away from me.

"Where. Is. Gabe?" I finger the head of the cane, tracing its smooth surface and worn dents the size and shape of my bones, smaller and younger at the top, bigger and harder at the bottom. Each dent, a piece of my life that was beaten into submission. Each stroke of the cane rips away another of my layers, until I am no more than a naked essence. Not unloved. Not loved. Just Jesse.

"That man is a presidential pain in the ass. You deserve each other. Too bad he's already dead." Her gaze slips to the side, and I know she's lying. "Don't you want to know about the bomb?"

"The bomb? I made the call. And then, I waited."

Her cheeks tighten.

"The bomb didn't go off. I thought at first the bomb had been disabled, but then I realized." I point the cane at her, and she shies away as if she's been on the receiving end before. "There is no bomb. You used it to make me think I was crazy. You used it as a distraction to get to Gabe." I thump the cane on the ground, near her knee. "This is the last time I ask you before I show you all I've learned from you over the years. Where. Is. He?"

The cane has a life of its own. It taps against Momma's shins with each syllable, gains strength from her gasps of pain. "You really think there's no bomb, Jesse-girl? I never wanted to blow up the ship. But you? You deserve everything that's coming your way." Her lips quiver, and despite her pain, her voice lifts up.

I falter at her words, at the knowing in my bones. There is a bomb. It's in this room. And it'll likely be just enough to blow me and Momma to pieces.

The cane wrenches from my hand, and Momma looms over me, cane raised high above her head.

My heartbeat *boom booms* in my ears. I scramble backwards, knocking over a chair, my breath gasping, cold sweat stabbing my spine.

"Your father and I gave you everything you ever needed, and you turn on us? You dare to raise your hand to your own mother?" The cane crashes down, and I jump out of the way. She swings it sideways, making contact with my thigh. I roll to the ground, ribs hindering my lungs. Doesn't matter. Pain is temporary. Life is temporary. Only death matters.

And I won't die like this.

I spring from a crouch and hit the light switch. Darkness floods the room, and I sink into the shadows.

Momma laughs. "So, we're playing hide and seek in the dark? Just like we used to, right, Jesse-girl?" She starts to hum that old lullaby. The one Daddy used to sing. *"Down, down deep, in the big ocean blue, swims two little fishies, a Me and a You."*

Terror creeps into my mind, terror that has been ingrained into my brain and my nerves and my muscles. Old sensations pound my memory, make sweat moisten all my bends and angles.

"Where are you, Jesse-girl?" Her voice taunts, and her cane taps. "Don't know what's happened to you. You used to be so docile. Used to love me so much. And now..." The cane swats against the couch.

I back away, fumbling for a weapon. She's going to kill me. I've thought it before, but never has the thought resonated through my entire body like it does in this moment.

"Now I have to resort to blackmail." She giggles, and her laugh is off-kilter, like her pull-string has worn out. "That poor puppy never saw me comin'. Neither did his stupid, slow owner. It was all so easy, and you...you fell for it! You never were smart enough to figure out a trick. Always just crazy enough to believe yourself capable of anything."

Something cold and hard rushes through my body. My hands dig into the carpet and clench around a coil of wire, left over from Momma's bomb. "You killed that dog. You killed that man." My voice hushes, no more than a broken whisper, but it doesn't matter. The pieces finally fall together. Not just for this week, but for my life. "I've never killed a dog." Blood drains from my head. "It was you, all along. Not me." The darkness seems to eat my voice. "I never did any of it."

"Ding, ding, ding," she says, slowly and methodically, tapping the cane closer and closer.

The past week rushes through my mind, all those moments that didn't quite connect. "You made me believe I did it. You held me hostage. You—"

A swoosh of air rushes over me. I jump up, but I'm too slow. The cane crunches into my shin, and pain explodes my world.

"You're a sick little girl, betraying your parents the first chance you get. Your father knew way back then what you were. He tried to teach you, show you the way to be a woman. And you didn't learn. You never learn." She lumbers over me, her skin pasty-pale and twisted into a nightmare. "Don't you remember the end of the song, Jesse-girl?"

I shake my head, cover my ears. I don't want to hear, I don't want to feel, I don't want Daddy to catch me.

She hums again, dragging the cane up my battered leg and digs it into my ribs. *"Down, down deep, in the big ocean blue, little fishies jump and little fishies fin, but all the little fishies swim swim swim."*

She leans on the cane, and my ribs *pop, one, two, three* and my world dims. Daddy's face swims to the surface, and I remember.

I remember the end of the song.

I wasn't hiding when he sang the song. That's where I wished I was. Prayed I'd be magically transported. Under the bed to hide with the monsters, because maybe the monsters would protect me from him. Daddy would sing the end of that song, and he'd find me and he'd drag me down the hallway as Momma huddled in a ball on the floor watching, blood dribbling from her mouth. He'd dress me in bows and ribbons, pink frills and lace, and Momma would pound on the door.

She used to try to fight him off.

But he beat the fight out of her. He beat her until she crossed the boundary of survival and into denial. Into blaming the victim.

Because if it was my fault, it was no longer hers.

Something inside me shifts, slides off the edge, fractures.

"I remember now," I whisper, but Momma hears. She stops singing and takes away the cane.

The coil of wire from Momma's bomb tightens between my hands.

I can no longer run. There are no safe places, and we've long lost the path to forgiveness. Death is the only option left to us now.

Momma turns her back, gearing up for her next round of punishment. She thinks I'm broken. She thinks I'm fragile. I grit my teeth against the pain and leap to my feet. I wrap the cord around her thick neck, twisting it in my palms until blood trickles down my wrists, all before she can think again.

She gurgles, and the sound numbs me. I twist tighter.

"Where's the bomb, Momma?" My voice goes low, hoarse, and rabid.

She claws at her throat, and I know, like a cat knows a good person from a bad, that the broken thing inside me is shattered beyond repair. I should stop. I don't want to.

I lean close to her ear, and my lips graze her stretched-out lobe. "Tell me where the bomb is, and I'll let you go."

She nods and points to my closet. Of course she kept it near. She wouldn't want to be too far from the vehicle that would take her to Daddy. I twist the coil of wire again, and it pops into my skin.

She struggles.

"Looks like I'm not the only one who falls for tricks," I whisper against her pearl-decorated ear, her soft skin grazing my cracked lips.

Her feet kick out and we fall to the ground, but I don't release my hold. I tighten. This is my escape. My only escape. She kicks again, and no more.

I hold on for a minute longer, to be certain. Her chest stills, and Daddy's breath whispers against my ear, "Well done."

I let go. The room fills with the rustling of her clothes and her boneless *thump* to the ground, and then, there is nothing but silence and emptiness. My legs tremble. My hands shake. My body vibrates from shock.

I've killed her. I killed my mother.

My body stills.

I've killed both my parents.

Daddy was an accident.

But Momma had it coming.

I suck down a deep breath, and my mind clears. I crawl to the closet, busted leg dragging behind me. Under a pile of clothes, a red light gleams. A timer ticks down. Three minutes left. Three minutes left until the time the ship left us on the dock in Cozumel, giving up on finding Daddy in the water, alive. I glance around the suite, but there's no detonator.

What now?

I wrap my hands as best as I can and fight through the pain. I take the bomb, the two little blocks of C_4, warm next to the timer, and place it in Momma's lap. I wrap her hands around it, holding it in place.

This is the best I can do.

Someone pounds on the door. "Miss David, are you in there?"

There are seconds left on the countdown. I throw myself at the door, swing it open, and plow into Delice and her team. "Get down!"

The bomb explodes behind us, flinging pieces of Momma all around.

DISEMBARKATION

Down, down deep,
In the big ocean blue,
Little fishies jump and little fishies fin
But all the little fishies swim swim swim.

35

GABRIEL

THE FIRST THING THAT PULLED GABRIEL OUT OF THE darkness was the sound of a machine steadily beeping. Was Jesse's mother back? Was she going to hit the button again? He struggled against his ties, then caught the scent of lavender.

"Jesse?" He expected his voice to bounce off the bathroom tiles, but it was so soft that it got lost.

"I'm here." Her voice floated over him, like dancing music notes and stars.

He fought to open his eyes. He was in a bed, centered in a room painted a light shade of yellow.

"You're in the hospital, in Galveston. You've been out for a couple of days. They weren't sure you were going to make it." Her words spilled out in a rush. She wrapped her hands around one of his and stared into his eyes. "How are you feeling?"

He coughed. "Like I've crammed two weeks of basic training into one day." Even his lungs were sore. "Your mother—she wants to hurt you, Jesse. You have to stay away from her." He struggled to sit up, to get out of bed.

Jesse reached to the side of the bed and raised him to sitting. "Momma's dead. Killed herself with her own bomb." Her eyes slid to the side, and he knew that wasn't the full story, but it didn't matter. Jesse was safe, and free.

He looked her over. Purple circles draped her eyes, and her hands were wrapped tight in gauze. Her mother's boot covered her foot, and her mother's cane leaned on the chair next to her. "*Cara rota!* Jesse, did she do this to you?"

"Momma was busy that day. I'll be fine." She shrugged off his concerns and helped rearrange his pillows.

He sank back into them, exhausted. "Tell me everything."

Jesse bit her lip but nodded. "You know that Daddy died twenty years ago. And that Momma blamed me. And you."

Gabriel nodded, letting her go at her own pace.

"I was nine," Jesse continued. "My father was...he wasn't a good dad. He..." She licked her lips. Her fingers trembled against the wooden chair arm, and her words came out stilted and stuttered. "I had reason to get away from him. We were on a snorkeling excursion in Cozumel, and I jumped off the boat. I thought I could swim to shore and live in paradise, far away from him and Momma. I thought I could swim fast enough to escape, but"—her hands clenched around the chair—"he caught me. I struggled and kicked and fought.

The rip tide caught him and carried him out to sea. You know the rest.

"Momma never forgave me. And she never forgave Luxury Lines. Or rather, you. Momma's always liked the personal touch, and as near as I can figure, Luxury Lines was too big, too impersonal. So you became the face of Luxury Lines. She could blame it all on you. She brought a bomb, used it to trick me, get you alone, then tried to kill both me and her with it. I fought back, and she wouldn't stop the bomb and she was going to kill me. I saw it in her eyes." Her voice broke, but she shook her head, continued. "I escaped, and she killed herself anyway."

Jesse looked out the window, watching a seagull glide by.

"When you found out about the bomb, you called in the bomb threat, right?"

Jesse nodded. "Momma also killed that dog. And that man," she whispered, stared down at her hands.

The heart monitor skipped upwards. "That was your mother? Mr. Reese's death wasn't an accident?"

She sucked on her lip and shook her head. "I told your CSO and captain everything. I'm not sure they believed me, but they let me go. The FBI has let me know I'm a *person of interest* and not to leave the country."

"I'm so sorry, Jesse. Just let me know who to talk to, and I'll tell them everything. This was your mother. All your mother." Gabriel reached for her hand, and she placed hers in his.

"Thank you." She wiped at her nose.

The door opened, and a nurse walked in. "Well, it's good to see you awake finally." She smiled brightly.

Jesse got to her feet, leaning heavily on her cane. "I told you he'd pull through." There was a familiarity to her tone that told him Jesse'd been at his bedside frequently over the past few days. "I'll check on you later, Gabe. Get some rest."

Gabriel watched her walk through the door, and somehow, he knew he was forgiven. Jesse had given him what *Papá* never had the chance to. Maybe this time, he could accept it.

Maybe this time, he could take *Papá's* advice and not just be his best man but be his own man.

Maybe if he was lucky, he could be her man too.

36

JESSE

Brian pulls up to the curb outside the deserted beach. "I'll wait for you here," he says, his English accent soothing this early in the morning. I get out and step into a stiff sea breeze. Sand blows against my pants, crinkling the drawing in my pocket that I've taken to carrying with me always. There's a recent addition, and already the paper is turning soft from being handled. Someday, I'll have to replace it with something more permanent.

The thump of Momma's cane feels like I'm grinding against sandpaper. I hobble down a broken pier that juts far into the bay, until there's nothing but ocean beneath the wood, and my driver's car looks toy-sized behind me.

The sun rises over the shoreline, and I lean over the pier, the sea-rotten wood digging into the bruises on my ribs. The pain centers me. The breeze ruffles through my hair and pops chills onto my neck. Galveston peeks into existence, turning gray and lightening with every second, as if a giant eraser is rubbing away the night.

It's been quiet since the night Momma died. The blackouts have stopped, as if the other me was a bully I finally stood up to. Facing Daddy's death and my own conscience has granted me a clarity I've never before experienced. Daddy's at peace. Content with the deal I made him. The smile has been captured, the little girl I saved is safe, and now, there is just this.

I touch the cane one last time. Then I raise it high in the air, tilt it back, and throw it as far as I can.

It twirls in the sunrise, flashing silver once, twice, before it winks forever away, sinking into the endless sea.

I climb back into Brian's car and pull out my phone. "Ready for some pictures?"

He leans back in his seat, and I show him pictures from my trip. All the smiles I've captured. All except one.

37

GABRIEL

Visiting hours closed an hour ago, and Gabriel still pathetically watched the door for Jesse to appear. It'd been three days since he last saw her, and her lavender scent had long vanished. Where was she? Across his small hospital room, the television flipped from a commercial to Channel 12's logo, and the theme song to the nightly news echoed into the room.

"We bring you tonight a rather gruesome story from a place many consider to be the doorway to paradise. Rebecca Jones is on the scene. Rebecca?"

Gabriel turned the volume up, television a relatively new distraction for him. Especially the news. So dark and full of drama. The background of Galveston Bay, peppered with cruise ships, filled the scene behind the tiny blonde reporter.

"Thanks, Natalie. I'm here at the Port of Galveston, where many travelers are gathered to take a cruise to paradise. But those travel plans must be delayed briefly while authorities wrap up their investigation. A body was discovered floating in the water early this morning. Many believe it to be the body of Frank Hanson, a Luxury Lines guest reported missing a week ago."

A week ago? That was the same sailing he and Jesse were on.

"Do authorities suspect this was an accident, or a case of foul play?"

The reporter hesitated, waiting for the feed to come through. "Unfortunately, the authorities are ruling this a homicide. My source tells me that the victim's face was mutilated in some way, then dumped overboard. It's a sad day for this family. He leaves behind a pregnant wife and a daughter."

The screen flashed to a picture of a family, a family Gabriel recognized. The little girl who almost drowned. Who Jesse saved.

"A sad day indeed. Thank you, Rebecca. Now onto high school football."

Gabriel's world narrowed and darkened, the only light came from the television. Words bombarded his ears over and over —*face mutilated, homicide.*

A flash of Mr. Hart's shredded lip flared across Gabriel's memory.

Jesse.

ALSO BY CHRISTINA DELAY

Truth Truth Lie

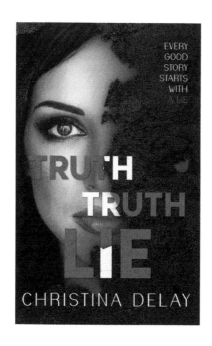

ACKNOWLEDGMENTS

No book sees the light of day without a community standing behind it, and so it goes with this story.

A huge heaping of gratitude to my ride-or-die, my 'fixer', Julie Glover. I would not be the person I am, the author I am, or be able to produce the books I do without you. *Thank you* for putting up with me.

To my wonderfully smart, never-holds-back beta-readers: April Karpus-Weddle, Carol Costley-Storey, Jason Beymer, and Rob Eveling...thank you for sharing your insights, catching my mistakes, and making this book shine.

To Lance Chaney...thank you for making me slow down time. Your imagery helped kick this story off in exactly the direction in which I was aiming.

To my Cruising Writers... I began writing this story on one of our cruises many years back—you may recognize some of the places or scenes from our various cruises together. You guys have filled and refilled my creative well over and over again. Thank you for being a part of my circle.

To my readers - you guys! Your notes of encouragement, your questions of when the next book will be released, your sharing of my books with your friends...I am so very grateful to you and to the time you spend with me and my stories.

And finally, my family. This book would not be done without you telling me to work on my book, without your willingness to let me have my writing space, nor without your sweet encouragement. I'm a very, very lucky mom and wife.

ABOUT THE AUTHOR

Christina Delay is an award-winning author of psychological suspense, as well as young adult fantasy written under the pen name Kris Faryn.

A wanderer by heart, Christina's latest adventure has led her and her family—a supremely patient husband, two adorable patooties, and mischievous, senior citizen cat—to the southwest of France.

When not planning their next quest, Christina can be found writing in her garden, hosting writing retreats in the Caribbean and other exotic places, sneaking in a nap, or convincing her patooties to call her Empress.

If you love books about complex characters who never know when to quit, with a good bit of will-they or won't-they tension, check out her books on ChristinaDelay.com.

instagram.com/authorchristinadelay

facebook.com/authorchristinadelay

bookbub.com/authors/christina-delay

amazon.com/author/christinadelay

goodreads.com/christina_delay

Made in the USA
Coppell, TX
06 May 2024

32074398R00196